Female Friends

Fay Weldon

HEAD
of ZEUS

First published in 1975 by William Heinemann Ltd

This paperback edition first published in the UK in 2014 by Head of Zeus Ltd

Copyright © Fay Weldon, 1974

9 7 5 3 1 2 4 6 8

A catalogue record for this book is available from the British Library.

Paperback ISBN: 9781784080761
eBook ISBN: 9781781858004

Printed by Clays Ltd, St Ives Plc

Head of Zeus Ltd
Clerkenwell House
45-47 Clerkenwell Green
London EC1R 0HT

WWW.HEADOFZEUS.COM

one

Understand, and forgive. It is what my mother taught me to do, poor patient gentle Christian soul, and the discipline she herself practised, and the reason she died in poverty, alone and neglected. The soles of her poor slippers, which I took out from under the bed and threw away so as not to shame her in front of the undertaker, were quite worn through by dutiful shuffling. Flip-flop. Slipper-slop. Drifting and dusting a life away.

There is a birth certificate in Somerset House – where all our lives and deaths are listed, and all our marriages and our divorces too – which describes me as Evans, Chloe, born to Evans, Gwyneth, *née* Jones, and Evans, David, housepainter, of 10 Albert Villas, Caledonian Road, London, N1, on February 20th, 1930. Evans, Chloe, female. There is as yet, no death certificate there for me, though looking through the files which now crowd those once seemingly endless Georgian rooms, I shocked myself by half expecting to find it there.

Sooner or later, of course, that certificate will be added.

Understand, and forgive, my mother said, and the effort has quite exhausted me. I could do with some anger to energize me, and bring me back to life again. But where can I find that anger? Who is to help me? My friends? I have been understanding and forgiving my friends, my female friends, for as long as I can remember.

Marjorie, Grace and me.

Such were Chloe's thoughts, before she slept.

two

'There is no point in raking up the past,' Chloe's husband Oliver says to her the next morning, as she sits on the edge of his bed and watches him pour coffee from a French pottery jug. This is the day Chloe's life is to change – in the way that the lives of calm people do change, through some alteration of attitude rather than of conduct. To Chloe, it seems an ordinary enough morning, except that she woke with a feeling of cheerfulness, conscious of the notion that she was finally to be allowed out of mourning for her mother's death; and that now, when Oliver says that there is no point in raking up the past, she quite violently disagrees with him.

As for Oliver, he is glad that the night is over, not because he has slept badly but because he has slept too well, and been savaged by nightmares. They hover permanently round his brass bedstead and if he sleeps too deep, or too trustfully, they pounce.

Oliver wears no pyjamas. He is a slight, muscular, hairy man and the hairs on his chest are turning grey. Once he sat up in bed against brave white sheets, shiny black body hairs lying smooth against an olive skin, and thick dark head hair springing up in tight curls from his temples, stimulated, Chloe used to think, by the passion of his opinions and the fury of his dislikes.

Now Oliver props himself against brown easy-care Terylene and cotton pillow-slips, and his grey chest gives him a dusty and defeated look, and even his furies have mellowed, and the hair on his head, now sparse, falls downward in a perfectly

2

ordinary way. His family do not notice the change in him. They imagine he is still king in the outside world, as he is in his own territory; but in fact he abdicated from that empire long ago. He rules at home and nowhere else.

Oliver has breakfast brought to him on a tray. He does not eat breakfast with his family. His nerves shrink from noise and good-humour first thing in the morning. When the thoughts and feelings of the night are still with him, the shriekings and posturings of the children – so many of them not his own – seem like some horrific charade especially set up to mock him.

So while Françoise prepares the children's breakfast, it is Chloe's custom to take Oliver his tray. After breakfast he will go to his study to write, or try to write, his novel.

'No,' agrees Chloe, lying in her teeth, 'there is no point in raking up the past.'

He is not to be placated even by instant agreement.

'Then why,' he asks, 'do you suggest I have nightmares because of something which happened to me in the past? It's much more likely to be Françoise's dinners. She will cook with butter. Instead of offering me psychological platitudes, why not try getting her to cook in oil?'

'Françoise comes from Normandy,' Chloe says. 'Not the South. The butter habit is very deep.'

'You don't think she's trying to kill me off with cholesterol?' He is half joking, half serious. The nightmares have not yet fully retreated.

'If she wanted to kill anyone,' says Chloe, 'surely it would be me.'

But Oliver is not sure. There is a coldness in Françoise's

3

eyes, as she lies beneath him, which belies the obliging languor of her limbs and the sweet moanings of her breath. He says as much to Chloe, but this time Chloe does not reply at all.

'You're not in a mood, I hope,' says Oliver, meaning that he himself trembles on the verge of one.

'No,' says Chloe, kindly. She pulls the blind high and looks out across the garden. It is March. The winter weather has broken: the sun shines on the green tips of the daffodils, just beginning to show through the black earth. Beyond the green wall of the yew trees she can see the copper spire of the village church, brilliantly tipped with green verdigris. She is elated.

But now the sun is shining into Oliver's eyes. He protests, and Chloe lowers the blind again to save him discomfort, but not before she has seen, on the blank pillow next to Oliver's, a long dark hair, Françoise's. Chloe removes the hair, and drops it in the wastepaper basket. Oliver does not like untidiness.

'I'm sorry if I was bad-tempered,' says Oliver. 'If you mind about Françoise, you know you only have to say.'

'Of course I don't mind,' says Chloe, and as far as she can tell she doesn't.

But something has changed in her. Yes it has. Listen to what she is saying.

'I think I shall go up to London today,' says Chloe, who hates cities, crowds and cars.

'What for?'

She has to think before she can reply.

'To see Marjorie and Grace, I suppose.'

'What for?'

'They're my friends.'

4

'I am very well aware of that. Why do you choose such odd friends?'

'One doesn't choose friends. One acquires them. They are as much duty as pleasure.'

'You don't even like them.' He is right. Chloe sometimes dislikes Marjorie, and sometimes Grace, and sometimes both at once. But that is not the point.

'How do you know they'll be free to see you?' he goes on. 'Other people won't just drop everything because you happen to remember they exist. You're very egocentric.'

'I'll have to take that chance.'

'The fare is monstrous.' Oliver says. 'And who will look after the children?'

'Françoise will.'

'You mustn't impose on Françoise. Her function is to cook and clean and run the home. It does not include childcare.'

He waits for his wife to say what else it does not include, but Chloe merely says, mildly,

'The children are old enough to look after themselves.'

And so they are.

three

At half past nine Chloe suffers a spasm of fear at the prospect of going to London, and annoying everyone, and by five past ten, with the assistance of some inner fairy godmother, finally stirring from sleep, has regained her courage. She telephones.

Inigo, Imogen, Kevin, Kestrel and Stanhope are out on the

lawn, marking up a badminton court for the season's playing. Chloe's fleshly children are the youngest and eldest. Inigo is eighteen, Imogen is eight. Chloe's spiritual children, Kevin, Kestrel and Stanhope, come in between. Their cheerful, easy profanity drifts across the garden as Chloe tries to get a line through to London, and once in London to the BBC, and once at the BBC, through a succession of receptionists and secretaries, to Marjorie.

Who'd have believed it, thinks Chloe? That these children can use the words so lightly, which once were hurled, with such malignant ferocity, across their cradles. Bitch and bastard, Christ and cunt.

Although Chloe is fleshly mother only to Imogen and Inigo, all the children, she likes to feel, owe their existences to her. Four of them, Kevin, Kestrel, Stanhope and Imogen, share a common father – one Patrick Bates. Inigo has Oliver for a father. Stanhope has Grace for a mother. Kevin and Kestrel's mother Midge (Patrick's legal wife) is dead. Imogen supposes, wrongly, that Oliver is her father. Stanhope is not told, for reasons clear to his mother Grace but no-one else, the true identity of his father. And as guilty adults have a way of protecting children from truths which are probably less painful than the lies, the children live in supposedly blissful ignorance that Stanhope and Imogen are not only half-brother and half-sister to each other, but to Kevin and Kestrel as well.

Or so Chloe believes they live.

Eventually the voice at the other end of the line is Marjorie's.

'Why are you ringing?' asks Marjorie. 'Are you all right? What's the matter?'

6

'Nothing,' says Chloe.

'Oh,' says Marjorie. Is there a faint disappointment in her voice? 'Did you have trouble getting through? I've been in four different offices in four weeks. If I was a man they wouldn't dare. Do you know what they're making me do now? The most boring series they can think of. Whole departments have toiled weeks to produce it. They told me so. A thirteen-part adaptation of a novel about the life of a middle-aged divorced woman, victim of modern times and a changing society. It is my punishment for asking to do *Z-cars* for a change. I *like* cops and robbers so they give me human suffering, not to mention staff directors who're so permanent they can't fire them.'

Chloe has little idea of what Marjorie is talking about, but is obliged to admire her for her capacity to cope with, and earn money in, the outside world. Marjorie, however, has neither husband nor children, which to Chloe seems a great misfortune, and emboldens her to ask, insignificant though she feels she is, a housewife up in London, knowing nothing of directors or contracts, if Marjorie will have lunch with her that day.

'Is that French girl still with you?' inquires Marjorie.

'Yes,' says Chloe, as one might say, and what of that?

'In that case I'll have lunch with you,' says Marjorie, 'and put off two bad directors and a worse writer. Because you know what will happen. She won't just be content with your husband. She'll want your children and your house as well. You'll be eased out within the year and end up with nothing.'

What a simple view of life, Chloe thinks, the unmarried have. What can Marjorie know about it? She says as much.

'I read scripts all day,' Marjorie replies, 'and it is the kind of thing which always happens in them. You might say I knew life well by proxy. And fiction, or so my writers swear, is nothing compared to real life. Watch out for poison in the soup. The Italiano, then, at twelve-thirty.'

She rings off, with that talent she has for giving with one hand and taking away with the other, without telling Chloe where the restaurant is.

four

Marjorie, Grace and me.

Who'd have thought it, when we were young, and starting life together, that Marjorie could ever have taken charge, would ever have stopped crying, fawning, placating, and would have developed these brisk satirical edges? Let alone earned £6,000 a year.

Poor little Marjorie, with her pear-shaped body, her frizzy hair and oily skin, her sad, astonished eyes and her sharp mind, sawing raggedly through illusion like a bread-knife through a hunk of frozen fish. Battling through rejection after rejection, too honest ever to pretend they were not happening.

Marjorie has not cried, she tells me, for twenty-five years. She got through all her tears in childhood, she explains; she used them all up then. (Grace, on the other hand, dry-eyed then, is tearful now. Perhaps we all have our quota to get through. My mother would say so.) Along with Marjorie's tearducts, it seems, the rest of her dried up too. Womb, skin,

8

bosom, mind. She shrivelled before our eyes, in fact, after her Ben died, the love of her life, long ago. Only once a month, punctually with the full moon, she practically bleeds to death, all but soaking the ground where she stands.

Poor little Marjorie, obliged by fate to live like a man, taking her sexual pleasures if and when she finds them, her own existence, perforce, sufficient to itself. Childless, deprived of those pilferings into past and future with which the rest of us, more fertile, more in the steady stream of generation, enrich our lives. Yet still with her woman's body and her rioting hormones to contend with.

five

It is ten-fifteen. If she means to get to the Italiano by lunchtime, Chloe will have to catch the eleven-fifteen to Liverpool Street Station. And before she can leave the house, thus unexpectedly and disturbing the smooth running of its routine, she must pay the expected penalties.

First she must explain her actions to the children, who will want to know where she is going and why, and with what gifts she will return, before giving her their spiritual permission to leave. Thus:

Imogen (8) London? Can I come too?
Chloe No.
Imogen Why not?
Chloe It's boring.

9

Imogen No, it's not.

Chloe Yes, it is. I'm only going to talk to my friends.

Inigo (18) If it's boring why are you going?

Chloe It's nice to get away sometimes.

Stanhope (12) It's nice here.

Kestrel (12) Will you bring something back?

Chloe If I can.

Kevin (14) Male or female friends?

Chloe Female.

Inigo I should hope so too.

Imogen Why can't I come? There's nothing to do here. The others are only going to play boring badminton.

Chloe You can help Françoise.

Imogen I don't want to help Françoise. I want to go with you.

Stanhope If you see mother, send her my regards. Is that who you're going to see?

Chloe Your mother's moved house you know. She must be very busy.

Imogen If you're going, can we have fish and chips for lunch? From the chip shop?

Chloe It's very expensive.

Kestrel So's going to London.

Chloe Very well.

Inigo Will father drive you to the station?

Chloe I shouldn't think so. He's working.

Inigo I'll run you down, then.

Oh, lordly Inigo. He passed his driving test a week ago.

Then there's Françoise, muttering into the marinade. She's a stocky, hairy, clever girl, not so much pretty as lascivious

10

looking. The look is an accident of birth, more to do with a low brow and a short upper lip than a reflection of her nature.

Françoise What about the children's lunch?
Chloe They want fish and chips.
Françoise It is very extravagant.
Chloe Just for once. Inigo can take you down to the village in the car.

Françoise aquiesces. She even smiles.

Chloe The marinade smells lovely.
Françoise The meat will be only soaking for four hours. This is not sufficient. It should have been immersed last night, but I am fatigued, and in consequence forgetful.
Chloe If you like to have tomorrow off—
Françoise Tomorrow I must prepare the *lièvre* for Sunday's dinner. It is Oliver's favourite dish. What is *lièvre* in English?
Chloe Hare.

Françoise has done an advanced English course but never stops learning.

After Françoise there is Oliver. But Oliver has hardened his objections to her going into indifference. He is working in his study and actually, for once, typing. Usually, should she disturb him in the middle of the morning, he is merely contemplative, staring out of the window.

Oliver So you're off, are you?

11

Chloe Yes. Is it going well?

Oliver I'm writing a letter to *The Times*. They won't print it.

Chloe Why not? They might.

Oliver No they won't, because I won't post it.

Chloe You won't want to read to me today? Because I can always put off going.

It is Oliver's custom to read completed passages aloud to Chloe, before making a second draft of what he has written.

Oliver Don't be silly.

He turns back to his typewriter. It is not encouragement to go, but it is permission.

While Inigo takes the mini from the garage Chloe rings Grace at her new Holland Park number and asks her where the Italiano is.

'You're much better off not knowing,' says Grace.

'Please. I'm in a hurry.'

'Up a concrete walk-way at Shepherd's Bush. Stick to the pasta and avoid the veal.'

'And Grace, would you please speak to Stanhope. It's school holidays. Easter. He arrived yesterday. Shall I bring him to the phone now?'

'I'm busy packing,' says Grace. 'I'm going to Cannes with Sebastian this evening. I'll send Stanhope a postcard. He'll like that. He doesn't really want to speak to me, you know he doesn't. I embarrass him dreadfully on the telephone. We really don't have anything in common. You do nag, Chloe.'

'He's your son.'

'You only ever say that when it suits you. I suppose you've got Kevin and Kestrel there too?'

'Yes.'

There is a pause. Many people hold Grace responsible for Midge's death. Midge, who was Kevin and Kestrel's mother.

'What a martyr you are,' is all Grace says. 'And I suppose the French girl is in Oliver's bed by now?'

'Yes. As it happens.'

'Congratulations. So now's your chance. You can throw Oliver out of the house and divorce him and live off his money for ever.'

'I don't want to.'

'What? Divorce him or live off his money?'

'Either. I really must go. I'll miss my train.'

'I think it's all rather sick,' says Grace. 'Do they make you watch?'

'Don't be silly,' says Chloe, shocked.

Grace has a passion for detail. She will probe into tragedy and atrocity and insist on full details of childbirth, rape, heart-attacks, road accidents, suicides and murders, long after the teller is sick of the tale. 'Yes, but what did he say? Did she scream? Did the eye-balls burst too? Where did he put it, exactly, and how? Did the steering-wheel show through his back? Yes, but *where* did they burn the after-birth?' Grace knows all about after-births and how, by law, they have to be burned. And how if the mid-wife at a home delivery can't find a suitable fire, she must carry it off to a hospital incinerator.

Otherwise witches might get it.

'If they don't let you watch,' says Grace, 'it's not just sick, it's boring. Can you come round this afternoon after your lunch?'

'Yes,' says Chloe, though her heart sinks. Why? Grace is her friend.

'Who are you having lunch with?'

'Marjorie.'

'I thought as much,' says Grace. 'Only Marjorie would be seen dead in the Italiano, and dead she will be if she touches the minestrone. Give her my regards and say I hope she keeps her moustache out of the soup.'

And she gives Chloe her new address and puts the phone down.

Grace, who is well over forty, lives with Sebastian, who is twenty-five. Chloe feels herself to be morally superior to Grace.

six

Grace, Marjorie and me.

Who would have thought it, when we were young.

Grace, so talented, so bold and desperate, now lives off men. Well, it is the way the world was arranged, most women do, and we all have to live somehow.

Grace complains of debt and recalcitrant lovers, but always seems to have a house to sell, a Rembrandt print to pawn, someone to take her out to dinner or fill her bed for the night. The rest of us fear poverty, deprivation, abandonment, separation, death. Grace fears the lack of a good hairdresser.

She has no doubt been trained to this end, like one of Pavlov's dogs, by a series of unpleasant experiences, but she was, I suspect, a more than willing victim in the experiment.

Grace is beautiful and frequently disagreeable and it is the latter quality, I sometimes think, which is more of an attraction than the former.

Grace remains beautiful as she grows older – it is as if she gains nourishment from her temper tantrums and her tears. She looks dreadful when she cries. I have seen her many times, her eyes red and swollen and ugly: her mouth swollen by blows, her neck marked not with love bites but the strangle marks she no doubt provokes. See her the next day, and who would have thought it. All is smooth and glossy again: a necklace round the firm white neck, the eyes clear, mocking and indifferent.

Grace wounds easily, but heals suspiciously quickly.

seven

Marjorie, Grace and me. How foolishly we loved.

Grace loved her Christie, arch-villain of a decade, and after that herself (and she is, as they say, her own worst enemy).

Marjorie loved and still loves her mother, who frequently forgot not just her name but her very existence.

I, Chloe, loved Oliver.

We all, at one time or other, loved Patrick Bates, and Marjorie still does, much good may it do her.

These days I hardly know what the word love means. My

mother, I remember, once told me it was the force which keeps people revolving round each other, in fixed orbit, and at a precise distance, as the planets revolve around the sun; and the moon, that cold creature, around the earth.

My mother, poor dead soul, loved her employer, in secret, for twenty years, and he never once made physical love to her, so such a vision of love came easily to her. And it is certainly true that with the force which attracts us to other people comes a force which similarly repels – keeps us forever dancing and juggling in our inner spaces, like motes in a sunbeam, never quite close enough, always too near, circling the object of our affection, yearning for incorporation and yet dreading it.

I remember love's enchantments. Of course I do. Sometimes something happens, like the sun across the garden in the morning, or a song, or a smell, or the touch of a hand – and the body remembers what love was like, and the soul lifts itself up. certain once again in the knowledge of its Creator; and the whole self trembles again in the memory of that elation, which once so transfigured our poor obsessed bodies, our poor possessed minds.

It did us no good.

eight

Marjorie, Grace and me. How foolishly we loved, and murderous we are. We have had six children between us, but have done to death, as if to balance the scales, some six of our nearest and dearest. And though the world does not acknowledge such deaths as murder, we know in our hearts that they are. No-one lies dead in a coffin but that our neglect has sent them there, or else it was our death wishes, sickening the air about them while they lived. Or perhaps we have overlain them with the great weight of motherly or wifely love, and crushed the life and spirit out of them.

Our fault.

Grace killed her Christie. It was the morning after his third marriage, to California: Grace had kept him awake all night by first telephoning, then ringing his front door bell, then shouting obscene instructions to California through the door, until the police removed her. The next morning, exhausted, he drove his new Maserati off the M1 and was killed, not instantly, but horribly. The alimony stopped with him, and Grace was left with nothing (in Grace's terms) but a run-down house in St John's Wood. California, that flower child, had shrewd lawyers and a marriage settlement which withstood almost instantaneous widowhood, and was overnight a millionairess.

Marjorie killed her Ben, with whom she was living (in the terminology of those days) in sin. Ben, changing a light-bulb one evening, reached out to take the new one from a slow-moving Marjorie, fell off his chair, hurt his neck, and later went down to casualty to see why it was hurting.

He'd been there three hours when the hospital rang and asked Marjorie to collect him, so she went along and was met by an old man in broken shoes and a white coat, who led her into a chilly tiled room, where the full moon glittered through opaque glass. He pulled out a drawer from the wall and there was Ben, lying dead. He'd cracked a vertebra when he fell,

17

they told her later, and by some remote chance the two pieces of bone, grating together as he waited in the queue for attention, had snipped some vital nerve.

Marjorie was six months pregnant and it was her clumsiness, undoubtedly, which had caused Ben to stretch too far and fall. The baby was born prematurely, and died.

Two deaths to Marjorie's account. She wasn't even asked to Ben's funeral – his family, too, assumed it was all her fault, murdering seductress that she was. And the baby didn't have one. The doctor just wrapped it up and took it away, as the vet does with a dead animal.

As for me, Chloe, I killed my mother, sending her into the hospital to have a hysterectomy she never really wanted. The womb, that little organ, so small when not in use, in her case past functioning, was cancerous after all and not merely, as I insisted, plugged with fibroids.

And it is amazing how once the word is said, the disease, dormant until the moment of recognition, proliferates and spreads. It is as if the body catches an idea and then can't get it out of its mind. Mother didn't want to go into the hospital: it was my idea. I was irritated by her passivity; I felt it must have a physical cause, somewhere in the roots of her female nature. If they'd only cut it out for her. I thought, excise it once and for all, she would be better, would look after herself, stop suffering, stop forgiving and understanding me. my children, my husband, and my friends, and her own oppression.

But all my mother did was die, as if that tiny, useless organ was the very mainspring of her being.

18

nine

Inigo drives his mother Chloe to Egden station. He drives without hesitation or fear, calmly and sensibly, clearly regarding the machine as a useful tool and not as an outlet for any suppressed and disagreeable aspects of his personality.

She cannot think what she has done to deserve this paragon, with his broad shoulders and friendly eyes, smooth olive skin and glossy black springing hair, so like his father in looks but so unlike in temperament, who deals with her affectionately, and his father with a respectful deference only slightly tinged with mockery: who passes his exams, takes drugs in moderation, avoids his enemies and understands his friends, who are multitude; and now not only drives her to the station, but offers to.

Perhaps, she thinks, out of the flat Essex countryside, which to her is featureless to the point of oppression, ripe only for cabbage-growing, air-fields and urban development, Inigo has wrung whatever is calm and good: or else, more like it, has made his own pocket of grace and beauty in which to grow, since God has declined to do it for him.

Even the hedgerows of her childhood have gone now, uprooted in the cause of progress and cabbage-cropping machinery. The sun has gone in. The early promise of the day has gone. The few trees left stand brown and crusty with old creepers: the fields are untidy with the winter's debris.

What fate, Chloe wonders, has condemned her to live her life in these few square miles of England? First, long ago, as Gwyneth's daughter, in Ulden, with Marjorie and Grace for friends. Then, after a brief respite, as Oliver's wife in Egden, ten miles down the railway line.

And where the Egden supermarket now stands, was the cottage-hospital where Grace was born, first and only child of Edwin and Esther Songford. Or so they assumed – Grace had a tendency to deny their parentage, and with it her duty towards them. And not without a withered shred of justification too – for a year or so after Grace's birth the market town of Egden and its outlying villages rocked to a scandal which closed the cottage-hospital entirely, the elderly and eccentric matron having conceived a fresh scientific system of tagging new babies according to their toe prints, which resulted in confused nurses and almost certain mis-identification of the infants, and the necessary reallocation, more than three years later, of six children amongst six couples, on the strength of blood-tests, physical appearance, established temperament and, of course, parental instinct. To the delight of the press, both national and foreign. Six for sure, and how many others not for sure? It was Grace's fancy to allocate herself in her mind, throughout her childhood and afterwards, to many a rich and noble couple. The belief that one has been switched at birth is common enough in little girls – and give Grace an inch, like a mad matron, and she'd take an ell, and never wash up for her mother, not even on the help's day off.

The Songfords lived in Ulden, in a solid Edwardian house called The Poplars. It had a good-sized garden, a wind-break of poplar trees, a swing for the children, a tennis court, large attics. a gardener, a daily, a pantry full of bottled fruits and jams, living rooms with chintzy curtains and squashy sofas,

Persian rugs, Chinese carpets, much bamboo furniture, Eastern bric-à-brac, mementos of the Indian army from which Grace's father had been cashiered, and one small bookcase containing the *Encyclopaedia Britannica* in twelve volumes, some guide books, an atlas, two novels by Dornford Yates, and three thrillers by Sapper and the *Light that Failed* by Rudyard Kipling.

It was to this house that Marjorie was evacuated, in 1940, coming on a train which stopped in Ulden by mistake. As for Chloe, she was on the train by mistake and it was only by this first fortunate accident that she and her mother Gwyneth, on her way to a domestic job at the Rose and Crown, were able to alight at Ulden.

When we are children, so much happens by mistake. As we grow older, and see a pattern to things, we are obliged to agree that there is no such thing as an accident. We make tactless remarks because we wish to hurt, break our legs because we do not wish to walk, marry the wrong man because we cannot let ourselves be happy, board the wrong train because we would prefer not to reach the necessary destination.

As for a train which stops at the wrong station, disgorges sixty children at the wrong place, and changes the course of all their lives, what are we to say to that?

ten

Picture the scene now, that autumn morning in 1940, as the train which carries Marjorie and Chloe approaches Ulden. Grace is waiting at the station with her father who is uncrowned king of the village, a princess dressed like a prince, in trousers and sweater, contrary to her mother's spoken request, but in accordance with her mother's deepest wishes. Her mother wanted a boy.

Chug-chug, puff-puff, across the flat fields. It's like a scene from Toy Town. The day is hot, and calm, and blue. There's panic in London, but not here. War clouds may be lowering somewhere over to the South East, but here they're nicely silver-lined with protected farm prices and agricultural subsidies. Full employment in the area at last, laying run-ways for Spitfires on Ulden Common. And out of that cloud, clear into the sunshine, comes the train with two coaches. Its white smoke drifts prettily over the fields, where they're taking out the daffodil bulbs and laying down potatoes.

Inside the Toy Town train, the picture is not so pretty. The coaches (all that could be spared) are crowded with terrified, weeping, rioting, vomiting and excreting children. There are no WCs. The floors are aswill. These are the evacuees from London. They have been briskly labelled and sent off for their own safety, out of the way of Hitler's bombs. Many haven't been able to say good-bye to their parents, most don't know what's happening to them. Quite a few would certainly rather be dead than here.

Little Chloe, of course, sits well-behaved and upright amidst the uproar, with her hand firmly in her mother Gwyneth's. Mothers are clearly a precious commodity on this particular train. And as for Gwyneth, she is feeling quite faint with distress. She is surrounded by misery and filth and deprived of her usual tools for coping – water, soap, bucket, and cloth.

Moreover, being on this train by accident, having mistaken Platform 7 for Platform 8, Gwyneth has been separated from two trunks in which are all her worldly possessions, neatly packed, folded, and interlarded with tissue. What now most preoccupies her is that in the elasticated silk pocket of the smaller trunk, along with the birth certificate and the careful roll of her husband's tiny landscapes, is his medical record card. This she stole from the hospital where he died, and this she is always fearful will be discovered by someone in authority and used as evidence of her crime. All the same, she has not been able to bring herself to destroy it. Now she wishes she had. Supposing the trunk is searched, the card found, and herself sent to prison? What will happen to Chloe?

What will happen to Chloe? It has been the theme song of Gwyneth's life for the past ten years.

Gwyneth resolves to destroy the card the minute the trunk reaches the Rose and Crown. She is starting a new life as barmaid and general domestic help, in return for board and lodging for herself and Chloe, and five shillings a week pocket money.

It is as well Gwyneth is so fond of cleaning, for being a widow with a child, this is the direction in which her future clearly lies.

eleven

Opposite Chloe and Gwyneth, sits a plain, thin, tearful child, with pale, deep-set, slightly squinty eyes peering out from beneath a creased brow. Marjorie. She has a mass of frizzy hair, which is kept back from her forehead by a battery of brown metal hair clips. She is not accustomed to the language and behaviour of the other children in the coach. Until recently Marjorie has lived a protected life. Then her father Dick upset everyone by volunteering for army service and her mother Helen took her away from her private school in the country, and enrolled her in the local state school which promptly closed. Now, re-opened for just one week, the school has been evacuated, and Marjorie with it.

Or, as the lovely, highly-principled Aryan Helen, Marjorie's mother, wrote to her handsome, tormented, highly-principled Jewish husband, Marjorie's father, only the night before:

'We're all in this together. It's best for Marjorie to take her chance with the others. I believe she's going somewhere in Essex. The country air should be good for her spots – I'm afraid London aggravated them shockingly. I'll be down to see her as soon as possible, though you know what the trains are like, and actually I've offered the house as a hospitality centre for Polish Officers and am acting as hostess, so you can imagine how busy I'm going to be. Don't worry – I've packed all your books and papers safely away in the attics – and cleared the library for the dancing. Poor fellows – what a dreadful business this war is: they deserve all the relaxation they can get.'

Dick, posted somewhere in Scotland to supervise the manufacture of Wellington Boots for the WRAC (the Women's Royal Artillery Corps), can hardly object to anything. If Helen did not consult him before removing Marjorie from her school, neither did he consult Helen before joining the army. He just came home one evening, late at his own party, and said, 'I've done it' and the next day he was gone. What kind of conduct was that?

If Helen has put his books and papers up in the attics, where the roof leaks, then it is his fault for not attending to the attic roof (as she has repeatedly asked him to do) but going to political meetings instead. If she wants to be unfaithful on the library floor (dancing always makes her sexy, and they both know it) or even on his bed, or even in the corridors in front of the very servants, then she will, and he deserves it, and he knows it. For Dick slept with a friend's wife – the second woman he'd ever made love to – the night Marjorie was born, and the friend's wife, in a flurry of either guilty malice or boredom, told Helen. All this Dick knows, and so is helpless.

Dick scarcely knows his daughter Marjorie. First she had a nanny, then she went away to school. He assumes she will be all right. She is not pretty, and he is sorry for her, but now the Army is his life. He can fight Hitler. Helen he cannot fight.

As for Helen, she simply cannot think what she did, during all those lovely laughing years of childless marriage, to deserve Marjorie. Who is plain and who fawns, and at whose birth she lost her husband.

Now little Marjorie, labelled, rejected and forlorn, sits and stares at Chloe's small gloved hand lying so securely in Gwyneth's, and starts to cry. Chloe, longing for the safety of a label round her neck, sickened by the noise and the smell of vomit and worse, begins to cry as well.

Gwyneth begins to cry too. She takes her spotless hand-kerchief from her pocket and dabs her daughter's face, and her own, and Marjorie's too, seeing it to be there.

And so the train arrives in Ulden. It was, as we know, meant to go on to Egden, and only the relief train on Platform 6 to stop at Ulden, but the driver has misread his instructions.

twelve

On the platform, Grace's father Edwin heads the welcoming committee. He is a stout bald man with a braying laugh and what used to be known as a fine military bearing. That is, he stands with his shoulders back and rigid, and his chin high. Thus bold and brave, properly pulled together, showing no sign of weakness and distress, he held out his hand for the cane his father wielded when his school reports were bad – as they always were – thus standing he took the proud parades of his later life, and thus he stood when the Court Martial dismissed him from the Service he had been born and bred to. It is an unhealthy way to stand, thus rigidly, and his back is often bad.

Edwin is nearing fifty now, and has made, he believes, a good adjustment to civilian life, although still, sometimes, even after fifteen years, he finds it strange to wake in a chintzy house to soft female voices, and not to the clanking of boots and the rattling of weapons and commands. Then he will lie late in bed, desperate, waiting for death, with Esther clattering the breakfast dishes more and more frantically below.

His eyes are blood-shot, hooded and close together in a

narrow face. His nose is long and thin: he has a handle-bar moustache which bisects his face with its sprouts of coarse reddish hair, and droops to hide the sensitivity of his mouth.

He is a busy man, though he is unemployed. Cashiered he may be – and the village knows it – but gentry he is, and he has his village obligations to fulfil. The flower shows, the fêtes, the sense of service, principles uttered in the pub. He has endless trips to London to make, to see the London lawyers who stand between him and an inheritance. He has his badly invested capital to worry about, and the problem of never eating into it, in the face of his wife's alleged extravagance. He has his own quite violent fits of anxiety and depression to cope with. Now he has the Home Guard to organize. And every night, he has the Rose and Crown to visit, where he holds court in the Cosy Nook from eight-thirty to closing time. He holds his liquor well, like a gentleman. Or so he believes.

His wife knows otherwise, but says nothing. Grace is Edwin's only child. It is a source of sorrow to both of them that there are no more children, but they have reached, these past years, such a state of sexual deadlock, so how could there be?

As for Grace, standing on the platform, she is in a bad temper.

thirteen

Grace does not want to share her home with an evacuee. And she is disappointed in her father for so meekly succumbing to the authority which says this is what she must do. She had hoped, moreover, to be sent away to boarding school when she was twelve. Now, with the advent of the war, and her father's inheritance even less likely to materialize, and his shares tumbling, it seems she will never be allowed to leave home.

And if she has to attend the village school – and it looks as if she will – her humiliation, she knows, will be profound. She doubts her own scholastic capabilities, not without reason, and suspects the grubby riff-raff may well do better than her at sums and spelling.

Grace is a lean, pretty, arrogant child, with a wide face, regular features, green eyes, silky red hair and the creamy matt complexion which sometimes goes with it. She resembles neither her father nor her mother. Nervousness makes her rude, and frustration makes her desperate, and for as long as she can remember, she has felt nervous and frustrated.

Thus the conversation goes that morning, at The Poplars, over a breakfast lovingly if clumsily prepared by Esther Songford, Grace's mother, Edwin's wife. Esther serves porridge, eggs, bacon, kidneys, toast, mushrooms – she was up early picking them so at least they are fresh, even though they are over-cooked – and Jackson's Breakfast Tea.

Rationing, of course, so far, affects only the mass of the urban proletariat. The well-to-do find their eating habits unaffected. It takes more than a paper war to alter the servile habits of grocers. The real one, presently, is to turn them into all-powerful tyrants, only too happy to be revenged upon their once mean and arrogant betters. In the meantime, it is not shortage of food but short tempers which makes breakfast at The Poplars an uneasy affair. Grace is pink with fury.

Edwin Stop sulking, Grace. We're having an evacuee and that is that. We have to set an example.

Ester She's not sulking, Edwin. She's just a little quiet. Please don't shout at her. Grace dear, eat up your porridge and don't aggravate your father.

Grace It's burnt.

Esther Only a little bit, dear.

Edwin (Sneering) Like the curate's egg, I suppose. Good in parts.

Esther I'm afraid it's the saucepans, Edwin. They've worn so thin. They really must be replaced. I'm ashamed to ask Mrs Dover to clean them.

Esther has been asking for new saucepans for seven years, in vain. Edwin controls the household money flow with stringent care. He is not so much mean, as fearful of sudden penury; living in dread of military, social or natural cataclysms which will sweep away pension, profits and property overnight. He fears the working classes, and the creeping evil of socialism, seeping under the doors of privilege like flood water.

And as Edwin walks the country lanes, swinging his blackthorn cane, the very model of a healthy-minded Englishman, he is not raising his face to meet God's good sun, as you might think, but sniffing the air for the first scent of the enemy's Poison Gas – expected to envelop Britain at any moment.

Edwin A bad workman blames his tools, Esther. I'm afraid new saucepans are out of the question now, of course. There's a war on. The metal is needed for guns. I'm surprised you should be so unpatriotic as to suggest it.

Esther Oh dear. I didn't think of it like that. I'm so sorry. I'll eat your porridge, Grace.

And Grace pushes her plate over, without gratitude. Mothers, in her view, are born to scavenge, to incorporate the evidence of their culinary shortcomings.

Grace Me? Share with some snotty-nosed urchin from the East End! Molly (a friend) says they had evacuees at her aunt's and they brought fleas and nits and wet the bed and never take off their vests at night and smell. You can't, daddy. Not in my house.
Esther Our house, Grace. We'll manage somehow. Think how much you've got to teach them. You must pass on your good fortune. Poor little things, separated from their mothers. Some of them have never even seen a sheep or a cow, let alone a farmyard, in all their lives. Daddy's quite right. We must all pull together, Grace dear, even the children.
Grace Why?
Esther To defeat Mr Hitler.
Grace Well I hope he wins.

Has she gone too far? Yes.

Edwin Grace, go to your room.
Grace But I haven't finished my breakfast.

She goes, all the same. She is frightened of her choleric father, especially at breakfast time. So's Esther.

Edwin Esther, you have let that girl get totally out of control. Let's hope an evacuee brings her down a peg or two. I've put your name down for a girl.

Esther Oh. I was rather hoping for a boy to help with the garden.

Edwin Garden! There isn't going to be a garden from now on. There's going to be a vegetable patch. I'm afraid this war's put paid to your flower shows and your prizes, Esther. No time for your frills and fancies any more.

Esther reels.

For Esther, having more sense of future than her husband, spends much time working in the garden, which flourishes in her care. The soft lawns, the neat flower-beds, the many roses – which make Edwin wheezy – have been her concern, her territory, for many years. Now it seems that Edwin feels at liberty to invade it.

Invasion is most surely in the air. And indeed, throughout the war years, the battle is to rage to and fro across the garden, sometimes Edwin's onions and carrots winning, sometimes Esther's herbaceous borders.

Esther, this first morning of declared hostilities, is most upset. She goes into the kitchen and tries not to cry into the washing-up water as she scrapes the burnt porridge saucepan clean.

Who is this Esther, Edwin's undoubted wife, Grace's alleged mother, Marjorie and Chloe's second mama? She is a vicar's daughter. She has a sense of service, and the feeling that for the children's sake, at least, she should remain brave, cheerful and uncomplaining. And like her husband she suffers

31

from a sense of loss. He lost his pride and his career. She lost her faith, waking up one morning to the dour sense of her father's dislike of her, the knowledge of his preference for his sons, and the feeling that God, even if He did exist, was certainly not good. These days it is Edwin, and only Edwin, who makes her unhappy, but he, like her father, is the fact of her existence, and she has become used to it.

She married late, at thirty, after her parents died and left her a little money. She has a faded prettiness, rather large, rather popping eyes, a lot of rather wispy hair, a lax skin. She works unceasingly, and inefficiently, about the house.

She sleeps apart from her husband because after Grace was born (and it was a difficult birth and she had hoped for a boy) intercourse was painful. Their physical union had been, at the best of times, distasteful to her, and difficult for him.

These days, just sometimes, when Edwin has drunk rather more than usual at the Rose and Crown, he will come into her bedroom and face both her distaste and his own probable inadequacy, and despise himself afterwards for his animal nature, and hardly be able to look her in the eye in the morning; the mother of his child so abused and debased, and he himself responsible for it. He would knock himself down, if he could, for the cad he is, and failing that, is ruder than ever to her.

Such a morning is this, and he hates her, and will grow carrots in her flower-beds, yes he will.

And she will not fight him, she will merely weep into the washing-up water. There is such a virtuous obstinacy about her, such a gentility in her bulky tweed skirts and shapeless twin sets, such an unawakened beauty in the body beneath them. This sense of his wife, so unused, drives him to great heights of irritation. He is apopleptic, sometimes. He thinks his heart will stop. As for her, she knows perfectly well that she wrongs him with her niceness, her sweetness and her moral supremacy. But what can she do? Sink to his crude masculine level? Never. She is too angry with him on such mornings.

She will grow roses and make him sneeze and wheeze.

So the day does not start well for Grace, or Edwin, or Esther. Now, at the station, Grace holds her father's hand – not because she has forgiven him, but because, amongst so many milling women and children, any male is valuable and must be seen to belong to her.

fourteen

Ulden station is usually a quiet and orderly place. It seldom sees more than five passengers at a time, and the station master, Mr Fell, a patient and domestic man, has both time and inclination to cherish it. The platform is clean and tidy, the name of the station is spelt out in flowers against a well-trimmed, grassy bank, and the Victorian waiting-room is lit by gas and warmed by a coal fire. Technically, the waiting-room is for the convenience of First Class passengers only, but in the winter months Mr Fell opens it to Third Class passengers as well.

Today the station is noisy, crowded and confused, and Mr Fell is suffering from an attack of asthma and gasping for breath in his office. The church bell rings out a kindly and welcoming peal – the last one for some time, since the Government is the next day to ban all bell ringing in case it assists the Germans in some way; the train which should never have stopped (as only Mr Fell knows, and he is too breathless to say), lets off steam; the Evacuation Officer reads out, undaunted, the names of children who do not exist.

Children cry, adults protest, dogs bark.

Edwin Songford, as is his custom, takes over. He silences the Evacuation Officer, the bells and the steam. He administers brandy from a hip flask (silver and leather, lined with glass) to Mr Fell, and establishes what is long since obvious, that either the train has stopped at the wrong station or contains the wrong children.

Evacuees had been expected from Hackney, in the East End. These children come from Kilburn, in West London.

Undaunted, indeed encouraged – for the reputation of the East End evacuees, who cannot tell an armchair from a WC, and who are followed everywhere by cunning, foul-mouthed, ferocious mothers, whom neither manners, lack of a bed, nor Government decree can keep away, has already spread amongst the more respectable classes of England – Edwin instructs the assembled villagers and gentry to select their own West London children according to taste. There is a rush for the strongest boys, and the most domestic looking girls.

Marjorie is left.

Grace, looking at her, sees the child most likely to depress her mother and irritate her father. She tugs Edwin's arm.

'Let's have that one,' says Grace.

34

'We'll have to,' says Edwin. 'It's the only one left.'

And wham, bam, so our lives are ordered.

But perhaps, if we look deeper, people are nicer and fate is kinder than we at first assume. Perhaps Grace did not choose Marjorie from spite, but because she perceived a child who expressed outwardly what she herself felt inwardly, and she wanted to help.

And perhaps it was not cupboard love which drove Chloe to choose The Poplars as her second home, and Esther as a second mother, and Grace and Marjorie as her friends, but her recognition of their grief, and their inner homelessness. It was not that she used them, or that they used each other, but simply that they all clung together for comfort.

Well.

fifteen

Ulden station is closed now, axed by Dr Beeching's axe. The railway track is used by ramblers. An amazing collection of wild and garden flowers grows along it, memorial of that long dead eccentric who once travelled the length and breadth of England's railways, scattering flower seeds by sackfuls, feeding them out of the carriage window into the rushing Edwardian wind.

Egden station, down the line, remains. Here Inigo leaves the adult Chloe, and she catches the train to London with two minutes to spare.

Inigo said she would.

Chloe arrives punctually at the Italiano. Marjorie does not. Marjorie is late, having, no doubt, important matters to delay her. Chloe is not sure whether to be glad for Marjorie, or irritated on her own behalf.

Marjorie, as a child, is all too anxious to please. If she is brave and good, she thinks, and does not complain, and is unfailingly helpful, her mother, whom she loves, will come and take her back home. It is a direct challenge to God, but God does not appear to notice, although Marjorie goes to church with Esther on both Wednesday evenings and Sunday mornings. (Grace, an early atheist, refuses to go to church: or at any rate faints whenever she does, which comes to the same thing.)

And still Helen does not come, to claim her child and take her home.

Marjorie, it is soon acknowledged by all, and whatever her motives, proves a better daughter to Esther than Grace, her natural daughter, ever was.

Marjorie makes the beds, appreciates the cooking, runs Edwin's bath, skips in and out of rooms prattling and eager, learns the piano, comes top in examinations, buries her head in Esther's lap when she is miserable, brings her wild flowers when she is happy, asks for advice about what to wear and what to say.

And still Helen her real mother does not even write a letter, let alone come to take her away.

Marjorie is frightened of Edwin, but masters her fear sufficiently to learn the disposition of the allied and enemy forces, and so be his companion as, year in year out, he follows the progress of the war through Europe, Africa, Asia on the maps on the library table.

And still Dick, her real father, does not come to take her away. How can he? He is in France, and if he writes to her, care of her mother, who is to say whether the letters arrive at their destination, or whether her mother simply forgets to forward them?

As for Grace, she is not interested in the war. Grace has disowned her parents, those plain and boring people now so fond of Marjorie, the cuckoo in her nest. Grace decides to be a changeling. She sulks, she lounges, she complains. She fails to make her bed; she makes trouble instead. She is artistic, and is proud of it. She draws. She paints. She models. She stares in the mirror, and has hysterics in the moonlight. She makes Chloe her confidante. Chloe, for all her mother is a waitress, is genteel, and clever, and funny, and regards adults – excepting only Gwyneth her mother – as equals and enemies. But she does not betray her opinion, as Grace does. And Edwin and Esther regard Chloe with relief, see her as a civilizing influence on Grace, and welcome her to the house. She appears quiet, polite, deferential, and clean. And she acts as some kind of helpful catalyst on Grace and Marjorie.

In Chloe's presence, Grace will behave quite civilly towards Marjorie, and even show her some degree of affection.

In the garden, Marjorie learns how to grow Christmas roses, and protect their pale bruised petals from the slugs and the wet.

Grace deigns to grow Brussels sprouts, under her father's instruction, and wins First Prize in the 1942 school competition.

Chloe, whose home is a clapboard room shared with her mother behind the Rose and Crown, learns how to prune the roses which so aggravate Edwin's asthma.

And still Helen does not write.

Marjorie works hard at school, and comes top of all her classes, except games, art, music and PT. She inspires pity and admiration both. She gives her sweet ration away, mostly to enemies, sometimes to friends, aniseed ball by peppermint drop, and if she is buying love, poor little thing, so, it is bought.

And still Helen does not come.

sixteen

Now, braver by far, Marjorie keeps Chloe waiting. Chloe is shown to a table between the kitchen door and the toilets. She asks for a Campari while she waits, and is given a Dubonnet. Chloe does not protest. Chloe understands the dilemma of the waiter, and forgives him. Chloe is in any case automatically on the side of the waiter, and not the diner.

Gwyneth, likewise, doing her bit at the Rose and Crown in those early years of the war, seldom protests.

Gwyneth is not unhappy, although usually exhausted, and always spends the morning of her day off in bed. She rises at six-thirty and seldom goes to bed before midnight, and has one day off a week.

In the mornings, fresh and restored after her heavy sleep, Gwyneth is energetic. She enjoys throwing open the bar windows to let the warm stale air out and the fresh cold air in.

She enjoys rubbing away at the beer rings on the tables, and later, when furniture polish runs short, all she says is 'never mind! What's wrong with elbow grease!' and rubs the harder.

Gwyneth even enjoys the admiration of men, so long as there's a bar between them and her: and since presently there is both an army camp and an airbase within ten miles of Ulden, the Rose and Crown is full of men in uniform, both officers and ranks, admiring her. She has a pretty, gentle face and a full bosom and dainty feet.

Gwyneth objects to nothing, not even clearing up vomit or washing out the WCs on a Sunday morning after a wild Saturday night. These are the droppings of the saviours of her country, after all. Someone has to do it, and when men are drunk, they miss. It is a fact of life.

Gwyneth can cook, and wait at table too, and when Mr and Mrs Leacock decide to do cooked lunches, Gwyneth does so, forgoing her midday break.

Gwyneth charms the customers and is never a source of scandal.

The Leacocks can't think what they did before Gwyneth was there to help.

They worked harder, actually.

'Shouldn't you ask for a raise?' Chloe once tentatively suggests to her mother, on one of those rare occasions when Gwyneth actually complains in her presence about the tenor and texture of her life. The Leacocks have opened a snack bar in the Cosy Nook, and it is not the extra work it means, but their failure to so much as mention their intention to Gwyneth, which now aggrieves her.

Gwyneth is shocked at the notion of asking for more.

'If they think I'm worth more they'll offer it,' she says. 'Besides, think how good they've been to me. Not many people will take on a mother with child. We're lucky to have a roof over our heads, Chloe. And there's a war on, and it's not fair to think of oneself. I'm just being silly, and it's the time of the month, that's all it is. A snack bar in the Cosy Nook would do very well, I'm sure.'

'Couldn't you ask the Leacocks to get another girl?' persists Chloe. 'You can't do everything yourself.'

'It wouldn't be fair. The girls should be doing warwork. What if some poor airman had to go without a parachute because I was being selfish?'

'Then couldn't you leave and get another job?' asks Chloe, who is tired of wearing dresses made of gingham tablecloths, discarded because of the cigarette holes. Gwyneth dressmakes for Chloe on her afternoons off.

Well, yes, Gwyneth knows it would be sensible, but she is terrified of change. She has the feeling that though here may be bad, the other side of the hill may be a good deal worse, and that in any case patience and suffering will surely be rewarded by God.

He's shown no sign of it so far, alas.

You might think, indeed, that God has taken a special dislike to Gwyneth. First He kills her father in a mining accident, and her mother of grief. Then He presents her, nice young Welsh girl that she is, living with her Nan and top of the class in Home Economics, with a handsome young miner, David Evans by name, to love and marry.

The Heavenly Hypocrite (Marjorie's description) smiles on the wedding, sending a blue and perfect day. Only, a month or so later, to fan to a burning flame a talent in her husband that has so far smouldered quite unnoticed, leading him to the conviction that he does not want to die in the pits, but to live in London and paint pictures, and keep the company of artists and writers.

Having led them to London and the Caledonian Road, He then makes Gwyneth pregnant and ill, in spite of her constant chapel-going, and thus renders it impossible for her to work, or David to earn a living other than by house painting. Then He sends bad weather – and since He also started David working in the pits at the age of twelve and weakened his lungs – David develops TB, declining steadily year by year, and is finally taken to the Heavenly Arms when Chloe is five, leaving Gwyneth strictly on her own.

And of the paintings which David did in the sanatorium, all, either from inclination, or from shortage of strength, or time, or canvas, only one measured more than 5″ × 3″, and that one was 6″ × 4″, and was in any case taken in payment by the landlady for the final week's rent.

Then Gwyneth, because she has Chloe, and nowhere to go, and no money, and her Nan is dead, has no alternative but to move into the first home which God offers her, sending her as He does David's friend Pat the Irish Pacifist to love and care for her.

Gwyneth is not unhappy here, with Pat in a caravan on Canvey Island. She can bring up Chloe in peace and fight a never-ending battle against the mud which rises like a tide around the caravan; and wash Patrick's clothes. And God has ensured that Pat's sexual energies should be increasingly whittled away by drink and talk, so that her sense of sin of being unfaithful to her husband – for that is what he still is, dry bones that God has made of him – is not too painful.

All the same, when war breaks out, and Pat is interned as a danger to the State, and the caravan is broken up by policemen looking for incriminating evidence, it is something of a relief to find God has decreed she move again.

A clergyman puts her in touch with the Leacocks.

One way and another, now, Gwyneth feels it is better to stay where she is and not provoke God to any further excesses.

Besides, Gwyneth is in love with Mr Leacock.

As for little Chloe, she goes to the village school, sits between Marjorie and Grace, and learns Latin and Greek and the intricacies of the feudal system while men in aeroplanes fight their masters' battles in the sky above her.

And after school, all going well, if Grace hasn't quarrelled with her, and if she's speaking to Marjorie, Chloe will go back to tea at The Poplars, where Esther makes her welcome. It is common knowledge in the village that Gwyneth is exploited, and that Chloe, fatherless, has a hard time. The woman in the sweet shop slips her peppermints and her teachers seldom scold. Chloe has been warmed and comforted and made cosy by misfortunes as far back as she can remember.

After tea Chloe will go back home to the Rose and Crown, and the room in the yard which she shares with her mother. Here, on the small table which fits tightly between the two hard beds, Chloe does her homework. A curtained corner serves as a wardrobe. They have few possessions. Under her mother's bed are her father's paintings, safely enclosed in a roll of cartridge paper. The paintings are of the pit-head he so hated and feared, but which might have been a lesser evil than the fogs and chills of London. Perhaps he came to this conclusion before he died, because the paintings, so scrupulously and minutely done, seem to be of some loved and magical scene.

And underneath Chloe's bed, in a cardboard box, with the family birth, wedding and death certificates, is Gwyneth's photograph album. Gwyneth as a child, surrounded by parents, cousins, uncles, aunts. What became of them? Chloe does not know, except they are lost and scattered. And the wedding photographs too, on that especially brilliant day, the shadows of the bride and groom sharply etched against the chapel wall.

Chloe studies the photographs carefully, but rarely. She is frightened lest the black and white dots of her father's photograph will eventually replace her own fragile memory of him. And so they do, of course, in the end.

Chloe knows his fever chart by heart. She keeps the stolen medical card beneath her mattress. His temperature was normal on the day he died, she notes – TERMINAL, someone has scrawled upon the card, in red.

Good-bye, father.

At seven, Chloe has supper in the Rose and Crown kitchen with her mother. It is not a lavish meal. Well, there's a war on. Gwyneth could help herself to pies from the snack bar but is unwilling to take advantage.

After supper, Chloe helps to wash the beer mugs. She is not paid for her work, but as the Leacocks say, it keeps her out of mischief.

And Gwyneth likes to spend this time alone with her daughter: she can instruct her in the ways of the world.

How is Gwyneth to know that the platitudes she offers, culled as they are from dubious sources, magazines, preachers and sentimental drinkers, and often flatly contradicting the truths of her own experience, are usually false and occasionally dangerous? Gwyneth retreats from the truth into ignorance, and finds that the false beliefs and half-truths, interweaving, make a fine supportive pillow for a gentle person against whom God has taken an irrational dislike.

'Red flannel is warmer than white,' maintains Gwyneth.

'Marriages are made in heaven.'

'Marry in haste, repent in leisure.'

'Hard work never hurt anyone.'

'The Lord helps those who help themselves.'

'See a pin, pick it up, all the day you have good luck.'

'The good die young.'

'Never have a bath when you've got the curse.'

'A blow on the breast leads to (whispered) cancer.'

'The Lord looks after his own.'

'You can always tell a lady by her shoes.'

And so on. Chloe, polishing glasses, tired and sleepy, listens patiently and tries to make sense of it all. She is a good girl.

Gwyneth, disturbed by the amount of time Chloe is

spending at The Poplars, worried in case Chloe is making a nuisance of herself, is emboldened to ask for an extra half-day off so she can spend more time with her daughter. At which Mrs Leacock, that bright, hard-eyed bustling little woman, a devout Catholic, utters a shriek of dismay, calls on Mother Mary, and takes to her bed with a pain in her chest, and for a day or two a cloud comes over Mr Leacock's kind and ruddy face, while he considers the request. He seems not so much annoyed, as grieved.

Gwyneth is horrified to have caused so much trouble. She withdraws her request, but the Leacocks mull over it for weeks. They seem unable to let the incident go, gnawing at it as if they were starving and had been at last offered a bone.

If the problem is money, Mr Leacock says, Chloe could be allowed to clean the guests' shoes – there are eight guest bedrooms by now – for two shillings a week.

'It's not the money—' says Gwyneth—

'If the problem's tiredness,' says Mrs Leacock, descending the stairs all of a tremble, 'I can get hold of some Ministry of Food Orange Juice. They're selling some off cheap in Stortford – too much preservative so the babies won't drink it – but perfectly all right for adults. That'll perk you up.'

So Gwyneth doesn't get her extra afternoon off. But before Chloe starts work on the shoes each morning, she is given a spoonful of thick orange syrup, tart with sulphuric acid, from the crate Gwyneth now has to find room for under her bed.

One winter morning, groping for Chloe's mouth in the dark – blackout curtains are tacked over the windows at night – Gwyneth laughs.

45

'You have to laugh,' she says. 'It's a funny old life.'

Ha-ha.

So now, when the Portuguese waiter brings a Dubonnet instead of a Campari, in a not very clean glass, Chloe says nothing. She is aware that he especially dislikes women customers, seeing it as a humiliation to have to serve them. She is aware that he is overworked, underpaid, exploited and helpless in a strange land, and that the greatest insult of all is her awareness of these things.

And still she sits there.

seventeen

At twelve-fifty Marjorie arrives at the Italiano. She is dressed in expensive leather but manages to look not so much erotic, as fearful that the weather might turn. Chloe, who is tall and very slender, and has small hands and feet, and a refined and gentle face, and short cropped dark hair, wears a pale silk blouse, and pale suède trousers. She spends a lot of Oliver's money on clothes, ever fearful that the days of tablecloth dresses, holed by cigarettes, might return.

'You're looking more like a boy than ever,' says Marjorie. 'Do you think you should?'

Marjorie carries a bright green plastic launderette bag, stuffed full of damp washing.

'And we can't possibly sit at this table,' says Marjorie. 'Are you mad? We're practically in the Gents.'

'Don't make a fuss,' begs Chloe, but Marjorie has them

removed forthwith to a table near the window. She stows the launderette bag beneath her chair, and beams at the waiter, but he remains hostile. They order *antipasto*. He brings dried-up beans, hard-boiled eggs in bottled mayonnaise, tinned sardines and flabby radishes prettily arranged in bright green plastic lettuce leaves.

Marjorie eats with relish. Chloe watches in wonder.

'Why don't you kill her?' asks Marjorie, meaning Françoise. 'I can let you have some tablets.'

'I am perfectly happy, Marjorie,' says Chloe. 'I don't suffer from sexual jealousy. It's a despicable emotion.'

'Who told you that? Oliver?'

'We all live as best we can,' says Chloe, 'and surely we are entitled to take our sexual pleasures as and when we want.'

'Yes, but they're getting the pleasure and you aren't.'

'I'm not a highly-sexed person, these days.'

'Who says so? Oliver?'

But Chloe can hardly remember, of her and Oliver, who said what first.

'I behaved very badly towards Oliver,' says Chloe. 'If this is his revenge it's very mild. I can endure it. I would rather not talk about it. Whose is the washing?'

'Patrick's.'

'I thought you'd stopped that kind of thing,' says Chloe.

Marjorie is looking tired. It is one of her bleeding days, Chloe can tell. Her face is drawn and tired, and her hair is a wayward frizz.

'Someone has to do it,' says Marjorie.

'Not necessarily,' says Chloe. 'He could leave it until the

council issued a compulsory fumigation order.'

'Patrick's not as bad as that,' says Marjorie.

'I may be looking like a boy,' says Chloe, 'but doesn't it seem strange that you, a high-powered television producer, should be doing Patrick's laundry? You aren't married to him. You don't even sleep with him.'

'How do you know?' inquires Marjorie. 'Though of course you are right. How can I have a sex life? I bleed all the time. What upsets me is the way his other lady friends behave. A lot of them must have automatics and I don't see why they shouldn't take their turn. If they're strong enough to go down those steps – and lately the local hippies have been using the area as a shit-house – they're strong enough to face his washing. All my stuff goes to the laundry – but I haven't the nerve to send his as well. It's not the money which stops me – it's the humiliation.'

'If you don't mind,' says Chloe, 'I'd rather not talk about Patrick either. It's unlucky.'

Patrick Bates lives in a filthy basement room and paints pictures in the half-dark. They fetch a good deal of money – although not quite so much as they did at the height of his fame, ten years ago. Patrick is reputed to be very wealthy, although he swears he burns the money instead of banking it. Certainly he spends very little. Since the death of Midge his wife he has become more and more eccentric. He danced on her grave when she died.

Patrick's paintings were always small: now they are becoming miniature. He will confine a whole seraglio on a canvas marked out by a bread-and-butter plate and use cosmetic brushes to apply the paint. He is a miser. He scrounges food and clothes. He looks older these days than the forty-seven he is. His cheeks have sunk over toothless gums – he won't spend money at the dentist. He pulls out his own teeth if they ache.

Chloe has not seen Patrick for nine years. Not since she went to visit him to ask for some money towards Kevin and Kestrel's upkeep – Oliver was chafing under the burden of supporting them – and came away with Imogen instead.

Now she prefers not to talk or think about Patrick. She wants him out of her life. She wants him to keep away from the children. He is elemental, disruptive and mischievous. He has moved through her life like the Angel of Death, disguised sometimes as a malicious gnome and sometimes like Pan himself.

'What was he doing, the Great God Pan, Down in the reeds by the river?' she says now to Marjorie. They learned the poem by heart, at thirteen, competing for an elocution prize. Chloe won.

'What indeed? We have all always wanted to know that,' says Marjorie tartly. 'And as for Patrick, you ought to talk about him. He is all those children's father.'

'Sometimes half a father is worse than no father at all,' says Chloe. 'And they have dozens of his paintings on the wall, so his presence is always with them, along with his genes. Oliver will keep buying them, in spite of everything. And you can get so many on a wall, I sometimes think there will be no end to it.'

'Patrick will drink himself to death, and then there'll be an end to it,' says Marjorie.

Chloe is not sorry to hear this.

49

'And then Oliver will have the largest collection of Bates paintings and Bates children in the whole country. He'll like that.'

'It's not funny,' says Chloe. She wishes she had not come up to London.

'Perhaps Oliver wishes to corrupt the children,' persists Marjorie. 'And that's why he buys so many. Apart from just wanting to annoy you, of course.'

Patrick paints women in all shapes, conditions and positions. Chloe has never considered them to be a depraving influence in the house. Oliver told her, in the days when he played poker with Patrick, and told her things and she believed them, that all Patrick's latent generosity was revealed in his work.

'Why should Oliver want to annoy me?' asks Chloe.

'Heaven knows,' replies Marjorie. 'If it was in script form I could tell you. As it's real life I have no idea.'

She becomes gloomy, quite suddenly, as was always her way.

'I hate my life,' she says. 'Everything through a glass darkly, and the only reward lousy lunches in lousy cafes with friends too busy making a mess of their lives to care what happens to me.'

'I care,' says Chloe, who has known Marjorie too long to be embarrassed by such speeches. 'I thought you liked your work, anyway.'

'My work? My work is nothing. Flickers on a screen. I've worked so hard to get where I have and now it seems to mean nothing. Just four different offices in as many weeks, arguments about whether or not I'm entitled to a carpet, and an executive producer over me instead of a producer. They'll never trust me.

Why should they? I can't take their beastly flickers seriously. It's not real life. I tell them so and they look offended.'

'You are living the life you chose,' says Chloe. 'You should have married and had children.'

'I didn't, so I couldn't. I shall never have what I really want. I am one of nature's dead-ends. I am a walking Black Hole. I have a hollow inside me. a bottomless pit, and you could shovel all the husbands and children in the world into me, and still it wouldn't be filled up. It's the same with you, and the same with Grace. We none of us will ever get what we needed, I wish a bomb had dropped on us, and put us out of our misery.'

Marjorie, Grace and me.

What was it we needed?

Not much. Perhaps only the fathers and mothers with which we started. Perhaps to own and not to disown us. Mothers to love us, and put themselves out on our behalf. To relinquish life as we grabbed hold of it. And smile as they did so.

Failing that, what do you get?

Marjorie, Grace and me.

Little Marjorie, tagging along, always reproachful. Just occasionally scouring the equanimity of the day with some excoriating remark. Should she be forgiven?

'The barmaid's daughter,' Marjorie calls Chloe, coming home from school the day Chloe wins the elocution prize. 'You can always tell she's coming by the smell of beer.'

It isn't true, of course. Gwyneth and Chloe are the most frequent washers Ulden has ever seen. They soap, they rub and scrub and poke, and rinse their bodies clean. They even trade in butter coupons for soap. Between their toes and behind their ears and under their breasts, and in their navels, above all in their navels, all is clean and pure. They rub and scrub away at guilt and resentment and restlessness, and in the end they wear them thin.

And how proud they are, the pair of them, enduring and forgiving to the end. They have a row of boxes on the window sill, each with its share of coins. For gas, light (their room is metered), books, fares, dinner money, pocket money. Sitting in their parlour, counting out their money. While the king sits somewhere else, on someone else's bed, eating bread and honey. Mr Leacock.

He drinks too much. His face is flushed. His hand is broad and firm. He lays it on Gwyneth's arm, and she trembles and smiles. Chloe sees.

'Poor man,' says Gwyneth. 'His wife isn't good to him. It's a dreadful way to live.'

Understand and forgive, says Gwyneth. Understand husbands, wives, father, mothers. Understand dog-fights above and the charity box below, understand fur-coated women and children without shoes. Understand school – Jonah, Job and the nature of the Diety; understand Hitler and the Bank of England and the behaviour of Cinderella's sisters. Preach acceptance to wives and tolerance to husbands; patience to parents and compromise to the young. Nothing in this world is perfect; to protest takes the strength needed for survival. Grit your teeth, endure. Understand, forgive, accept, in the light of your own death, your own inevitable corruption. What is there to want that's reasonable to want? How can wanting be reasonable, when soon you'll be dead? Await that day with composure and dignity, that is all you can do.

Oh mother, what you taught me! And what a miserable, crawling, snivelling way to go, the worn-out slippers neatly placed beneath the bed, careful not to give offence.

eighteen

The plastic lettuce leaves have been empty for a long time. The waiter avoids Marjorie's eye. Marjorie, who is always better in adversity, quite perks up. And thus the conversation goes.

Marjorie Will you be seeing Grace this afternoon?
Chloe Yes.
Marjorie (*Put out*) I'm glad you could find time for me, then. I'm surprised you bothered.
Chloe Don't be silly.
Marjorie I don't see much of Grace, these days. She's sorry for me and I'm sorry for her, but she always wins.
Chloe She asked after you.
Marjorie Big deal. Is she still with her infant porn king?
Chloe He isn't an infant. He's twenty-five.
Marjorie I suppose we must be grateful he's not seventeen. You're not denying he's a porn king? He makes skin flicks.
Chloe He doesn't. He makes very good, very sensitive films. When he can raise the money.
Marjorie Who says so? Oliver?
Chloe Yes.

53

Marjorie He's one of Oliver's hangers-on, I believe.

Chloe Why are you so against Oliver?

Marjorie Because I'm hungry and the waiter's being bloody. And because he makes you unhappy.

Chloe No he doesn't. Men don't make women unhappy. Women make themselves unhappy.

Marjorie Who says so? Oliver?

Chloe Yes.

The waiter takes away the plastic lettuce leaves and brings the spinach and Greek sausage Marjorie maintains is the speciality of the house. It has been kept a long time, under a hot grill, and the sausage frizzles on the plate, and the spinach, once aswill, is now riveted in a green crust. They eat.

Marjorie When you see Grace do tell her I'm without a gentleman friend.

Chloe Why should I?

Marjorie It will make her happy. I do want Grace to be happy.

Chloe grits her teeth and chews her sausage, and says nothing.

Marjorie I don't really mind Grace being happy. It's just she always has such a good time. I know it's at other people's expense, trample, trample on all and sundry. I just wish I had the courage. Perhaps I could have a baby, while there's still time and give it to you, Chloe?

Chloe No thank you.

Marjorie You see what I mean. I suppose she's just off somewhere?
Chloe Cannes.
Marjorie What a lovely way to live. Litigate in London and copulate in Cannes. She always did have everything.
Chloe Not really. You took a lot of it.
Marjorie What do you mean?
Chloe Esther and Edwin. You stole their affection.
Marjorie It wasn't what I wanted.

She seems quite startled. It makes a change.

'Isn't this sausage good,' says Marjorie, automatically, chewing hard. It is her habit, while marking time in her head, to praise whatever appears before her. 'Oh jolly dee,' Marjorie would cry, back in the Ulden days, as Esther served up the stiff red blackberry jelly everyone hated. 'Scrumptious,' as the boiled onions appeared, knobbly beneath the lumpy white sauce, which Esther made with lard, grey flour, milk powder and water.

And everyone suffers for Marjorie, so transparent are her pains, so noble her efforts to be good and happy.

Family life at The Poplars. Making England what it is. The backbone of the nation, set rigid against change.

Esther likes to save things from corruption. She makes cold sago pudding into soup by adding tomato sauce and salt. She makes jam from the over-ripe sodden plums in the grass at the end of the garden. She presses flowers to save them from decay. She turns and re-turns the sheets to stave off the inevitable holes. She prays and prays for her soul to be saved, and that Marjorie, Grace and Chloe should be good and happy. She prays that Edwin should be forgiven.

When Edwin is away fishing or seeing his solicitors, Esther is brisk and efficient. When he returns, she lapses into a vague clumsiness, letting the saucepans burn, the baths overflow: she trips and sprains her ankle.

There comes a time when all is not well with Edwin. His Home Guard troop is incorporated into a larger unit, and he loses his command. The blow drives him back into the Rose and Crown, from which, encouraged by military responsibilities, he has been diffidently emerging, like a mole into the light of day. And back in the Cosy Nook, alas, all is not as it should be. Sometimes a trooper or a common airman will take over the corner seat which he regards as his, and will not vacate it even on request. His perfectly ordinary and patriotic remarks extolling Churchill's conduct of the war will on occasions, if there's a particularly low crowd in the bar, be met by a gale of laughter. Sometimes, too, the beer runs out.

Edwin ages ten years in as many months. Alcohol traces pink stress marks over his face. His moustache turns grey. He suffers from fits of temper, depression, asthma, and acute irritation with his wife. And his stomach, normally tough enough to cope with even Esther's cooking, now revolts at the very thought of dinner.

He becomes an expert in domestic sadism.

Envisage one Sunday, not untypical of those months, when distress, frustration and despair swirled in Edwin's mind and distorted his view of the world and the people that inhabited it.

The sun shines. It is high summer. The sea calls. There is enough petrol in the tank to get the car to the coast and back. Esther has made sandwiches with real butter – having saved everyone's ration for a week – and bloater paste. Chloe has provided four hard-boiled eggs – given to her mother by a hard-drinking farmer, in the vain hope of preferential treatment on days when beer is short and the whisky run out. Grace has put on her best dress – red cotton spotted with blue, and Marjorie has swept out the Riley and polished its real leather seats. They have borrowed a beach-ball from neighbours, and with difficulty, for girls grow apace and clothing coupons are short, have acquired decent swimming suits for everyone.

Departure is timed for ten o'clock. As the hall clock strikes the hour, Esther and the girls assemble by the garage. (Edwin does not like to be kept waiting, at the best of times, and if he is, is quite capable of making the entire journey in total silence.) By ten-fifteen Edwin has not appeared.

Chloe, being the one least likely to provoke bad behaviour, is sent to the library to fetch him. Edwin sits staring morosely out of the window. He is dressed in his Home Guard uniform, not in the expected slacks and sports shirt.

'We're ready. Mr Songford,' says Chloe.

'Ready?' He seems puzzled.

'We're going to the sea,' she ventures.

'The sea? The country is on the verge of disaster, and we are going to the sea? What madness is this?'

'We're waiting,' says Chloe, humbly. Edwin strides out to the garage. Chloe trots behind. She is wearing her mother's white sandals. They both wear size two and have difficulty

57

finding shoes to fit their feet.

'So!' Edwin is jocular. His teeth gleam in a too wide smile. 'Is our journey really necessary?'

'Yes it is, daddy,' says Grace. 'Before I die of boredom.'

'We're all ready and waiting,' says Esther. 'And a lovely packed lunch! I can hear the sea calling us, can't you?'

'I polished the seats,' says Marjorie.

Edwin stands, and smiles, and waits. Esther falls into the trap. She always does.

'Are you going to wear your uniform?' she asks.

'Why, do you think I shouldn't? Am I not entitled to it?'

'Of course you are, dear. I just thought it might be a little hot. Such a lovely day!'

'You must allow me to be the judge of my own body temperature.' Edwin's face begins to flush. A vein in his temple throbs. The children move away, pack themselves and their belongings into the car, and hope against hope.

'I shouldn't have mentioned it,' says Esther. 'I'm sorry.'

'But you have mentioned it,' remarks Edwin. 'So shall we investigate the remark? You want me to be the only man on that beach not in uniform. I am afraid I am not the sort of person to take such things lightly. You have organized this outing, Esther, solely to humiliate me in front of every whipper-snapper we pass. I see through you, Esther.'

'But darling—'

'Too hot in uniform! You are impossible.'

He stalks back towards the house.

'Edwin,' she calls plaintively after him. 'Edwin, where are you going?'

'To my study.'

'What for?'

'To write letters. Should I not?'

'But we were going to the coast,' she is in tears. 'I've made sandwiches.'

Edwin shuts himself into his study. The girls clamber out of the car, embarrassed and disappointed. Esther pulls herself together, and says, brightly,

'I'm afraid daddy's tired. Shall we have a lovely picnic instead, down by the river? We can carry the basket. It isn't far.'

But they shake their heads. They won't. The day is spoilt.

Edwin remains in his study. Eleven passes, and twelve. What slim chance there is of his relenting, evaporates. The heat is oppressive. The house is silent. Esther fries the sandwiches for lunch. Grace draws. Marjorie does her homework. From under the study door drifts a miasmic cloud of hate, gloom and resentment.

Chloe goes home at tea-time to the Rose and Crown, and returns the eggs to her mother.

They are not good days for Edwin, or for anyone.

Sometimes Esther wonders if she could learn to drive, but the first obstacle, that of asking Edwin to teach her, is insurmountable.

Envisage now another scene, one summer Sunday some twelve years later, when Grace is in the middle of her dream marriage to Christie. (Grace had a dream marriage the way other women have – or don't have – dream kitchens.)

Into the Mercedes, waiting in the drive, are packed Grace's two little children – a pigeon pair – the Spanish nursemaid, a picnic hamper packed by Harrods (*alia tempora, alii mores*) and a case of champagne for the charming friends they mean to visit that day in their cottage on the Sussex coast.

Grace leans, all warm and contented, against the long bonnet of the Mercedes. Her high plump bosom is delicately revealed by the low-cut white cotton dress which she wears. She stares at the sky, and watches the birds. Does she think of the past, of her mother and father, and other outings, in other years? Probably not. Grace makes few connections between then and now.

But here comes Christie, leaping down the steps, all vital executive energy and financial acumen. Six feet one inch, broad-shouldered, clean-shaven, with a clear-cut Aryan face, her highly desirable husband.

He stops short, seeing Grace. She smiles at him. It is a slow and languorous smile; she offers him a remembrance of past pleasures; she has not smiled at him like that before, nor will she again.

The night before has been rich with strange untoward sexual events (thanks to a careless remark dropped by Grace's gynaecologist) as new to Grace as to Christie, who had thought the missionary position – he on top of her – with his eyes closed, to mark the limits of married conduct, and anything else the mere substance of pornography. Women, like men, the gynaecologist told Grace, have orgasms, and though her mouth could scarcely bring itself to utter the word aloud, so rich, strange and dangerous a concept it seemed, she had whispered the information into Christie's ear as they lay together in their marital bed.

In the morning, this feat accomplished, she is languid, replete and gratified. But what is Christie saying? Why is he calling her names? He who so embraced and pleasured her in the night – and yes, at breakfast ate his bacon and drank his coffee in so unusually companionable a way – what are these words he uses now? Exhibitionist, slattern? What has she done? Her dress? Exposing her breasts like a tart?

But the day is hot. She chose the dress because the day is hot, and that is all, she swears – and not, as he alleges now, to seduce their host in his Sussex cottage, husband of her dearest friend. Christie is cruel, unjust, sadistic. Her happiness crumbles. The children cry. The nursemaid is white with horror.

Now, it is true that the host much admires Grace's bosom. It is true that she would like to annoy her friend. It is true that the events of the night before and the power she then exerted over Christie, and which he now so fears and resents, have extended her erotic fancies towards all the men in the world, and not just her best friend's husband. Christie is not so wrong as he in his poor cold heart suspects he is. So far as Grace is concerned she is totally innocent. She chose the dress because the day is hot; her eyes fill with tears. Christie has ruined her day, her life, her future. She stammers hurt and bitter words, and he stalks off silently to his office.

It is the first Sunday in seven months he has taken off from work, and see how she has ruined it?

Grace tells this story often, as evidence of Christie's malevolence and general impossibility, and her own fortitude, for her response to the incident was, very sensibly, to learn to drive, and to pass the test first time. And since Christie would not let her drive the Mercedes in case she damaged the gearbox, she sold herself for fifty pounds to an Armenian violinist in his bedroom in the Regents Park Hotel, in order to buy a car of her own. Or so she said.

Though Christie's second wife Geraldine, the social worker, said very differently.

'I know for a fact,' she said to Chloe once, 'that Grace only passed the test on the fourth try. As for sleeping with an Armenian for money, that is typical of one of Grace's sick fantasies – and part of her mental illness, I'm afraid, and further evidence, if any is necessary, that she is not fit to see the children at weekends. The Regents Park Hotel! Women just don't behave like that, and if they did, I'm sure the hotel porter doesn't let them in. It's a very respectable place. I've been there to tea. And fifty pounds! Who would pay that much for Grace? Armenians are a very shrewd race, the market price for prostitutes is three pounds, and our currency is not all that difficult to master. She is quite frigid, poor Grace, according to Christie, and that of course is part of her trouble.

'As for that Sunday, Christie didn't go to the office in a temper, but because he'd had a phone-call to say one of his buildings was falling down, and he was needed on site.'

This last statement certainly had the ring of truth. Christie was a civil engineer and his buildings were frequently falling down.

Chloe quite liked Geraldine, and was sorry for her, believing Grace when she said that Christie had married Geraldine, that respectable young woman, merely to gain custody of the children. And though Geraldine, at that time, possessed to a marked degree the cool and irritating smugness of the untried and childless wife, who knows that a little goodwill, a little common sense and a little self-discipline will solve all problems – be they matrimonial, social or political – Chloe knew that life and time would soon cure all that.

As indeed they did. Once the children were safely and securely adopted, and Grace had renounced all interest in them, Christie drove Geraldine out, and a long and humiliating process it was, and entered his day-long marriage to the greedy if blissful flower-child California; and thus Geraldine found herself the mother of two children whom she neither liked particularly nor had the means to support, and was no longer heard to make remarks such as –

'No such thing as a bad child, only bad parents.'

or

'People have only themselves to blame.'

– and was much the nicer for it.

nineteen

By the time the waiter takes away their empty plates the Italiano has almost emptied. Marjorie, nevertheless, consults the menu and orders *zabaglione* for Chloe and herself. Marjorie never gives up, never saves herself, thinks Chloe. She invites trouble, in order to face it. She struggles in some monstrous swimming-pool of dire events, forever almost drowning, forever bobbing up again, reproachful and gasping for breath, and forever declining to stretch out her hand and be saved.

'How's your mother?' inquires Chloe. It was Helen who pushed Marjorie into the pool, in the first place, and that's why she won't get out.

Yes. Listen to her now.

'Mother? Mother's marvellous!' says Marjorie. 'She'll be seventy next week. She was in *Vogue* last month. 'Didn't you see? No? I thought you'd be sure to read *Vogue*. She gives fashionable dinner parties for the gay political crowd. All very camp. I don't know if she knows that's what it is, but it's something for old ladies to be appreciated by somebody, isn't it, and they all adore each other over the lace napery and the flower pieces and the *Coq à la Tunisie* cooked by a sublime little Suliman imported from the Bosphorus.'

'I hope he washes the napery,' says Chloe, to whom tablecloths have always been a burden, for her husband Oliver cannot digest food without one, and she has no washing machine.

'I do them for her,' says Marjorie. 'I collect them on Sunday, do them by hand in luke-warm suds on Sunday afternoon, dry them in my little yard, and send them back in a taxi on Monday morning from the office. I wish I could move in with her and look after her properly but you know how independent she's always been.'

'You do quite a lot of washing, these days,' says Chloe. 'What with your mother's table cloths and Patrick's undies.'

'What else do I have to do in my spare time?' asks Marjorie. 'And who else would do it?'

The *zabaglione*, astonishingly, is rich, warm and good. The waiter even smiles as he offers it. Perhaps it was shame, rather than resentment, which had so afflicted him. Marjorie smiles back. She has, after all, won a victory.

'She could pay a laundress,' Chloe ventures.

'Oh no.' Marjorie is shocked. 'She has to be very careful. You know how worried the elderly become about their futures – having so little of it left, I suppose. She's even having to sell the Frognal house.'

'Not before time.' Chloe has not liked Helen since she overheard her commenting on Esther's liberalism in letting her daughter associate with the village children. Chloe, that is, the bar-maid's daughter. Or so Chloe assumed.

The Frognal house, scene of Helen's early happiness with Dick, has been unoccupied for the past fifteen years, while Helen toys with the notion of selling it. Occasionally hippies or squatters move in, and move out again, of their own accord.

'She has a sentimental attachment to it,' says Marjorie. 'It's hard for her.'

'I expect it's past repair now,' says Chloe. 'And that's what she's been waiting for. It will have to be pulled down, there'll be planning permission for flats, and she'll make a fortune.'

'It's not like that at all,' says Marjorie. 'Nothing could destroy that house. It's solid concrete. She's not a calculating person at all, she just needs the money.'

Over the years Helen has sold the paintings Dick bought in the twenties. She has done very well from them. Unfortunately the first editions, which would have fetched even more, were left under the leaky roof and eventually disintegrated.

When Dick left for the war there had been only one loose tile on the roof, but the anti-aircraft batteries on Hampstead Heath had shaken the ground and loosened thirty-two more. Or so a fire watcher, up on the roof with his bucket of sand, waiting for incendiaries, had once told Helen. And she, going up to the attic one rainy day, looking at those mildewing pages, could not bring herself so much as to move the volumes from beneath the drips.

His books. His fault. And only one chance for anyone.

'I don't know why you don't live at Frognal,' says Chloe to Marjorie, although she knows quite well why, and how painful the reason is. But as Marjorie gets warmer and happier Chloe finds herself becoming more and more disagreeable. 'All that space going to waste.'

And 'I hope your mother asks you to her smart parties in return for all that washing,' knowing full well that Helen doesn't.

And finally, 'Do you wash Patrick's sheets as well as his undies? The ones he uses with Lady This and Lady That while you wait outside?'

Marjorie seems pained rather than angry.

'You're not usually like this,' she says. 'There is something the matter. That's why you wanted to see me. Well, we all know what it is. You've stayed married to the wrong man for twenty years, for reasons that have more to do with snobbery, greed and fear, than anything else.'

Chloe is silent. Presently Marjorie says,

'I wonder why I keep coming to this dreadful place? The service is appalling, the food is rancid, the waiter is round the bend, and they put us at this draughty table on purpose.'

'That's right,' says Chloe.

Marjorie begins to laugh. Chloe begins to snivel.

'Oh Marjorie,' says Chloe.

'Oh Chloe,' says Marjorie. 'Nothing ever changes.'

'Yes it does,' says Chloe. 'It must.'

But it doesn't really. This is what it's like now and then it was much the same. You ask for bread, and get given stones.

twenty

At last! Helen comes down to Ulden to visit her daughter Marjorie. How beautiful Helen is, how elegant, how timeless; how she charms Esther Songford and how she flirts with Edwin, laying a scarlet fingernail on his dusty lapel, mesmerizing.

She comes in a chauffeured car. She is all cream and roses. Her stockings are purest silk; her underskirt, just briefly showing, is lined with lace. Her eyes are wide and innocent in an oval face, her pale hair waves sweetly round her ears.

(Dick, far away, cold and hungry, dreams of Helen in the arms of enemy officers on the Library floor beneath a leaky ceiling, and well he might. Helen does not dream of Dick.)

'Oh my dears,' she says, 'my dears.' And she embraces all and sundry, but Marjorie somehow less than anyone. And

67

Esther, who seldom touches anyone, is gratified and enchanted by the smooth warmth of Helen's hand; and the feel of another cheek in soft proximity to her own, so gentle and affectionate, amazes her.

'The times are so dreadful,' mourns Helen, 'this war is such a shocking business. I am grateful to you for looking after Marjorie. She has settled in so happily here.'

'She can stay as long as she likes,' says Esther Songford. How clumsy she feels, in her old brown skirt and cardy; how earnestly she wishes for Helen's approval.

'Well—' says Edwin.

'Just until we find somewhere out of London – such a frightening place – and I will send a guinea a week,' says Helen. 'It is the least I can do. It is difficult for me, of course. I am very much alone in the world. My husband's parents. I am afraid, disown his child. They are Jewish, you see, and very orthodox; and of course disowning her does save them money! I am sure it is no more than that. It hurts me, all the same.'

This is the first Marjorie has ever heard about her father being Jewish. Well, she shouldn't be listening at key holes.

'We'll look after her,' says Edwin. 'Poor little Marjorie. By Jove we will, it's the least we can do. Feed her up, make a man of her, put the colour back into her cheeks.' He is distressed by notions of discrimination and unfairness. He is a nice man, to everyone but Esther. 'London's no place for a child, these days. I heard the East End's taken a battering.'

'The spirit of the people is incredible,' says Helen. 'They sing down in the shelters while all hell rages above them. I'm working day and night, you know. Well, we all have to work, these days. I help young mothers to cope. So many temptations, poor things. If a husband is conscripted, the wife's allowance is only twenty-eight shillings a week! It is quite shocking. How can anyone keep a family on that? Well of course they can't – and with so many soldiers on the loose in London. I'm afraid one fears a complete breakdown in morality. No, London is no place for a child.'

'But mother,' says Marjorie, in the room somehow, pulling at her mother's sleeve in the way that most infuriates, 'all the other evacuees have gone back. I'm the only one left in the village.'

'Marjorie,' says Helen, 'please don't look gift horses in the mouth, when the Songfords have been so good to you. It's dreadfully rude.'

Marjorie goes scarlet. Tears burst from her eyes.

'I'm afraid she's something of a grizzler,' says Helen. 'It's her heredity, I'm afraid. A kind of permanent wailing wall.'

'She's a dear girl,' says Esther stoutly.

'Well that's that,' says Helen, 'I must be off.'

'You can't stay to tea?' asks Edwin. 'We couldn't tempt you with a slice of nut cake?'

'I'd love to, but duty calls. I'm at my Young Wives Sanctuary tonight,' says Helen. 'I shouldn't have come at all really, abandoned them, but I had to make sure Marjorie was settled and happy.'

'Please stay, mother,' blurts Marjorie. 'It's only lunch-time.'

'Darling heart, don't pester. We have to be back in London before dark. There's a blackout, you know.'

The chauffeur opens the door for her. He is blond, young, healthy, handsome, and in some kind of uniform, though whether of private or military service would be hard to say.

Edwin sees her into the car, tucks her fur rug round her.

'This war,' she says, hesitant and intimate, 'this war. So extraordinary. It's changed my life. I was so selfish before. A blessing in disguise. What a place the world is – oh what a place!'

He gapes, enchanted.

The engine purrs. Marjorie comes running up.

'Mother,' she says, 'what about father? Where's father?'

'I simply don't know,' says Helen, 'but that means nothing. Letters, these days, just never get through. You can't rely on a thing.'

'But mother—'

Helen smiles sweetly and pats her daughter's cheek and winds up the window and is gone.

But she has stirred something in the Ulden air.

'Extraordinary,' says Edwin to Esther over late-night cocoa. Esther makes it with water, not milk.

'What is?'

'Her age.'

'What's extraordinary about that?' asks Esther.

'She must be the same age as you, and look at her and look at you,' and Esther is as distressed as Edwin, unsettled and restless, has meant her to be.

Silk petticoats lined with lace! Blond chauffeurs!

'When I grow up,' says Grace to Marjorie, before they go to sleep, 'I'm going to be like your mother.'

Marjorie snivels in the next bed and doesn't reply.

Lies and scarlet fingernails!

Half a mile away, in the room behind the Rose and Crown, Chloe lies awake in her bed. The sheets are coarse and the blankets are thin: the iron bed has rusty springs: the mattress is made of lumpy flock. Little Chloe wonders if she is doomed to live like this for ever. From the open windows of the Cosy Nook comes a gust of beery smoke and song. Down there her mother smiles, and serves, and cleans, and wipes, and disguises her distaste. Doors slam and voices shout. Out in the yard, caught short, beer-loaded men excrete, urinate and vomit. On Saturday nights, when the factory girls come down Stortford, the whole yard seems to heave and grunt with embracing couples. Chloe reads the Bible by torchlight.

'Remember now thy Creator in the days of thy youth, when the evil days come not—'

But supposing they do?

Next time Helen has to come by train, and not by car. There is no petrol. But she is accompanied by a gallant Polish officer. He clicks his heels and bows and speaks no English. Now Helen too is in uniform. It is of enigmatic origin, and its khaki bulkiness serves to enhance her fragile charm. She looks as if she is in fancy-dress.

She is pale and trembly, and leaves the Polish officer for Esther to cope with, and takes Edwin off for a walk in the woods. And thus, more or less, the conversation goes:

Helen I feel you are my friend, I feel I can confide in you. And Esther too, of course. But somehow – a man, you know how it is

71

when one needs advice. You don't think Esther minds me carrying you off like this? I wouldn't want to offend her for the world. I'm so indebted to her.

Edwin She's got the Polish fellow. Fair's fair.

Helen Yes. And the children. She loves the children, doesn't she! Edwin, I've heard from Dick at last. I thought he was in Scotland, but no, they sent him to France. It must have been a mistake because no-one in their right mind would have sent Dick on active service. He's far too much of an intellectual, and Jewish too. Sergei says they make terrible soldiers! Dick belonged to the Peace Pledge Union, you know. So did I, actually, but I think I was very much under Dickie's influence. Is it a dreadful thing to say – but since he's gone I've discovered myself. I was a Socialist, too, you know. Yes, I really was! I used to think the People were perfectly sensible, they just lacked education and one's own advantages, but I begin to think they're really very stupid. Sergei – he's a Count, actually – says Communism is doomed by virtue of the stupidity of the working classes. At least I think that's what he says – we talk in French. We both have a smattering. But the thing is, you see, Dick's a prisoner of war, and I feel so ashamed. I know it's not his fault but I can't help feeling he's taken the easy, well, actually the Jewish, way out. So passive and sneaky. He'll be cosy as anything for the duration, being an officer and a gentleman, and safe as houses while the rest of us go through the bombings and the hardship. I wouldn't be surprised if he didn't volunteer with just this in mind. It was such an odd thing for him to do. Do you think you could possibly break the news to Marjorie for me? I find it very difficult to talk to her about her father. You know he was unfaithful to me while she was being born and I nearly died?

72

Edwin finds it an incredible notion. So, plainly, does Helen.

Poor Dick, offered warmth, understanding and solace by Helen's best friend Rhoda, a bouncy, rompy, ridiculous girl, chosen by Helen for light relief. What should Dick have done that night of Marjorie's birth? Turned away by the nursing home matron, as he was – birth no business of his, a female concern, his own wife swelling and bursting and all the fault of his own brutishness, the doctors saying no sex during pregnancy bad for baby, and no sex for three months after the birth – bad for mother, and Helen always more than ready to believe anything that suited her?

What should Dick have done, Rhoda's friends (ex-friends) and Helen's, asked? Why, turned his back resolutely on Rhoda, of course (sexual urges not being considered the driving force they are now, and seen as a weakness, not a strength), held his tongue, his breath, and kept his patience, and saved everyone from ruin.

So poor wounded Helen believed, who had bared her beautiful breast simply, one might imagine, in order to receive the blow, and who in any case always had difficulty distinguishing a symptom from a cause (she believed, quite sincerely, that Marjorie's spots were the cause of her misery, and not the result). Hurt turned to moral outrage, thence into habit, and now at last to her advantage.

Edwin You poor plucky little thing.
Helen All the same, I want to preserve the child's faith in her father. I think that's so important. If I see too much of her, I am

73

afraid my rancour may spill over and damage her innocence. There is simply nowhere for her to go. My parents are in Australia, and as for Dick's – well, they always thought themselves too good for me, you know. Can you imagine, people like that? Sergei says their sort should be interned, the Jews are the real traitors. London is quite dreadfully dangerous now, but I must stay, I can't run away, it is simply not in my nature. Mr Churchill says we all have to stay put, and help, and London needs all the help it can get, you've no idea! One half of the population refuses to leave the shelters, and the other half won't go down. The first lot risk dying from disease, the others being blown or burned to bits. And the breakdown in morality! I'm working with the fallen mothers. I ask them back to tea, we play records; I show them that life can still be civilized, we don't have to descend to the level of brutes. And such a trial keeping that enormous house clean — it's almost impossible to find a cleaner, let alone keep one, without paying something monstrous. One woman asked one and sixpence an hour and she had dreadful varicose veins, she couldn't possibly have earned it... now, Edwin, you naughty boy, we'd better go back. Esther will be wondering what we're up to. I am so lucky, to have such good friends, and such a good home for Marjorie.

And they go back to the house, and Helen sweeps the Polish count away from an inspection of Esther's roses, and pecks Marjorie good-bye, and Edwin quite forgets to tell Marjorie that her father is a prisoner of war, and Esther has a bad time for a day or two, while Edwin finds fault with her appearance, her cooking, her extravagance, her handling of the children, her very existence, and finally, provoked beyond endurance

74

by her bewildered, suffering face, digs up her antirrhinum bed and lays down onions.

Chloe and Grace help.

twenty-one

In the summer of 1943 Marjorie goes up to London for the day, to visit her mother. It's a Sunday. The Frognal house, built in 1933 by a leading architect, rather in the fashion of a concrete boat, with portholes instead of windows, now stands like some dingy ark stranded in a jungle of creepers and shrubs. All the young gardeners have been called up and all the old ones can find better-paid work.

But Helen is cheerful. She still entertains: there are more than enough guests. Assorted Polish officers on leave in London, one or two reformed friends left over from the Peace Pledge days; former struggling painters, now official war-artists, previous avant-garde writers, now earning good money as war correspondents – all take refuge in her house. Tradesmen, warmed by Helen's charm, supply extra food in quantity and the hospitality is lavish.

Helen cannot leave her guests to meet Marjorie, who makes her own way to Hampstead from Liverpool Street Station on a bus which takes her through the still smouldering rubble of the City, and from the top of which she sees, half hidden by bricks, what she thinks at first is a sack and then realizes is the top half of a body. She wonders whether to draw the attention of the conductor, and then changes her mind. Someone must know. She does not want to look silly.

She tries to tell Helen about the body, but Helen is too busy to listen. She is telling her friends what an independent girl Marjorie has become, by virtue of living in the country and going to the village school. Marjorie, laying the table for lunch, overhears her mother talking to a friend, thus:

Helen Poor dear Dick! I don't know what he'll miss most in his prison camp. Sex, or culture. Can you imagine Dick without the Left Book Club, or the *New Statesman* or *Apollo*? All they ever get to see in those places is *Tit-Bits* and *Esquire*, I believe, sent in by the Red Cross. I'm afraid his mind will quite wither up and dry without its accustomed stimuli, and that's not the only thing that will! He was never a one for inner resources.

Marjorie Mother?

Helen Run along, Marjorie.

Marjorie You mean father's a prisoner of war?

Helen Yes of course he is, dear. Mr Songford told you.

Marjorie finds her father's POW address by searching her mother's rosewood desk. Every week she posts a lengthy letter to this address, copying out pages from *Apollo*, and the *New Statesman*, and whole stories out of *Penguin New Writing*; Chloe helps, churning out page after page when she should be doing her homework, and Grace – 'quite the little artist' as her teacher says – copies Henry Moore sketches and Paul Nash paintings on to airmail paper, and these too are enclosed. (Grace has an amazing facility for graphic mimickry: she will pick up a pencil and dash off a copy of someone else's original,

76

with half indifferent, half contemptuous pride.) Whether the letters get through, none of them knows. Certainly there is no reply. It doesn't seem to matter.

'I expect they've tortured him to death,' says Grace, one day over tea. 'You know what the Germans are.'

'Be quiet, Grace. He's an officer and a gentleman,' says Esther, comforting, 'that kind of thing only happens to the ranks. Don't upset poor Marjorie.'

But Grace does if she can, and no wonder, Marjorie's school report is startling. At the end of her first year in the Grammar School she's top of everything, with Chloe running second. Grace gets the Art Prize and 'Could do better if she tried' for nearly everything else. And though Grace does have normal parents, and lives in her own house in a fairly normal way, these, with the years, appear less and less desirable attributes. Grace is limited to the reality of Edwin – choleric, open-pored and fallible. Marjorie with her missing father, and Chloe with her dead one, live in a world of might-have-been and might-yet-be.

Marjorie sends her school report to her mother, and gets a reply in which Helen quite ignores the report but says she is going to the States for a year to work for a Free French organization in New York – Will she tell Mr and Mrs Songford, please.

Marjorie does. The guinea a week has long since ceased arriving.

'You should be doing some kind of warwork,' is all Edwin says to Esther, 'sitting round here on your backside all day.'

Esther rarely sits. It's all patch and mend and make-do,

these days. Every available blackberry is bottled; turnip pulp must be added to the jam to make it go further; custard must be set with golden syrup, not eggs – there are no eggs available; even here in the country, officials pounce, it seems, while they're still falling from the hen. Only the supply of cabbage is unlimited. And, of course, the garden vegetables.

'I'm singing for the troops at the concert,' says Esther, roused to defiance at last by the injustice of his fault-finding. Before she married, Esther had plans to be an opera singer. Edwin is horrified.

'You'll make a fool of yourself,' he says. 'And me.'

But Esther persists, and Edwin tries to get the organizers to cancel her appearance. But they won't, and Esther sings. She stands up in front of all those men, this middle-aged lady with her red, swollen hands and lost ambitions, and sings, of all things, a Brecht song. 'The Ballad of the German Soldier's Bride':

'And what did he send you, my bonny lass,'

it goes,

'From Paris the City of Light?
From Paris he sent me a silken dress
A dream caress of a silken dress,
From Paris the City of Light.
And what did he send you my bonny lass,
From the deep deep Russian snows?
From Russia he sent me my widow's weeds,

From the funeral feast my widow's weeds,
From the deep deep Russian snows.'

Her voice is clear and firm and young, her delivery exact and
confident. There is silence after she finishes. Then applause,
on and on. She seems gratified but not surprised by the
response she gets. She won't sing an encore.

'That's enough,' she says. 'That will last me for ever.'

It has to.

'Sometimes,' says Gwyneth to Chloe, 'you rub brass and
find gold. Not often, but sometimes,' and for once what she
says sounds true to Chloe.

Edwin does not hear his wife sing or witness her triumph.
He slips a disc a couple of hours before she is due to appear on
stage, and takes to his bed, and afterwards is in too much pain
to listen to anyone's description of the event.

twenty-two

'I know what the matter is with you,' says Marjorie, as they
wait for their coffee, 'and with me. It's the Stay Put poster. It
has embedded itself in our minds.'

Oh yes. The Stay Put poster, on the notice boards of
Church, Pub, School, Women's Institute and Station, along
with the Ministry of Food recipes for carrot cake and cod-
and-potato pie.

'What do I do?

– If I hear news that the Germans have landed? I stay put. I say to myself "our chaps will deal with that". I do not say "I must get out of here" whether at work or home, I just stay put.'

'I stay put at work, and you stay put at home,' says Marjorie. 'What good little girls we are.'

Snip, snip, snip, goes the shopkeeper's scissors round coupons and points. Little packets of margarine, smaller ones of butter, tiny squares of cheese pass over the counter. Melon jam and milk powder. That's all for this week. Ration books get flabby with use. Identity cards to children, are a source of pride. So that's who one really is! The suicide rate plummets. The standard of health soars. If you can't fill up on chips, you have to on carrots. War babies grow inches taller than pre-war ones. Britain's finest hour!

The buses are filled with turbaned women on their way to work in the munitions factory. The sweet-shop lady's son is killed in action. The baker's brother loses a leg. The gardener who once helped Esther with the herbaceous borders is posted missing. Regulars at the Rose and Crown, laughing, handsome, horse-playing young men from the air-field, fail to turn up at their usual time. Other young men take their place at the bar, leaning and crowding in the same way, ordering the same drinks. It is hard to tell them apart.

Sometimes Gwyneth lies in bed at night and cries. Why? Chloe does not know. For herself or for the world. In the morning she is brisk and competent again. Chloe and she follow the early-morning exercise classes on the radio as best they can in their tiny room. Chloe breaks her little finger hitting the wall as she swings her arm. Well, there's a war on. Hardship is no longer one's own responsibility.

A German bomber is shot down, and explodes a mile or so from the village. The charred remains, metal and human, are cordoned off. A week later Marjorie comes across a severed human arm, still in its uniform sleeve, in a ditch.

Always Marjorie.

'It's nothing to do with staying put,' says Chloe. 'I love my husband.'

'Love!' says Marjorie. 'What's that? At your age?'

She gets up, goes over to the Cona coffee machine, and helps herself and Chloe to coffee. The waiter is nowhere in sight. Chloe longs to leave, but Marjorie has no intention of giving up.

'One gets driven too far,' says Marjorie. 'Like Edwin Songford. Did you know he once raped Grace? She would walk round the house with no clothes on.'

Chloe blenches.

'Grace will say anything to liven up a conversation,' she says, faintly.

'What's more,' says Marjorie, 'she says that when her father was a little boy in India his father wired him up to a machine which gave him an electric shock if he masturbated, and that's what rendered him impotent for ever.'

'Then how did he rape her?'

'She didn't go into that.'

'And how did she get born in the first place?'

'You take everything so literally, Chloe,' Marjorie complains.

'And the reason he was cashiered, was because he cut a hole in the floor to watch his commanding office copulating with his lady in the room below.'

'Poor Edwin,' says Chloe. 'Why is she so dreadful about him?'

'Because he's alone and senile on the Bournemouth coast and if she had a good word to say for him she might feel obliged to go and look after him. But it is not beyond the bounds of possibility that the rape story is true. Grace was very provocative and very inquisitive, and the whole set-up was there waiting. In primitive communities, I may say, the wife who finds her sexual duties distasteful will rear one of the daughters to take her place in the marital bed. Remember how Esther kept insisting Grace wasn't developed enough to wear a bra, so she used to bounce about the house, when the rest of us were decently encased in solid boned uplift bras?'

'Nobody bounced in those days. One died with shame if a nipple showed through. Anyway, you're talking about incest, not rape, and I don't believe a word of it. Life just wasn't like that.'

'Yes it was,' says Marjorie. 'You just never noticed. You walked past that ditch twice without seeing that pilot's arm. I was the only one to see it.'

'Perhaps it was only there because you expected it to be,' says Chloe, desperately.

'According to Grace,' Marjorie goes on, 'it happened after I'd gone back to London to stay in the Frognal house, and Edwin was worrying about Grace's purity. He'd come back from the Rose and Crown and gone to her room to check that she was there, and she wasn't. So he blamed poor Esther for it, and she went to bed crying, and he sat up waiting with a bottle of whisky. When she finally came in about three, all flushed and mocking and furious – you know what she was like – he followed her up to his room and took off his belt to thwack her and his trousers fell down and that's when it happened.'

'I suppose,' says Chloe gloomily, 'that if you have a fantasy as detailed as that it might as well be true. If she's determined that he raped her, the facts of the matter are irrelevant.'

'That is simply not true,' says Marjorie, 'and you know it. A fact is a fact, and a fantasy open to Freudian interpretation.'

'Whosoever lusteth in his heart,' says Chloe, 'as my mother used to say.'

'No wonder you can't keep Oliver in control,' says Marjorie. 'Why *do* you put up with Françoise?'

'Because she makes Oliver happy,' says Chloe.

'And what about you?'

'She doesn't make me unhappy,' says Chloe, cautiously.

'She ought to,' says Marjorie.

And what do you know about it, thinks Chloe, furious. Unmarried as you are and always have been and always will be, so sure you are of ought and oughtn't.

'You're like your mother,' Marjorie goes on, blandly. 'You put up with too much. Endurance is a disease, and you caught it from her.'

'It's a question of alternatives,' says Chloe. 'How would my mother have lived, except by putting up with things? And what could Esther have done, except stay with Edwin? How would she have lived? Women live by necessity, not choice.'

'Women who don't earn,' says Marjorie.

'I tried to earn,' says Chloe. 'I did, and that's when the trouble started. And Esther Songford didn't have too bad a life, in spite of what you say. Married people don't, it just looks dreadful from the outside.'

'It doesn't look,' says Marjorie. 'It is.'

'She had an inner life, which nothing could touch.'

'That's not true,' says Marjorie. 'It was touched, and braised and destroyed. Esther hurt dreadfully when Edwin mocked her, or Grace was rude to her, I know she did. I had to watch her being brave.'

'It wasn't like that,' says Chloe. 'She had all kinds of pleasure. Her flower garden and the house, and making do. And when Edwin was out she'd get quite skittish.'

And indeed, Esther would sometimes act like a kitten on a windy evening, prancing and dancing and singing around the kitchen, to the mingled delight and embarrassment of the girls.

'Who's afraid of the big bad wolf?' she'd sing, but when the front door opened at eleven-thirty, and Edwin returned from the pub, she would be, and with reason.

twenty-three

One Sunday morning Chloe comes early to The Poplars and finds Esther sitting crying amongst last night's washing-up. Her right eye is black and puffy and her lip is bleeding. She wears an old green corduroy dress and the fabric has faded to a soft richness. Her eyes are magnified by tears and distress has smoothed out her face. She looks like a very pretty child. She speaks to Chloe. thus:

'I'm afraid I fell downstairs, Chloe. I'm a little shaken. Will you put on the kettle? Shall we have a nice cup of tea? I can't abide a dismal atmosphere in a home, can you? And it's up to the wife and mother to set the tone, I always think. By and large men are gloomy creatures, always taking offence, and you have to keep chivvying and cheering to keep things going. How nice you look this morning, Chloe. Always so spick and span – such a good girl. I'm afraid Grace is still snoring in bed, and so's her father. It's the Rose and Crown does that, and I do find it unpatriotic. Pouring beer down the throat all evening and lying in bed all next morning and so bad-tempered in between! Still, I mustn't complain. I was lucky to get married at all; I wasn't all that pretty as a girl, and I met Mr Songford quite late on. I always wanted to be a singer, you know, but I didn't have the looks, and of course my parents would never have heard of it. Young Corporal Bates wants me to sing at the garden fête – 'Now Is The Hour' – but I'm afraid my husband won't hear of it. In fact I'm afraid he objects most strenuously to Corporal Bates himself – well, his views are rather extreme – and won't hear of him having the fête in our garden, he says it must be at the vicarage as usual. I've tried to explain about how so many of the ranks are Irish Catholic, and that it's not suitable, but I'm afraid he's not the most reasonable of men. I'm so sorry for poor Corporal Bates: he tries so hard, and he really is a perfect gentleman, in spite of everything. I'm sure never in his whole life has he raised his hand to a woman.'

But even Chloe, schoolgirl that she is, knows that Corporal Patrick Bates is no gentleman. The Angel Lucifer before the fall, perhaps, but more an upstart than a gentleman.

Patrick Bates kisses and tells, and worse.

Patrick Bates is twenty-two. His father (he says) was an alcoholic criminal, murdered in a drunken brawl. His mother (he says) is a prostitute in Manchester. And Patrick himself, the child of this ill-omened match, was (he says) brought up by a maiden aunt in Morningside, that genteel suburb of Edinburgh.

Patrick Bates is afraid (he says) of nothing – not of husbands, fathers, brothers or his own nature. He is stocky and strong. He has brilliant blue eyes, coarse reddish hair, and a member (Grace whispers) both powerful and long.

Patrick Bates has the mature ladies of the village in an erotic ferment and the young girls giddy with love. What is this special power that Patrick has, beyond looking deep into the troubled eyes of ladies, and offering them his concentrated and admiring attention? Not, one may be sure, the size of his member (for only Grace, in all the village, knows or cares, let alone speaks, about such things).

Marjorie, later, was to say women felt themselves to be sexually worthy in Patrick's presence. So intense was his curiosity about all things female. Marjorie maintained, that it quite overrode a woman's consciousness of being too old, too young, too big in the bust, or too small, too inexperienced or over-experienced, too tight of cunt, too loose, too ready to respond, or too slow, in the simple knowledge that she was female, and that that was quite enough for Patrick.

86

Grace was to say it was because he didn't see women as sex-objects, rather himself as one.

Chloe felt, in those days, that he was simply kind, and interested, and concerned. Only later, as youth and optimism fell away, and he got the sweets he wanted and found them ashes in his mouth, did the rumbling wheel of Patrick's existence jam somehow at its summit, and turn into reverse, depleting the pool of goodwill, stirring up the muddy violence of his beginnings, leaving him revealed as mean, and mad, and malevolent.

Patrick Bates is Entertainments Officer at the local Airforce camp. Because the vicar has high blood-pressure it is Patrick who for a while organizes the village hops, whist drives, vegetable shows, waste paper and scrap metal collections, and so on. He seems surprised to find himself doing it, but as an occupation it is clearly preferable to being say, a rear gunner, whose remains are regularly hosed out of returning aircraft. Patrick has not come so far, so fast, to end in so humiliating a manner, and says so, publicly, in the Cosy Nook.

It is a mark of his popularity and charm that he can say so and still be bought drinks.

Only Edwin Songford, strangely, suspects him in those days, sees the destructive glint behind the smile, and senses the ultimate parasitical design, and has some vague vision of a ravaged future. But who will, these days, trust Edwin Songford's judgement? The world has changed: Edwin has not. Edwin's belly is swollen with beer; nightly he waxes hysterical at the notion of socialism, strikes, employment for women: he wishes to extend the death penalty to cover black-market and homosexual offences. When he speaks of his doubts about Patrick, who will listen? Only Esther, who has to.

Mrs Songford accepts her cup of tea from Chloe.

'Thank you, my dear. My throat is very dry. It has been since that concert. I think I over-strained it then. I daresay Edwin is quite right – one makes oneself a laughing stock. Better not to make the effort, really. And I do worry about my throat. My mother died from an unpleasant disease – one of the spreading kind. It affected her throat. My father used to like us to chew every mouthful sixty-four times, in order to preserve our stomach linings. He was the best of men, but in retrospect I think a little eccentric about diet. And there was no talking at meals. Of course there was nothing mother could do about that, she'd married him, but all the same it was a dismal household. One has a duty to be cheerful and I do try, I don't want to end up like mother, and I tell myself my troubles are nothing, compared to what our poor fighting men have to put up with.'

One of Esther's troubles is Grace, now burgeoning into adolescence. Grace creeps out of The Poplars at half past ten, when her mother is already in bed and her father is dragging out his last drink at the Rose and Crown. She waylays Patrick as he leaves the public bar. She walks back with Patrick to the gates of the Army Camp.

What happens on the way?

Who is to say, but Grace has a sly and rounded look, and Chloe begins to hate her, not for the last time in her life, but with more intensity than ever after.

88

In Patrick's company Chloe is paralysed. Grace flaunts herself before him: Marjorie entertains him: Chloe can only gaze, dry-mouthed.

All three girls are at the Chelmsford Grammar School. Navy pleated tunics, bunched round the middle (hardly waist) with a cord. White shirt. Striped tie. Panama hats in summer, navy felt in winter, and a detention if you didn't wear one. Darned black lisle stockings, stout shoes, and in winter, combinations.

Combinations (a word used in the plural, never the singular) were worn next to the skin. They started at the neck and went down almost to the knees. Stiff yellowy-white flannel, scratchy, the neck opening fastened with a row of flabby buttons and stiff buttonholes (tab-lined to prevent fraying) and with two buttoned flaps, one at the front, one at the back, for when the wearer went to the lavatory.

On winter mornings Graces leaves the house wearing her combinations, and takes them off behind the hedge at the bus stop, even when it is snowing.

Marjorie and Chloe prefer to be warm.

Marjorie has stopped writing to her father. Culture seems without meaning. The female spirit, at fifteen, has time for little else but self-appraisal. (Though the Grammar School does its best to deflect it with hour after hour of homework.) A letter comes from Helen in New York, with a PS saying that according to a message from a prisoner of war organization that has finally caught up with her, her father Dick is still alive and still has partial sight in one eye.

Chloe is in love with her history teacher as well as with

Patrick. Both loves are hopeless and agonizing, and, she is convinced, perverted.

They can never be spoken of to anyone. She learns to bear things inwardly.

Grace has no intention of bearing anything. She has prevailed upon her mother, at last, to admit that she is sufficiently developed to wear a bra. One is bought. It is marked with the Government Utility Kit Mark. It is stout and functional. For a day or two Grace goes about, like the other girls, with a shelf for a bosom.

It was not uncommon for a nice young man, in those days, on first seeing a woman's breasts – something which might well not happen until his wedding night – to be horrified by their appearance, having assumed that they were of necessity forward, thrusting, nippleless cones, uniform in every female.

Grace finds the shelf irritating. She boils and boils the stout, unloving fabric in a saucepan, until it is denatured. Then she dyes it black.

The sports mistress spots it one combinationless hockey day, showing quite plainly beneath the open-weave of her Aertex sports shirt.

And thus the conversation goes:

Sports Mistress Grace dear, I don't think that bra is quite suitable.
Grace What do you mean?
Sports Mistress Nice girls don't wear black underwear.
Grace Why not?
Sports Mistress Because how would one ever know whether or not it was clean?

Grace By remembering when you last washed it. Besides, if it was black, would it matter? In any case we should all save soap for the war effort. They say men prefer black underwear. Do you think that's true?

Sports Mistress Only a certain sort of man. The kind of man you will be interested in likes a woman to be spotlessly clean in mind, body and underwear.

Grace Do you really think so? Well, since it's all such a fuss, I won't wear a bra at all.

And she doesn't. Grace, everyone agrees, will come to a bad end. She is all but expelled for being an evil influence on the other girls, but her talent for drawing saves her. They even line the school corridors with her pseudo van Goghs.

twenty-four

Marjorie, Grace and Chloe. They bled in unison, punctually and regularly for five days once every four weeks, whenever the moon was full. It was a fact of their existence which used to make Grace furious.

'You're looking rather peaky,' says Marjorie, to Chloe, as at last they leave the Italiano. 'Do you have the curse, like me, or is it the life you lead?'

'It's the curse,' says Chloe. 'There is nothing wrong with the life I lead.'

'We were always in time,' says Marjorie, 'do you remember? Grace used to starve herself to get out of step but it never worked. Do you think it means anything? Do you think there's a kind of inner force which drives us all along? Perhaps we have a female group identity, as black-beetles do?'

'No,' says Chloe.

'Do you remember those sanitary towels we used to have? Made of paper which shredded when you walked?'

'I'd rather not remember.'

'Do you know what today is?' Marjorie persists. Chloe walks with her towards the Television Centre, past the rampant infertility of Shepherd's Bush Green, down towards White City. Their nostrils are filled with diesel fumes.

'No,' says Chloe. 'What is today?'

Ah, today.

Today Chloe's children – hers by virtue of blood, or obsession or love – mark out a badminton court on an English lawn. They are well fed: they do not have hookworm, trachoma, or TB. Through the television screen they have become acquainted with the concept of violence in all its forms: the nearest they get to its reality is a bomb hoax at school, or a crashed car seen in passing on the motorway. They show little astonishment at their good fortune.

Yet at their births, who would ever have predicted so good a future for them? And they show little understanding of Chloe's sacrifice in bringing them to this good end – if sacrifice it is, for do we not all do what ultimately we want?

So Oliver assures Chloe, when she complains about the burden of the children. And who pays, he asks? Not you, but me. Yes, thinks Chloe in her heart, but your money is easily earned. I pay with my time and energy, my life itself. Children take the mother's strength, grow strong as she grows weak.

Inigo and Imogen. Kevin, and Kestrel, and Stanhope. Poor Stanhope.

Today Chloe lunches with Marjorie. And afterwards, Chloe will go to visit Grace. Who would have thought, after all that happened, that they would ever consent again to enjoy each other's company?

Today Esther Songford is dead. Five bungalows stand where once the roses grew, not to mention the onions and the cabbages. A builder has bought The Poplars. He uses it as a storeroom for his materials, and waits for it to fall down so he can have planning permission to build luxury flats on the site. The motorway is coming. The chalkpit has been filled in; where Mad Doll's boys once struggled for their lives, and lost, the slip road runs.

Today Mr Songford lives in an Old People's Home in Bournemouth. Grace seldom visits him.

Today Patrick's canvases fetch from £750 (for the larger works) to £2,000 (for the tiniest). He paints women making love, giving birth, dying, dead, emerging dimly from an overwhelming wealth of domestic detail.

Chloe shows Patrick Bates her father's paintings, those near miniatures in 1947. He comes to the room behind the Rose and Crown to inspect them, one night at ten-thirty, while Gwyneth is still washing-up glasses. Chloe lies on her front on the floor, searching beneath her mother's bed, amongst the cases and crates, for the canvas roll. She finds them right at the back, pushed against the wall. By then she is almost completely under the bed, except for her seventeen-year-old legs.

93

The floor is so clean that Chloe's check dress is not even made dusty. Had Gwyneth been of a more sluttish disposition, Chloe might have given up the search earlier, and Patrick never seen her father's paintings, or Chloe's smooth stretched legs, for that matter.

Thus our destinies are made, for good or ill. Inigo, Imogen. Kevin, Kestrel, Stanhope: linking back to brave David Evans, sitting exhausted in a hospital bed, waiting for the taste of blood in his mouth, covering his tiny canvases with scrupulous care – obsession mingling with optimism. Courage is not in vain; the painful wresting of beauty out of ugliness is not wasted. Believe it to be forgotten, worthless, buried deep and rotting under clods of earth, yet it creeps out somehow, raises its storms of life and energy.

Patrick stares at David Evans' paintings and seems stunned.

'Yes,' he says. 'Very interesting.'

He looks again.

'Well, well,' he says. 'There's one way not to die.'

Chloe is flushed from crawling about on the floor.

'Would you like me to make you pregnant?' Patrick inquires, and it seems to Chloe that this is exactly what she wants. Patrick makes love to her there and then, upon her mother's bed, to Chloe's infinite amazement and gratification. It seems to her not so much a pleasurable experience as an overwhelming one – as much another world to enter into, as the one of sleep, when she has been awake, or waking, when she has been asleep. She suspects it of being a dangerous world, full of deadly pit-traps, but clearly the one the élite inhabit.

Patrick leaves within the half-hour, to get back to camp.

'Don't tell anyone,' he says. 'Forget all about it outside. Remember it inside. It's very good for you.'

The next morning, waking, she has difficulty in believing the event actually occurred. She stares at the faint well-sponged stain on her mother's coverlet, and wonders if perhaps she did spill her tea, as she told Gwyneth. Patrick, thereafter, ignores her, and suffering, she recognizes reality again.

She isn't pregnant, not this time. She doesn't care for that: it makes Patrick too unlike the Deity.

twenty-five

'No,' says Chloe, 'I don't know what today is.'
Today Françoise has been in the Rudore household for just nine months. For three months she has had carnal acquaintance with her employer. Chloe has had none for nearly a year. Is this hardship? Chloe does not know.

When Chloe sleeps in her husband's bed, there is no end to her expectations – not just that the empty spaces in her body should be nightly filled and rewarded, but all her inner space as well, by day.

Look after me, nurture me, love me, care for me, she cries to him with every waking and with every sleeping breath. Be perfect. Not perfect as you see it, but as I want perfection. Be perfect not just for me, but for our children too. All our children. Don't work, don't drink, don't be bad-tempered; these things deflect you from your task. Your task is me. Fill me, fill my empty spaces. Complete me.

Although, in her heart, Chloe knows she never can be filled. Some wounds have gone too deep, protective membranes have been torn and can't be mended. Love and concern will always trickle out of her, in the end, and leave her empty again, no matter how he fills, and fills.

But sleeping in his bed, she cannot quench her expectations.

Out of his bed, she can be serene. Badly treated, but at least free of expectation. Walking wounded, trudging away from the battle zone, not needing the pretence of being whole. What a relief! So long as the children notice nothing.

Of course they notice. Inigo and Imogen, Kestrel and Kevin. Stanhope too.

'Very well,' says Chloe, 'tell me what today is.' The ground beneath shakes as a juggernaut passes, off on its journey to the M4 and the West.

What a dim domestic heroine she is in danger of becoming, like her mother, like Mrs Songford, who at least died in disgrace. Like a million million women, shuffling and shameful to the end.

'Today eighteen years ago,' says Marjorie, 'I went to the hospital to collect Ben and I found him dead in a drawer. Today a week ago I went to the doctor, and he said I ought to have a hysterectomy, it was ridiculous the way I bled, and I don't know what to do. Don't you please tell me, either, Chloe, I don't trust your judgement any more. Not since Françoise. You don't know how that's upset me. I had hoped that you at least could be happy.'

What can Chloe say? She wants to cry, for everyone.

twenty-six

Today Grace lives with Sebastian, who is fifteen years younger than she is. Or rather Sebastian lives with Grace. Grace may have the income, but Sebastian has the talent, the charm, and the future. He picks and chooses whom he lives with. Grace, these days, tends to take what comes along. Sebastian is a film director, or would be if he could raise the money to make a film. He was taught film-making at his public school, and took a degree in visual communication at college.

Today Grace lives in a half-finished flat, on the top floor of a large terrace house in Holland Park. She has been living there for six months, the last three of them with Sebastian. Here Chloe goes to visit her.

Builders have been knocking three rooms into one, but have gone away, it seems, in the middle of the task. There are piles of plaster rubble and heaps of sodden wallpaper, inside and outside the flat, and strips of wallpaper are still stretched half-pasted on a trestle table. Tins of paint stand open and congealing. Chloe automatically replaces the lids.

Grace crouches on the floor in front of the fan heater, drying her thick red hair. She has cleared a living space by the window, spread it with rugs and cushions, set up the hi-fi, plugged in an electric kettle and a small wall refrigerator, and within these limits has set up her home.

'Don't clear up the mess,' says Grace. 'I may have to sue. Everything has to look as dreadful as possible.'

Over the years Grace has developed quite a taste for litigation. She who once stood in court and wept, and screamed, now has a liking for the experience. And thus the conversation goes, between her and her friend Chloe:

Grace And how was Marjorie's moustache? Or does she shave, these days?

Chloe She has better things to think about.

Grace What? The BBC? And how's Patrick? Does she say?

Chloe Much the same, mad and mean.

Grace Why doesn't she move in with him? What a waste of rent and rates.

Chloe He hasn't asked her to.

Grace She has this dreadful habit of deferring to the male. She's as bad as you, Chloe. Don't you just love this flat?

Chloe It's hard to say.

Grace I hate it. It's been a nightmare.

Chloe You didn't have to move. You could have kept the house in St John's Wood.

Grace No I couldn't. I sold it. I had to have the money. I couldn't keep the buyer out for ever. His wife kept having babies and he kept complaining and in the end he had me evicted, well, more or less. The squatter people were very unhelpful.

Chloe That house was all you had. When you've got rid of the money, Grace, what will you do?

Grace Die. I hate it round here, don't you? It's a real middle-class ghetto. Full of short-sighted women with frizzy hair dressed all in leather and carrying teddy bears. All the real people have been driven out. You can't think how filthy this flat was when I moved in. They had five children and the father was in prison and the mother had TB and the floorboards were sodden with piss. I tried painting them with lino paint but they still smelt so I got some builders in to replace the floors. It was when the boards were up that Sebastian moved in and said we might as well have the whole place done properly, so they started knocking down the partition walls, and then the Council turned up and said they weren't partition walls at all, but structural, and the whole thing was illegal anyway and what about Planning Permission, and then of course the builders got disheartened and left. I'd paid them in advance – that was Sebastian's idea, he said it was customary, to show you trusted them. And then Sebastian got this architect friend of his to do some drawings, and he met some more builders in a pub – that's their mess over there, they were film technicians starting a new career, well, you know what the film industry's like – and then the neighbours got up a petition to stop us spoiling the sky-line, and in the meanwhile the builders had been offered a film after all, and couldn't refuse – they were making it in Belfast and the original crew had walked out – well, you know how it all is. I don't have to tell you. Property is all very boring.

Chloe What happened to the mother with TB?

Grace Is that the only thing you care about?

Chloe Yes.

Grace I don't know. I never asked. She was moved to the outskirts by some kind of agency, I believe. I paid her a thousand to get out. It was a fortune for someone like her.

Chloe And which is Stanhope's room?

Grace You'll have to ask the architect. He has a plan for some kind of ceiling suspension for guests. I don't trust him, really. He's all quick imaginative sketches and lots of talk and never any measurements.

Chloe Then why employ him?

Grace He's Sebastian's friend.

Chloe It's your money.

Grace No it's not, it's Christie's. He's lying there in his grave – or at any rate his urn – cheering at the way I've mismanaged things. I've never earned a penny in my life, not in the pay packet sense. I wouldn't know how to start. I'd quite like to be an opera singer, mind you.

Chloe Like your mother?

Grace No, not like my mother. I'd forgotten about her. I couldn't bear to do anything which ran in the family. Is Stanhope musical?

Chloe He never mentions it, only football. He's your son, not mine. They send you the school reports; you could always look it up, I suppose, under Extra Activities.

Grace I never read school reports. They should be abolished. They're an invasion of a child's privacy. What a child needs from a school is anonymity.

Chloe In that case, perhaps Stanhope should go to a comprehensive school. It's what he wants to do.

Grace You always give in to the children, Chloe. How can a boy Stanhope's age know what's best for him? He's far happier at a boarding school. They've got good teachers and wonderful equipment and splendid playing fields, and he must have lots of friends by now.

Chloe He doesn't make friends easily.

Grace Then think how miserable he'd be at a comprehensive school.

Chloe You did tell him he only had to board 'til you had somewhere settled to live.

Grace Settled? Do you call this settled? And I don't trust that architect. I don't think Stanhope would be happy in a ceiling suspension, do you? No, he'll have to stay where he is. And I'm certainly not having him at a comprehensive; why does he think he wants to go?

Chloe He wants to play soccer, not rugby.

Grace There you are, it's ridiculous. Besides, with a stupid name like Stanhope he'd only get laughed at, down there amongst the yobs.

Grace changes her social attitudes along with her boyfriends, as a stick insect changes colour according to the bush it lands on. But the nervous craving for privilege keeps rearing its head. Though she is, at the moment, prepared to blow up Eton, or at any rate light the fuse for the dynamite Sebastian has laid, she will not have her son at a comprehensive school.

Chloe It was you who named him, Grace. You insisted on Stanhope, in spite of everyone's advice.

Grace The whole episode of Stanhope was ridiculous, I quite agree. I should have had an abortion. I should never have listened to you, Chloe. Stanhope is your responsibility. Do you like my dress?

Chloe No.

Grace wears a navy-blue silk dress, made circa 1946; it has an uneven hem and frayed seams. It clings rather sadly to Grace's small bosom, seeming to miss a more robust original owner.

Grace No? I do. I bought it down the Portobello. Marjorie's mother had one like this. Do you think it's the same one? I always wanted to be like Helen.
Chloe You've succeeded.

She does not mean it kindly.

twenty-seven

January 1945. Helen, back from New York, turns up unexpectedly at The Poplars. It is eight in the morning and there is snow on the ground. She presses a ten shilling note into Marjorie's trembling hand, and presents Esther Songford with a tin of salmon. Esther has put on a good deal of weight – her ankles are puffy and she is short of breath – but she manages to gasp her thanks.

'Is Esther all right?' asks Helen, all solicitude, drawing Edwin to one side. 'She looks dreadful!' Helen has left the engine of her Baby Austin running. She can't stay more than a minute. Her passenger, grey-faced and desperate, stands in the drive, stamping his feet to keep warm, refusing to enter. He is, Helen says, a Labour politician.

'Esther's just fat,' says Edwin. 'Too many potatoes. She's let herself go.'

'We must none of us let ourselves go,' says Helen. 'We must

get ready to win the peace, as we are winning the war.'

Helen is elegant even at eight in the morning. She wears a thin spotted navy dress with padded shoulders and a pleated skirt, and a fur coat, and her stockings are made of nylon – the first pair even seen in Ulden. She has the new wedgie shoes. Her hair is piled up over her forehead and falls smoothly away behind until it reaches the nape of her neck, whence it rises again in a semi-circular half-curl, like a seawave on the verge of breaking. Such an effect is hard to come by: but in these times hair must look as unlike hair as possible, as must complexions. Orangy pancake make-up hides every blemish; scarlet lipstick transforms the lips into a cupid's bow God never intended.

Helen looks lovely, and inhuman. Esther clutches her old dressing-gown round her, clasps the tin of salmon and sinks into a chair, taking the weight off her poor aching legs. She feels sick all the time.

'I've only a minute, my dears,' says Helen, as they cluster round her, like bees around the honey. 'Marjorie, you must move back to London this weekend.'

'But you can't, the V-bombs—' says Esther Songford, from her chair. Helen ignores her.

'But I can't leave now. What about my Higher Certificate—' says Marjorie, 'and my University Entrance—' Edwin scowls at her.

'You love your father more than school, surely,' says Helen. 'We have reason to believe he will soon be repatriated, on humanitarian grounds. He'll want his family about him after all he's been through. I must dash now. John's on his way to a very important meeting. I promised to drive him; so much more cosy than the train, but I'm afraid if I stop the engine we never seem to get it started again. I tell him it doesn't matter if he's late, he's so important they'll be perfectly happy to wait all day for him, but I'm afraid he's dreadfully agitated.'

And off she goes.

When Chloe tells Gwyneth that Marjorie's going back to London, tears come into Gwyneth's eyes.

'What's the matter?' asks Chloe, surprised. 'She's going home, isn't she?'

'This war,' says Gwyneth. 'What it's done to us all!' She has an unsightly rash on her hands. The doctor says it's due to washing-up water and vitamin deficiency, but what can she do about either?

'After the war,' asks Chloe, 'what about us? Will we go back to London?'

But Gwyneth doesn't want to go.

'You must stay here and finish your schooling,' she says.

Gwyneth is proud of Chloe; her neat, pretty, clever daughter is her one achievement. She thrills with pleasure at each success in school; she panics at the slightest headache. She is selfless in her concern for her daughter's welfare, expecting nothing in return, forever soothing, patting, encouraging, moulding, preaching patience and endurance.

So long, that is, as Chloe's interests and that of the Leacocks do not conflict. If this happens, the Leacocks win. Gwyneth loves Mr Leacock. Why else would she allow Chloe to get up at six on those winter mornings, risking health and energy, to do the guests' shoes, and lay up breakfast, and waylay the milkman to get extra milk – and even, as she grows older and cleverer, to stay up late and make up the accounts after the Rose and Crown is closed? All for nothing, unless you count Mr Leacock's smile.

'What an honour,' Gwyneth says. And believes it, and so does Chloe.

Gwyneth has nowhere to go. She is over forty now and has no savings. Her life at the Rose and Crown has settled into a tolerable pattern of exploitation and excitement mixed. She believes that Mr Leacock loves her. And indeed, on the rare occasions when he can contrive to be alone with Gwyneth, he certainly kisses her and tells her so. They were meant for each other, he says, but their love can never be, can never go beyond kisses. Gwyneth must not, no, she must not, leave his employment because he will be miserable if she does. And no, she must not ask for more money or a shorter working week or his wife will suspect him.

And Gwyneth, such is her guilt and such the excitement engendered by these secret meetings, is content to believe him. The years pass quickly: she is forever looking forward, forever watching for a sideways look, forever half fearing, half hoping that Mrs Leacock will see and suspect. And the more guilty Gwyneth feels about the husband, the more fond she becomes of the wife, that bright little bird-woman, pitying her for the drabness of a life which contains only an open and legal love.

Gwyneth believes she has only to speak the words and Mr Leacock will be hers; and forever procrastinates, and never quite speaks them. Thus, lonely women do live, making the best of what they cannot help: reading significance into casual words: seeing love in calculated lust: seeing lust in innocent words; hoping where there is no hope. And so they grow old in expectation and illusion, and perhaps it is preferable to growing old in the harsh glare of truth.

twenty-eight

'Of course I told Marjorie that father raped me,' says Grace. 'Marjorie would never be able to make up anything so interesting on her own account. They're all like that in the media – no imagination at all. Poor father. He was very drunk and very angry.'

In what serves for a bedroom, Grace packs. That is, she empties drawers upon the floor, selects garments and stuffs them into squashy leather bags, seeming to have as much an affection for old torn knickers as she does for Yves St Laurent jumpers.

'He'd taken off his belt to beat me – I think he once had a batman whose virility he admired very much, who used to say the way to keep women in order was to belt them. But all that happened to father was that his trousers fell down, and you know what those austerity underpants were like. I could see he had what I supposed – I was only fifteen – to be an erection. Usually his penis was a dim little thing snuggling in beneath his pot belly. Mother referred to it as daddy's winkie. We had baths together, you know, to save the hot water. Sunday mornings. Marjorie went in with mother, I went in with father. It was unpatriotic to have more than six inches of water in the bath – even King George himself did not.

'And here father was, pointing this great big swollen thing at me, like a gun. I told Marjorie he got me down on the bed and put it in, because that's what she wanted to hear, and I might have known she'd pass the word along, but I don't think he actually did. One would remember a thing like that, I suppose? Though in fact, in sexual matters, one remembers what one wants to forget. At the time I wanted it to be true. I told Patrick my father had raped me. I wanted him to take an interest.'

'Did he?' asks Chloe.

'Yes,' says Grace. 'He laid me in the ditch, there and then, to take the taste from my mouth, he said. And then he said tell no-one, or I'll go to prison, you're under age, look what a risk I'm taking on your behalf. Forget it outside but remember it inside, he said. It's good for you.'

'Patrick and his therapeutic dick,' says Chloe, sadly.

Occasionally, as Grace tosses about amongst her piles of clothing – as she used to toss about, as a child in piles of autumn leaves – she will lift a jersey or bra to her nose and sniff, and if she finds it offensive she will either throw it into the waste bin, if she considers it too far gone, or spray lavishly with cologne before returning it to its pile. Chloe is half admiring, half shocked.

'It's a relief to be able to talk about such things,' says Grace. 'All those years we had to keep quiet! Sebastian talks about everything all the time, every detail, as if nothing that happened was too terrible to mention. When we make love, which isn't often, thank God, he keeps up a running commentary. I don't like it at all.'

And indeed, Grace prefers the silent embraces of her youth, when there were no words for what she did, or what was done to her, or if there were, she didn't know them.

In those other days of speechless intertwinings, she feels, a darker force came into play, linking her more closely to the mindless patterns of the universe. Now this procreative essence shrivels in the light of knowledge. Fellatio, cunnilingus, sodomy – is this what is happening? Is this better than the night before, or what the Jaggers do? Grace would really rather not know, but to Sebastian such knowledge is all in all. Presently it will be the same for her. She knows it.

'I preferred it when fuck was a swear word,' says Grace.

'You ought to get this place cleared up,' says Chloe, nervous of what Grace might say next.

What does Grace have to offer Sebastian, Chloe wonders, since it's not her sexual cooperation? You could leaf through a whole month's supply of women's magazines and not find the answer. Certainly not his creature comforts, let alone a secure and supportive base from which to face the outer world. Apart from the builders' droppings, the floor is littered with books, crumbs, bills, mouse-traps, wine corks, empty bottles and old camembert boxes.

The toilet has recently overflowed and the floor has been only cursorily cleaned. Out on the balcony Grace has been building a curious part-shiny part-encrusted tower with the foil boxes in which Chinese take-away food has been delivered.

So much for talent.

Grace If you don't like the mess, don't look. You're a poor cowardly timorous thing, like your mama. You think if you don't clean up, no-one will love you.

Chloe (Lying) It's not that at all. It's if you don't clear up you get typhoid.

Grace (Happily) We have rats. That ought to look good in court. I feed them.

Chloe You must get in new builders. It's impossible to live like this.

Grace How can I? I haven't any money until I get damages from the last lot.

Chloe Grace, you must have some money. You've just sold the Acacia Road house.

Grace I've given it all to Sebastian. He has to make a feature film about a strike in the Warwickshire coal fields in 1933.

Chloe (Horrified) Grace!

How many times has she not spoken that word, in just those tones? Perhaps it is to hear it that Grace behaves as she does? Spoken by Chloe, a wail of concern.

Grace Sebastian says it's Christie's money anyway. It ought to be ploughed back as soon as possible into the society whence it was milked.

Chloe But that's nonsense.

Grace Do you think so? In any case I'm certain to get it back. I have a percentage of the profits.

Chloe What profits? You're crazy. If you want to invest in a film why didn't you ask Oliver first?

Grace Because I don't love Oliver. I love Sebastian. Anyway Oliver belongs to another world. He's too old. What a bourgeois soul you have, Chloe. You've gone quite pale.

Chloe What about Stanhope's school fees?

Grace Perhaps he'll have to go to a comprehensive school, after all. That should please you. But it will be from necessity, not principle, don't think otherwise.

Chloe God give me strength.

This is Oliver's favourite phrase.

Grace Don't get so agitated. Stephen said it was a perfectly good script. He told me I should put my money in it. He said the world was ripe, for protest films.

Chloe But Stephen is in advertising, not films.

Stephen is Grace's brother. He is twenty-seven.

twenty-nine

Spring, 1945. Hitler is in retreat. Esther Songford is fatter than ever, in spite of stringent rationing. Two ounces of butter a week, three of margarine, one egg and six ounces of meat. Bread and potatoes are on points, as are nearly all groceries. Only carrots and cabbage seem in infinite supply. Esther cooks both in the same water, to save fuel.

'You lumber round like an old cow,' says Edwin to Esther, and she cries. She would like to be young and lively and slim again, and not feel sick all the time. She would like to be like Helen, to please her husband. She doses herself with Syrup of Figs, in the hope that it will make her so. She has a vague belief that you become fat from eating hot food; and lets her dinner get cold upon her plate, to Grace's outrage and irritation. Anything irritates Grace, these days.

Edwin explains about proteins and carbohydrates: but Esther refuses to understand. She is not stupid, but is as irrational about food as she is about her insides.

One Saturday evening when Marjorie is back for the weekend, she, Grace and Chloe sit playing Monopoly with Esther. Esther sits well back from the table to give her fat tummy room. She wears a thin green cotton smock over a skirt which will not meet around her waist, and is pinned with a nappy pin.

A ripple runs under the smock. Esther's bulging stomach, beneath the thin cotton, can be seen to bulge and heave. There's something alive, inside.

'Look,' says Marjorie, her hand frozen in mid air, still holding the hotel she's about to put down on Pall Mall. (Marjorie's winning, as usual. Lucky in games, unlucky in love.) Everyone looks where she points.

'There's something in there moving,' says Marjorie.

Mrs Songford lurches to her feet: she is pale with shock and realization.

'I'm too old,' she says. 'I can't be. I thought it was the Change.'

But it's not, and she is, and Stephen is born in the cottage hospital some two months later.

The end of the war is a difficult time for everyone. The adrenalin level in the nation's bloodstream falls abruptly – depression is bound to follow. It does. Fear of oneself replaces the fear of sudden death: waking nightmares turn into sleeping ones again. No excuses left. Children have to move over to make room for fathers they cannot remember: wives have beloved husbands to feed and not just talk about: women have to leave their jobs and return to the domestic dedication expected of all good women in peacetime. Hitler is not coming, and neither is God; there is to be neither punishment nor salvation. There is, instead, a flurry of sexual activity which will land the schools between 1950 and 1960 with what is known as 'The Bulge'.

In the meantime, at home, there is a shortage of medical supplies – anaesthetics and blood for transfusions, not to mention doctors and nurses, are hard to come by. Midwifery, as always, comes low on the list of national priorities. Poor Esther, after a long labour unrelieved by anaesthetics, enjoined not to make a fuss by a severe spinster midwife, is delivered of a baby boy by sharp steel forceps. Esther haemorrhages after the baby has been put into the nursery, and everyone has gone off to tea, and dies unattended.

An accident, an illness, a death – and a family unit which has seemed secure and permanent can be seen to crumble, with a kind of gratitude, into nothingness. It seems that chaos and dissolution are the norm, and the good times just an accident between them. Days which seem hesitant and troubled as they are lived through, full of minor irritations and absurdities, can be seen in retrospect to be days of wine and roses. Monopoly! Flower shows! School reports! Blackberry puddings and arguments about onions!

They were good times at The Poplars, yes they were, and it was Esther who provided them, plodding dutifully through her days, though no-one thanked her at the time. Did she know she was rewarded? That for Marjorie, Grace and Chloe she provided a nourishment which was to see them through their bad times into good? Or did she see herself as her husband claimed to see her, a stumbling ineffectual creature, mentally chewing the cud of her days as once, at her father's behest, she chewed each mouthful of food, over and over and over again?

Grace is seventeen when the baby is born, and her mother dies. She is supposed to be going to the Slade in the autumn, to study the graphic arts. But what's to be done with this motherless baby, this squalling red-faced morsel with its bruised temples and its sticky eyes? Will Grace stay home and look after it?

No, Grace will not.

Edwin, distraught enough at Esther's death, finding his days empty, his socks unwashed, his food uncooked, his evenings at the pub flavourless for lack of her disapproval, takes refuge in rage and madness. He will not speak to Grace: she is, he says, unnatural and unwomanly. He refuses to pay for her tuition at the Slade; but Esther has left her daughter two hundred pounds he never knew she had, and this too he cannot forget or forgive. He is quite mad, for a time. Relatives say he must engage a housekeeper to look after the house and the baby, and by inference himself, but he will not. He will only be cheated and taken advantage of; he knows it. His pink face grows pale and wan: his paunch shrivels, for a time he looks as Esther does – dead.

Weeds run riot over the flower-beds. See how nature plots against him? By the time he recovers his sanity he has sold The Poplars, bought himself a bungalow in Bournemouth, sent the baby off to be brought up by Esther's elder brother's wife – an amiable widow, by name Elaine, who wears a shirt, tweed suit and brogues, and lives in harmony with Olive, a lady companion with a definite black moustache.

Elaine and Olive breed dogs outside Horsham; and here, except when swept off his feet by bouncing and clumsy labradors, Stephen is reared in happiness and contentment.

He grows, in fact, to some twenty stone, which in a young man of twenty-seven and five feet ten is not inconsiderable. He has Esther's pale pop eyes, much magnified by heavy spectacles, reddish hair and a cleft chin. He has an astute mind, and a commercial instinct. He works in advertising.

Grace used to be ashamed of Stephen. Stephen was, after all, associated with a traumatic time in her life, and could almost be said by his untimely birth to have caused many of her troubles. Stephen was fat, plain and not at all smart. Latterly, though, the gloss of advertising and the cheerful energy of the commercial world, rubbing off upon and somehow firming up his pallid skin, have made Stephen seem rather more attractive to Grace. She looks towards him with hope, beginning to see him as an asset, and not a liability.

Grace Of course, you realize that Stephen is Patrick's son?

Shock affects Chloe with a slight buzzing in the ears, a distancing of sound, a difficulty in hearing.

Grace It gives one some hope for Stanhope, to think that he's Stephen's half-brother. Perhaps we should steer Stanhope towards advertising? Or would Oliver object?

Chloe I do not believe that Stephen is Patrick's son. I cannot believe it. Your mother wasn't like that. Women didn't behave like that.

Grace All women are like that. All women behave like that. It's been proved, at last. They've just done a blood-grouping survey in a Hampshire Town, and discovered that a minimum of one in four children cannot possibly be the blood child of the alleged father. A minimum!

Chloe All I'd deduce from that is an inefficient local maternity home which doles out the wrong babies. Patrick was a boy at the time. Esther was old enough to be his mother.

Grace So am I old enough to be Sebastian's mother. Perhaps it runs in families. Stephen looks like Patrick, don't you think?

Chloe Beneath so much fat, who could tell?

Grace And he has this extraordinary creativity. He's always making or doing something, just like Patrick.

And indeed Patrick, as a young man, is possessed by a demon creativity. He must make something where nothing was before – a painting, a sing-song, a novel, a garden, an affair – forever

115

bridging the gap between nothing and something.

Grace And he knows everything too, just like Patrick did.

In 1945, it is astonishing what Patrick knows, which the rest of Ulden doesn't. He knows that the Bank of England financed Hitler, and that Churchill is an incompetent paranoiac: he knows that sex is not sin, and that gramophone records don't have to be small and fast, but could be large and slow, or even put on to lengths of tape, if only vested interests would allow. He knows that one day men will get to the moon, and that after the war to be born British will not be to be especially blessed by God. He knows what is happening to the Jews in Germany. He knows what will make Marjorie, Grace and Chloe happy.

For reasons, then obscure, he prefers to keep Marjorie unhappy.

Waltzing with Marjorie once, at the D-Day dance, he points out to her some six or seven of the most good-looking young men on the floor.

'Him and him and him,' he says. 'They're all in treatment for VD.'

Grace Anyway, you know what Patrick was. Anything in skirts would do. And mother had very nice legs, and you know how she was always bending over the flower-beds. Shall I take the blue bikini or the black one-piece?

Grace's body is still lean and smooth. She bronzes beautifully.

116

Chloe The one-piece.

But Grace has already sniffed it and tossed it into the waste bin.

Chloe Grace, you have to stop saying things that aren't true. I would have thought your life was difficult enough without you stirring things up.

Grace just looks at Chloe and smiles. And Chloe remembers Esther Songford, young and vulnerable, crying in the kitchen, and wonders. And Chloe considers Grace's past and present, and wonders. Perhaps Edwin Songford, the father, the ultimate provider, did once in fact ultimately provide what was required, in fleshly terms, failing all other. And perhaps Grace's lie – for lie she claims it was – is not the incest itself, but her horror of it.

Grace Sometimes you act like Mad Doll, Chloe. You won't believe what you know to be true.

thirty

Mad Doll haunts Ulden through the war years. She comes up on the London train at weekends, and walks through the village, stopping passers-by, knocking at doors, always smiling, always wheedling.

'Have you seen my boys, doll? Cyril and Ernest?'

She offers wild flowers to the women and kisses to the men, as if she thought she could bribe good news out of them.

'Cyril's jersey is green, dolly. I knitted it myself. Ernest's is maroon and on the small side.'

When it grew dark she'd give up and go home, sitting in the train quite calm and collected, like anyone else.

Cyril and Ernest are buried in Ulden churchyard. They were drowned on their second day in the village, running back to home and London in the middle of the night, crossing the ice of the chalk pit in the dark. Their school had been evacuated to Ulden, without warning to the parents; and no information either, once they'd gone, in case German spies found out. Mad Doll, they say, has slept with the school-keeper to find out where her children have gone, and even then he couldn't be precise. Essex, was all he'd say, and Essex is a large place.

Mad Doll arrives in Ulden the day after her children are buried. The vicar breaks the news of their deaths to her, but she seems unable to take it in. He leads her by the hand to the new grave, but she looks at it blankly and then says 'I'll give you a kiss if you tell me where they are. More than a kiss, if you insist.'

No wonder he suffers from blood-pressure.

She's a pretty girl, still only in her mid-twenties, though soon she develops a crabbed and aged look. Her husband is on active service, somewhere secret, and he is never to come back. He is posted missing, presumed dead. The manner of his death is kept secret too. She's become so used to secrets, poor soul, she's simply ceased to trust information.

thirty-one

Sebastian comes bounding up the stairs, lean, lively, and desperate, as if the hounds of old age would be yapping at his heels if he went more slowly. He seems pleased to see Chloe, to Grace's surprise. He clasps Chloe's stiff, self-conscious body to his thin, denim shirt, asks how she is, even asks after Marjorie.

'Having a hysterectomy,' says Chloe.

'My God, in the hysterectomy belt already!' says Sebastian.

Sebastian wears a wide belt with a brass buckle, in the form of a snake swallowing an eagle. How he mocks and masters the world! How he suffers and shrinks at the prospect of boredom and solitude. How untouched he is by the world's miseries.

All Sebastian owes the world, Sebastian believes, is his own existence, and the pleasure he takes in it.

Sebastian's buttocks are clearly defined in faded jeans. Chloe surprises herself with a sudden surge of sexual desire, which goes straight from eyes to womb, bypassing her brain. Is this, she wonders, what Esther Songford saw and felt, lifting her eyes from the geraniums to those of Patrick Bates?

Forget it outside, remember it inside. It will do you good.

'Marjorie's insides were always a source of trouble to her,' says Grace, ushering Chloe out rather hastily. 'She'd be better off without them.'

Well, thinks Chloe, forgiving, if your mother died in childbirth, giving birth to the half-brother of one of your own children, you too might find yourself viewing female insides as more trouble than they're worth.

'Grace,' says Chloe, lingering and anxious, 'your mother didn't know about you and Patrick, did she?'

'No,' says Grace. 'But I think she knew about father and me. That must have helped her die happy. She was always putting me in his way, you must have noticed, drawing attention to my tits or my arse, under guise of clothing coupons.'

'You imagine it.' Chloe is nervous.

'She didn't like me and she didn't like him, and it killed two birds with one stone. Like you and your Françoise.'

'What do you mean?'

'Pushing her under your husband's nose. I watched you do it, and I think you deserve what happened.'

She is all malevolence, suddenly, eyes aglitter. Chloe trembles, as she does when her reasonable world turns upside down.

'What harm have I done you?' she asks. 'Why are you like this?'

'You just existed,' says Grace. 'You and Marjorie. Great big cuckoos in my nest. It was you who killed my mother. You wore her out.'

And Grace goes inside and slams the door and poor Chloe, much upset, goes back home to Egden, to cope with Françoise and weed the geranium beds, before the light fades.

thirty-two

Marjorie, Grace and me.

We have our arcane secrets, our superstitions, our beliefs, fact and fantasy mixed. Our sexual fears, both rational and irrational. Our own experiences which we share with each other. They are altogether different from what the novels and text books told us they would be.

We got our certificates, our diplomas, our degrees. We had miscarriages, abortions and babies. Marjorie and I caught the clap. We still cannot name our secret parts. We know them blindly, by feel, and not by sight or name. They rule us.

Grace says women ovulate from sheer astonishment. That's why innocent girls get pregnant and experienced ones don't. Grace says she has a corroded cervix: she believes she has a soft and bubbly cyst somewhere inside which no doctor can discover: she says she's only twice had an orgasm in her life other than by masturbation, which she didn't discover until long after she'd left Christie, and even then didn't know that what she did had a name or that anyone else ever did it. Grace feels her bosom daily for cancer and daily discovers a good many different lumps. Grace does not trust the doctors who examine her insides. She suspects they take pleasure from the process. Well, she does.

Grace has had cheap back-street abortions and National Health abortions and an expensive post-Abortion Act abortion. She loves anaesthetics and feels only relief when the baby's gone and she's no longer nauseous. Grace tried a contraceptive coil but bled too profusely to keep it in. One woman in three does, says Grace. The pill made her sick. Dutch caps disgust her. These days Grace takes no contraceptive precautions at all. It is her Act of Oneness with the universe, or so she says. She relies on her age, her inverted womb and her imagined fibroids to protect her from pregnancy.

121

Grace enjoys getting pregnant, but not being pregnant.

Marjorie believes her reproductive energies were drained by her first baby, which she failed to carry to maturity.

Marjorie believes she is infertile, and will never know, because she takes oestrogen pills to regulate her monthly bleeding – not that it does.

Marjorie believes the age of the menarche to be dependent on the weight of the girl. Menstruation starts at ninety-four pounds. She, later to menstruate than any of her friends, need never have worried.

Marjorie believes it is just as well she is infertile – since any baby she had would be born monstrous. A disagreeable young nurse implied as much at the VD clinic she had the misfortune to attend, and Marjorie chooses to believe her.

Marjorie thinks if she had Patrick's baby it would perhaps be all right, but Patrick, alas, only uses her as a washer-woman.

Marjorie consults gynaecologists, goes to Health Farms, looks to authorities to tell her about the state of her insides, which she sees as a bloody, indeterminate mass and which behave accordingly.

Marjorie gives post-production parties at her flat and would sleep with anyone who cared to remain behind, except her insides will not allow, or very seldom. She bleeds too much.

I, Chloe, believe you shouldn't get your feet wet when you have a period, that pre-menstrual tension is the result of fluid retention in the brain, that sex is for the begetting of children. That some children are *meant* – and that the most unlikely people will come together to produce a child, and having done so will part again, astonished at what they've done: that some of the most robust and kindly couples can't help producing thin, weedy and miserable children and there's no fairness in any of it. That children do not change their essential natures between the day they're born and the day they leave home, and that there's precious little you can do to help or hinder on the way.

I, Chloe, believe that if you do not consider your reproductive organs they will function properly, and that the harsh light of inquiry is damaging to their well-being.

Feel your breasts today and have cancer tomorrow. A cervical smear now means the womb out soon. Experience shows it to be true, if not statistics.

I, Chloe, feel my function to be maternal and not erotic. I cannot concede that it's possible to be both, though reason tells me it is: and that is why I do not mind Françoise sharing Oliver's bed. It allows me my dignity.

Besides, a mother must be watchful. It is one of the laws of nature that one cannot be watchful and orgasmic at the same time.

thirty-three

Greenfly cover the honeysuckle like a surging foam. Chloe notices it on her return from London. The flies reproduce themselves like broomsticks in the *Sorcerer's Apprentice*. New small greenfly simply crawl out of the backside of older larger greenfly. Oliver told Chloe so, once, in wonder.

After spraying the honeysuckle with the non-toxic spray

that Oliver likes her to use, and watching a diminution of perhaps ten per cent in the level of the living foam. Chloe goes into the kitchen to face her family.

Françoise is at the Aga cooker, preparing the *boeuf-en-daube*. There is no machinery in the kitchen apart from the refrigerator, which is essential to the chilling of Oliver's champagne. Oliver dislikes the noise of domestic machinery: it jars his nerves. It is a symbol of the bourgeois content he dreads. He feels it to be more moral, with one half of the world starving and the other made wretched by the cult of conspicuous consumption, to have the dishes and clothes washed by hand; and the floors brushed on hands and knees; and closer to nature to have his food cooked over wood and coal, and not by electricity.

There are open grates in every room. This is in defiance of the Clean Air Act, it is true, but it is clear to Oliver that industry pollutes the air and not the private domestic fire. And as for cars (Oliver has two, a Peugeot estate and a Mustang) they contribute only six per cent to total air pollution and the attack against the private car, as is well known, is diversionary tactics backed by big business interests.

Chloe's hands, for years, have been sodden with washing water, ingrained with dust and soot, splintered by the wooden floors. She is no longer interested in arguing with Oliver. He is better at arguing than she is. And why argue? Everything Oliver says about the outside world is patently true. She knows for herself that the Aga cooks better than would an electric stove: that hands break down less frequently than dishwashers or clothes washers; that deep-freezers spoil the flavour of food and denature it, that vacuum cleaners damage the valuable rugs; that it is immoral to employ other women to do one's own dirty work; that central heating is enervating; that fitted carpets are a sign of growing old; that non-toxic greenfly spray does not kill butterflies.

Now it is Françoise's turn to live by Oliver's principle. In her parents' house at Rheims are many modern conveniences, even an electric carving knife – for the thin and economical slicing of excellent meat – and a mechanical vegetable chopper. Françoise has come to despise such gadgetry.

When Chloe returns, Françoise's face is wet with onion tears. Chloe is glad to see it. A whole layer of Gallic competence, she feels, is being peeled away. Beneath it lurks the universal woman, servile to the unreasonable will of the male.

Oliver believes himself to be supremely reasonable.

Oliver writes film scripts for major American film companies. His enemies (who are many) say they are slick. His friends (who are few) say they are competent. The scripts bring in a good deal of money. All Oliver wants to do is write novels. He would trade good money for good reviews any day.

Oliver is a scholarship boy at Bristol University when Chloe first meets him. He has emerged phoenix-like from the rubble of the bombed East End to read English literature. Oliver's parents are of Russian-Jewish descent. Oliver's mother has recently died of cancer, and Oliver's father is suing, out of public funds, a shop which sold his wife a fur coat the week before she died, and under which she died, and which the shop now declines to accept back in return for a cash refund.

'They could tell she was dying,' says Oliver's father Danny, six times a night for six weeks. Oliver counted. 'What sort of business sells a fur coat to a dying woman? You only had to look at her to tell she was dying.'

Oliver hates his father, hates his sisters, hates the East End, hates the governments which have rained bombs upon his head, killed his friends, and destroyed by blast the garden he has so lovingly created in the back-yard, between the dog kennel and the clothes-line. He has renounced them all, along with chicken soup, Yom Kippur and shaven Jewish brides.

One drunken night Oliver goes to a student's party. Picture the scene.

The student's smoky room (in these days anyone who can afford to smoke does so, and very few have heard of lung cancer, let alone made a connection between that illness and cigarettes, though no doubt as many die from it); the travel posters (Cyprus, mostly) around the walls; the guttering candles (and the wax melts in untidy stalactic clumps, not blindly and neatly, as now); Chianti in straw bottles; rows of smiling jolly blackened teeth; men in their early twenties, National Service completed, or even – oh romance! – Active Service, wearing baggy grey trousers, white shirts, no ties – or, daring! – sweaters in muted colours, and cropped hair; the girls straight from school, in neat blouses, and pleated skirts, their hair feather-cut short, or permed into icy waves, their make-up thick and matte, concentrating – according to temperament – upon losing their virginity, or keeping it, or somehow, best of all, magically, doing both.

Into this party, just after midnight, at the stage before conversation fades away and couples fall into horizontal innocent embraces, comes Oliver.

Oliver does not look English. Oliver is too dark, too hairy, too discontented – and, shall one say, too Jewish. Not that anyone here is anti-semitic, on the contrary, just the feeling goes, that Oliver seems troublesome to himself and other people. He argues with professors, insults those who try to help him, finds fault with the syllabus and the examination system – but that's what universities are *for*, surely – complains about the smallness of his grant, instead of being grateful for it like anyone else, and demands extra blankets and soft pillows for his bed – the comfort of which, after all, is underwritten by the long-suffering rate-payer.

Whatever, of course, the rates may be. Only a few have any idea, knowing or caring little, as they do, how their society is organized. Oliver knows. His father wailed and his mother choked every six months when the buff envelope arrived from the Town Hall. Town Hall? What's that?

Oliver drinks the dregs of such Chianti bottles as he can find. He does not like these people. He has come to the party only because he cannot sleep. He feels himself to be superior to the other guests by virtue of his tormented past and his lack of insularity. Yet they insist, he knows it, on feeling superior to him, patronizing him, allowing him in their midst as a kind of mascot, as if their complacency was to their credit, as his torments a joke.

And the girls! How he hates them, with their rounded vowels, their peeking bosoms, their daddies and mummies, their Aryan niceness. A proportion will even undermine him by obliging in bed, not wishing to be abused for purity or meanness – yet still, although on top of them he must plainly be victorious, they remain superior, kindly and patronizing. It is he who cries out in his spasm: the most they do is moan agreeably and tell him they love him, which he knows to be untrue. He can make them smart, he can make them cry; yet twist their soft spiritual arms as he may, he cannot make them angry, or nasty.

They are too nice. They are not human. Human beings rant and roister, fuck and feed, love and smother, shake their fists at the universe in thunder storms and defy a creator who is sure to get them with the next lightning bolt. These little English girls, with their soft, uncomplaining voices, and their docile hearts, whose worst crime has been a foul on the hockey pitch, are quite alien to him. He feels at liberty to behave with them as he pleases, and if in so doing he gets the better of the blond, smiling men, with their cool, intelligent, experienced ex-service eyes, so much the better.

Oliver's feet kept him out of the forces.

thirty-four

Dinner, it seems, is going to be late. If Françoise is still chopping onions then the *boeuf-en-daube* is far from ready. She wipes her eyes and turns them reproachfully towards Chloe. In the evenings, at the best of times, Françoise's face tends to lose its daytime alertness, and to collapse into disorder, as if the spirit behind it had given up. Tonight she is grey with fatigue, and the corner of her eye is twitching.

Good, thinks Chloe. Good, good. And then, what nastiness is this? See what Marjorie and Grace have done to me!

Chloe Is anything the matter?
Françoise No.
Chloe Did you have a good day?
Françoise Yes.
Chloe Were the children helpful?
Françoise Yes.
Chloe You seem a little tired. Would you like me to take over?
Françoise It is not necessary. It is all completed now.
Chloe Isn't it going to be rather late?
Françoise It will be ready to eat at twelve fifteen.

So Oliver, too, has had a bad day. It is not unusual for him, having abandoned one day as disagreeable, to postpone dinner until the next.

Chloe Then what about the children?
Françoise Oliver (*How she pronounces the name, with what sensuous Gallic charm – Oli-vaire!*) Oliver says the children are to have fish fingers. He says, in any case, it is a pity to waste good food on small fry.
Chloe I'm afraid it will make you rather late, Françoise. I'll stay up and clear away, if you like.
Françoise No. That is not necessary. It is what I am paid to do, and the literary spirit is a flame which must be fanned and not quenched. I am honoured to be able to serve.

129

There is a note of desperation in her voice.

Chloe You must get some sleep.
Françoise Oliver says that science tells us that the female needs less sleep than the male.
Chloe I expect science does.
Françoise May I confide in you, Mrs Rudore?
Chloe Of course.

What now?

Françoise Mr Rudore wishes me to sit English O-level examinations, and the classes are so distant and the buses are so far and few between I am quite *distrait*.
Chloe But your English is so good, Françoise. Really most colloquial.
Françoise Mr Rudore wants it to be better still, so that when he reads me his writing I can criticize in an informed fashion.
Chloe (Presently) Does he often read his work to you, Françoise? I had no idea!

Nor has she. Chloe is hurt and upset. A pain catches her under her ribs. Perhaps Marjorie and Grace are right. Perhaps she is surrounded by enemies – perhaps bed is the thin edge of Françoise's wedge.

Françoise Today was the first occasion I have been so privileged. He called for you, but you were not there, Mrs Rudore. You were in London, visiting your friends. The creative flame is so easily dimmed, that when he asked me to take your place in the easy chair I could not, in all correctness, refuse. He also asked me for my honest opinion, but when I gave it, he said I must have English lessons.

Chloe I hope you did not discourage him, Françoise.

Françoise Perhaps he is right. Perhaps I am useless and ignorant. It has always been the same for me. I am misunderstood, and not appreciated.

Chloe Françoise, we all appreciate you very much.

Françoise And I am alone in this country without friends and I do not mean to do the wrong thing. I am trying to please everyone; it is a bad habit of my personality. Perhaps I should go home. I feel you do not like me.

Chloe Françoise, of course I like you. You would not be here if I did not.

Françoise puts her arms round Chloe's neck, and lays her cheek on Chloe's hair. Françoise is taller than Chloe. It is a gesture both childlike and perverse, and disturbing to Chloe. In some way this flesh, so close to Oliver's, might be his. It is as if Oliver is touching her, and rousing her, through Françoise, yet still in the presence of a third person. Chloe stands still, neither accepting nor rejecting. When Françoise steps back, it seems the moment was after all innocent, of intent, or seduction, or even apology, and was indeed merely childlike. As a child will, she has recovered in the space of seconds from grief, guilt, and spite.

Françoise Ah, so you forgive me. All is well again. We shall all be happy. It is a great pleasure to see friends, especially those of long standing, is it not? Oliver says you and your friends are, as the saying goes, thick as thieves. We agreed, he and I, you were right to go. It is important to cultivate friendship, after a certain age.

Thick as thieves! What did they steal from each other, Marjorie, Grace and Chloe? Everything, in their desperate youth. Parents, lovers, children, a vision of themselves.

Chloe denies her friends, to that Gallic snippet, Françoise.

Chloe (Lying) They are not important to me.
Françoise What a pity! It is different for me, of course. It is not natural for someone of my age to have many friends. Lovers, yes. Friends, no. In any case, female friends are not to be trusted.

Françoise's fiancé ran off with her best friend, on the eve of her wedding.

thirty-five

At Helen's behest, Marjorie leaves The Poplars and moves into the house in Hampstead. The war is on its last ulcerated legs.

Buzz-buzz.
Is it a bee?
Is it a wasp?
No, it's a bomb.
A buzz-bomb, Hitler's last secret desperate weapon.

A Robot bomb, or doodle-bug, a Farting Fury or an unemotional V1.

It was all right so long as you could hear them buzzing. When the engine cut out you knew they were about to fall, and probably on you.

Marjorie, alone in Frognal, hears the same bombs as Oliver does in the East End. She welcomes the sound. Somebody, somewhere is thinking of her. Such is her frame of mind.

As for Helen, she's gone to Taunton, her current head-quarters. She wears a gay red cap and bright red lipstick, drives a general about, and books in at his hotels. The Frognal house depresses her, as much as it does Marjorie. The long low curving rooms are flakey with rotten plaster. The metal curtain rails, which criss-cross the ceilings like railway tracks at a junction, are rusty. They drop reddish flakes upon the pale unwaxed warping Bauhaus furniture. Creepers press and nod against the portholes. The roof still leaks: dry-rot has started, and the books and the bedding throughout the house are musty.

Helen feels that the fabric and condition of the house is nothing to do with her. It's man's work. Even so, she complains of its gloom. If she is in London she books in at the Connaught Hotel, where cucumber sandwiches are still served for tea, and keeps away from Frognal. Marjorie is there, of course. Well, someone has to be, in case the house is burgled. (Helen lives in fear of thieves, and rape. Her gentlemen friends, even generals, are obliged to look under the bed before she can compose herself for sleep.) Besides, Dick is still expected back.

A letter from the Red Cross says he is due for repatriation on humanitarian grounds. Prepare his bed, Marjorie.

So Marjorie lives alone in the pale, dusty, damp house. She studies for her High School Certificate through a Correspondence College. Latin, Greek and French. Helen complains of the expense, but pays the fees. She allows her daughter ten shillings a week for food and keep.

Marjorie goes to the shops on Mondays, buys her week's rations, posts off the week's work and goes home. Sometimes she does not leave the house until next Monday comes again. Once a month she goes to Ulden to spend a weekend with the Songfords. She cannot afford to go more often.

Once, when Helen is passing through London, she meets her at the Connaught for lunch, and eats kedgeree with a listless appetite.

Helen wears a cream shantung suit and a yellow hat. She does not seem to look older as the years pass, merely more immaculate. Marjorie wears one of her father's old grey jerseys, found in a drawer, and a brown skirt borrowed from Grace. She has put on a maroon scarf in deference to the fact that she is lunching at the Connaught. And thus the conversation goes:

Helen You're much too thin, Marjorie. I hope you're doing your bust exercises.
Marjorie Yes, mother.
Helen All that stooping over books! It's bad for your figure.
Marjorie It was never up to much in the first place.
Helen One is as attractive as one believes, Marjorie. I do worry about you. You're not lonely? All alone in that great house.

Marjorie There's no need to worry about me, mother. Please don't. I'm perfectly all right.

Helen Somebody has to be in the house, you see. I can't put in a caretaker, not these days. A good paid servant is as rare as dust. They say they're on war service, but my own opinion is they're taking advantage of the national emergency. And if you find someone to do it, it would be like putting the key into the burglar's hand! Now you're getting enough to eat?

Marjorie Of course, mother.

Helen Rations are very meagre, I know, but we all have to make sacrifices. Besides, you're slightly built so you should find them perfectly adequate. I hope you've brought your clothing book with you? Good! How many? Sixty-seven points? Lovely! I've seen such a nice winter coat in Harrod's sale, and being the cold person I am, it simply isn't safe for me to drive my generals about if I'm not nice and snug and warm. It's all right for you, safe and snug in front of the fire.

Marjorie I can't get any coal.

Helen For heaven's sake then, child, use your initiative. There's enough old wood in that garden to fuel a battleship for a month. And Marjorie, you won't leave crumbs in the kitchen, will you. I don't want the mice encouraged. How are your lessons going?

Marjorie Very well. I got an Alpha for a Latin prose.

Helen They have to give you something in return for all that money. I'm positive that all those tutors with degrees are either fakes or deserters, or worse. Or why aren't they working in proper schools? Don't look so dismal, dear, you have your father's return to look forward to.

Marjorie's heart shrinks at the vision of some blind, mutilated stranger stumbling towards her, up the elegant, unswept stairs, calling her by the name of daughter.

Helen Marjorie, what are we going to do about your hair? Your father will want to see you looking at your best. He has such an eye for a pretty woman, we all know that. Besides, it is a woman's duty to look her best, especially in time of war. It gives the men something to fight *for*. Perhaps if you tried brushing your hair a hundred strokes each side.
Marjorie I did try. It went all greasy.
Helen Better that than like a haystack.

Marjorie goes home. Helen gives her an extra ten shillings for which she is grateful. She spends it on stationery for her correspondence course.

Marjorie hopes a V1 bomb will fall on her soon. She begins to think the house is haunted. It takes all her courage to go through from the living room to the kitchen. It's as if some kind of invisible curtain hangs between them; she has to use all her strength to brush it aside. And in the kitchen a force rears up in front of her, saying go back, go away. She tends to do just that.

Marjorie eats her food, uncooked, in the dining room and gets her water from the bathroom.

Marjorie finds it more and more difficult to leave the house. She has nowhere to go, in any case. People in the street seem strange and distant, as if they inhabited another universe. Her voice, as she shops on Monday mornings, sounds hollow and undersea, a booming in her ears. And what she says sounds so nonsensical that she is surprised when the shopkeeper understands, and hands her food in exchange for money and coupons.

Marjorie is seventeen. She is in a nightmare. Some life comes to her off the pages of text books. And she manages a quite bright response to a Miss Janet Fairfax, MA, who corrects her Latin proses and from time to time adds an encouraging comment – well done! What a flair you have! How well you handle the living language, as well as the dead!

Marjorie thinks, she is probably a phoney. A fake or a lady deserter from the ATS. Or some maiden lady running a tea-shop and knowing nothing. But she is pleased, all the same. It makes a slight wall of warmth to help keep the cold out.

Marjorie goes home from the shops. She works, eats, clears the house up, barricades herself into her room after dusk. But whatever it is in the kitchen seems now to extend to the dining room. It is growing. She eats in the bedroom. The side of the house where the bathroom is seems less afflicted. The sun shines in through the portholes onto the staircase and makes yellow pools of light on the shallow stone steps.

Buzz-buzz. There it goes! Hitler's swan-song. Please fall. Spare someone else. Choose me.

No.

There is a private boys' school down the road. The boys were evacuated throughout the war but have lately moved back to London. Young men walk up and down past her windows: it is beyond the bounds of possibility to talk to them.

Marjorie wakes in the middle of the night. Something's in the room. The heart thudding, the hand creeping out to switch on the bedside light. Quick. No. Nothing. Just the knowledge

137

that it's there, in the room; come out from the kitchen. Why? Marjorie flees from the room, through the unseen curtain, which parts unwillingly to let her through. She sits all night on the stairs, with the light on and the full moon shining through the windows.

Marjorie begins to bleed. She doesn't dare move up to the bathroom to wash or back to the bedroom for paper sanitary towels. The stairs are stained for ever.

The next day her father returns. Dick. He wears a patch over one eye, and the other is opaque, but still has some sight in it. All the same, he walks with one hand rigid in front of him as if he were pushing away obstacles. He is gaunt; his head is prickly with newly-grown hair. Marjorie does not remember him: Dick clearly has other things to think about than her. A Red Cross lady comes with him. She is kind, and settles him in his bed, tells Marjorie not to worry, just to wait.

Where is Helen? Why, Helen's in the Shetlands, taking an American general on a visit to Northern defences. He'd always wanted to see Shetland sheep, in any case, having had a very expensive Shetland pullover in infancy. When else in his life will he have the chance? Helen drives him all the way, as obliging out of bed as in it. Marjorie sends a telegram at once – but the Shetlands are a long way, and the posts are not reliable, and it does not arrive.

That was Monday.

Marjorie comes to life and goes into the kitchen without thinking. She makes tea, and gives up all her butter ration so that Dick can have buttered toast. Dick lies on his back on the bed and sleeps, and rouses himself to eat, and then falls back again. Sometimes he just lies with his eyes open, blinking a little, thinking. What about?

That was Tuesday,

Buzz-buzz
Please don't fall.
No.

That was Wednesday.

Dick sits up, smiles, takes Marjorie's hand.

'Well, Marge,' he says. 'Perhaps we should call you butter.' He goes to sleep again. What a rare and precious commodity butter is.

That was Thursday.

It is night time. Dick gets up out of bed while Marjorie is asleep, goes up the blood-stained stairs (does he notice?) to the attic, to look at his books. He sees mildew and smells dry-rot. He comes down to the kitchen and has a heart attack and dies.

That was Friday.

Marjorie finds Dick on the kitchen floor. Helen comes back. The Red Cross say the death was to be expected, had they not made that clear? Helen says it is all Marjorie's fault for not calling her back. Well, she is very upset.

That was Saturday and Sunday.

Marjorie goes to Bishops Stortford to sit her Latin exam. How callous and cruel you are, says Helen.

That was Monday.

What a week!

Buzz-buzz
Shoo fly, don't bother me!

Marjorie gets Honours in all three subjects.

thirty-six

Marjorie, Grace and me. How do we recover from the spasms of terror and resentment which assail us, in our marriages and in our lives? When we lie awake in bed and know that the worst is at hand, if we do not act (and we cannot act) – the death of our children, or their removal by the State, or physical crippling, or the loss of our homes, or the ultimate loneliness of abandonment. When we cry and sob and slam doors and know we have been cheated, and are betrayed, are exploited and misunderstood, and that our lives are ruined, and we are helpless. When we walk alone in the night planning murder, suicide, adultery, revenge – and go home to bed and rise red-eyed in the morning, to continue as before.

And either the worst happens, or it doesn't. Or one is mistreated, or one is not, the answer is never made clear. Life continues.

Marjorie recovers her spirits by getting ill. She frightens herself with palpitations, slipped discs, stomach cramp. Snaps out of anxiety and depression and into hypochondria. She sits another examination, though with hands trembling and aching head. She writes another memo. Gets another job. Life continues.

Grace takes direct action. She throws out the offending lover, has hysterics, attempts to strangle, breaks up her home, makes obscene phone calls, issues another writ, calms down. Goes to the hairdresser and demands that the manicurist does her toe nails. Life continues.

I, Chloe, move in another tradition, like my mother and Esther Songford before me. Mine is the mainstream, I suspect, of female action and reaction – in which neglected wives apply for jobs as home helps, divorcees go out cleaning, rejected mothers start playgroups, unhappy daughters leave home and take jobs abroad as au pairs.

Rub and scrub distress away, hands in soap-suds, scooping out the sink waste, wiping infants' noses, the neck bowed beneath the yoke of unnecessary domestic drudgery, pain in the back already starting, unwilling joints seizing up with arthritis. Life continues.

thirty-seven

Grace is the first to marry, prancing back to Ulden with a ring on her finger, a white wedding behind her, and Christie at her side.

Who'd have thought it a year earlier, when Grace sets off for London and the Slade from Ulden station, with only Gwyneth, Chloe and the Vicar to see her off. Her mother decomposing in the churchyard, her father nutty in a nursing home, and The Poplars up for sale. Nervous, affectionate and chattery, looking thin for once, and not just slim.

'A pity Marjorie isn't here,' Grace says, as they wait for the Toy Town train. It is early October, and a damp and dismal day. Chloe is constantly surprised, these days, at Grace's softness. Grace even tucks her gloved hand under Gwyneth's arm and she is normally cool and distant with her friend's mother, who when all is said and done, in spite of her lilting voice and ladylike ways, is only a barmaid.

But after her mother's death, for a time, Grace becomes humbler and gentler, and grateful for affection.

'Remember the day Marjorie and you arrived,' says Grace. 'There were so many people around then. Now there seems to be no-one. Everything's running down.'

'It was a very smelly train,' says Gwyneth. 'And they were very upsetting, dangerous days. Times are better now.'

But they are nostalgic, all the same, for those days of innocence and growth and noise. The post-war world is drab and grey and middle-aged. No excitement, only shortages and work. The airfields are closed, the Americans gone, the troops have been demobilized. Even Patrick has left, taking his guilty excitements with him, leaving virtue and propriety behind. Cabbages grow wild in Esther's flower-beds, but the roses have taken over Edwin's bean trellises. Neither of them won, neither Edwin nor Esther. They were evenly matched in the end.

'You will look after yourself, Grace dear,' says Gwyneth. 'You're too young to be setting off on your own.'

The Vicar has found Grace a bed-sitting room in Fulham, her place is waiting at the Slade, she has two hundred pounds in the bank, she can't wait to be off, but Gwyneth worries.

'No younger than Chloe,' says Grace. Chloe is off to Bristol

University the following week. Gwyneth is trying to get used to the idea. For seventeen years the circumstances of her life have been dictated by Chloe's needs. Now she will be free, when she no longer has the strength to use her freedom.

'Still too young,' says Gwyneth.

'I can look after myself,' says Grace. 'Marjorie's in London. I won't be alone.'

'Now remember,' says Gwyneth, 'don't let yourself be alone with a man, then you can't get into trouble. It's a simple rule. I hope Chloe remembers it.'

'I'm sure there's a branch of the SCM at the Slade,' says the Vicar.

'The SCM?' asks Grace.

'Student Christian Movement. And at Bristol too, Chloe. They'll help you meet other young people socially under proper supervision. We're not wet-blankets, we old codgers of the cloth: we know girls want to meet boys and boys want to meet girls.'

Grace thinks of the muddy ditch in which she lay with Patrick. Chloe of her mother's bed, and the unlocked door, and Patrick.

'Yes,' says Grace, politely.

'Yes,' says Chloe, the same.

'I wish you'd put it off a year,' says Gwyneth.

When one mother goes, another moves in.

'Too late now,' says Grace.

Grace has burnt her boats. Her mother is dead, the baby sent off, her father is having a nervous breakdown. It is all Grace's fault and she can't wait to get out of Ulden.

'It's not too late,' says Chloe. 'You just don't get on the train.'

Chloe worries lest Grace meet Patrick in London. Perhaps even at the Slade. For did not Patrick, usually so secretive, once let fall that after the war he meant to use his ex-service educational grant at art school? Does Grace know more than she does? Chloe can't ask. Chloe and Grace never talk about Patrick, for fear of what they might hear, and this major silence sets up a whole chain of little silences between them.

Still, if you're going to be laid and left, it might as well happen in silence. The humiliation, otherwise, is extreme. Both feel it.

Chloe is wrong, as it happens. Patrick goes to the Camberwell School of Art, not the Slade, and sees more of Marjorie than anyone else. Marjorie has a large house all to herself, after all, and Patrick sees no point in paying rent. He finds her address in his pocket-book. Chloe had given it to him.

Patrick What a superb house. What decadence!

Marjorie I'd clear it up if I knew where to start.

Patrick It would be a shame to do that. I like it as it is. Are you here all by yourself?

Marjorie Yes. Mother's in South Africa.

Patrick Don't you get rather lonely?

Marjorie Yes.

Patrick The locks don't look too good.

Marjorie They're not. Sometimes when I wake in the morning the front door's ajar. And of course I can't use the kitchen at all because it's haunted.

Patrick What by?

Marjorie I'd think my father, except he died in there months after the haunting began. Unless of course these things have a different time scale from ours.

Patrick A ghost is the projection of a living person, not a dead one. If you stopped being so unhappy and depressed the ghost would go away.

Marjorie What makes you think I'm unhappy and depressed?

Patrick The spots on your chin.

Marjorie is fascinated rather than insulted. That the state of the mind and the state of the body might be inter-related is something that comes to her with the shock of truth.

Marjorie How do I stop being unhappy and depressed?

Patrick You get me to move in as the lodger.

Patrick smiles at her. How broad, strong, young and healthy he appears, and how simple, sensible, and straightforward his requests. You would think he was a farmer's son and not a criminal's.

Marjorie Mother doesn't like strangers in the house.

Patrick Your mother's in South Africa.

True, thinks Marjorie, with a flicker of, what, spite?

Patrick And I am not a stranger.

True. Patrick kissed Marjorie once, in 1946, leaning his strong hands against her small ones, pinning her against the trunk of a poplar tree, and who's to say what might not have happened if it had not started to rain, or indeed if it had been a different tree, and not a poplar, with its upstretched, unsheltering branches. How Marjorie had trembled. Patrick Bates, grown man, in His Majesty's uniform, and she nothing but Helen's plain and awkward daughter. 'Never mind,' he'd said then, as if he knew more about her than she did herself, and what can be more erotic than that. 'Never mind.'

Now Marjorie steps aside, and Patrick steps in. He looks at the ceiling of the long living room, and the criss-cross of curtain rails, from which hang moth-ridden brown curtains.

Patrick What's that patch of damp?
Marjorie There's something wrong with the roof, I think. It gets worse when it's been raining. I don't understand it. The roof's two floors up. How could the rain get down this far?
Patrick I'll see to it.

But he never does.

Patrick moves in with his paints and canvases and suitcases, and makes his home the living room. He goes to Camberwell by day, and paints in the evenings, still lifes at first, and presently Marjorie, at first clothed, and then unclothed. He makes no further demands on her. He does not wish her to cook, or wash, or clean for him. He prefers to eat baked beans cold from the tin, and once the possibility of so doing occurs to her, so does Marjorie. Neither of them, these proud, strong days, likes to be beholden to anyone or anything.

146

Marjorie's chin gets less spotty.

Helen moves to Australia. For two terms she fails to pay Marjorie's tuition fees at Bedford College, where she is studying Classics. The Registrar sends for Marjorie, and refers to Helen, in a perfectly kindly way, as 'one of these difficult parents'. Marjorie is most indignant on her mother's behalf, preferring to blame the mail for her shortcomings. At Patrick's suggestion she sells three Etty portraits for fifteen pounds each, to pay the bill. They were stacked in the wood shed in the garden, until he brought them in.

One night Marjorie, untroubled for some time, wakes in sudden terror, spirit breath upon her cheek, and runs to Patrick for comfort. He sleeps, fully clothed, in a roll of blankets beside the long, once luxurious, sofa. But he will not allow Marjorie in beside him, though he does not himself understand why not.

He sends her back to the troubled, heaving darkness of her room, which no amount of electric light seems able that night, to brighten.

'If you are the bride of darkness,' he tells her as they breakfast off cold tinned macaroni cheese, 'and I suspect you are, then who am I to come between you and your succubi? It is too dangerous.'

'But I get so frightened,' she says. 'And what are you talking about? I know it's only projection and neurosis and so on.' She does not love Patrick. She feels too close to him for that. He is father and brother in one.

'Just lie there and try to enjoy it,' says Patrick. 'Like any other woman. God knows what you and your other world

147

invader are breeding. It is not this house that is haunted, it is you. I don't want to catch it from you, your spiritual VD.'

'It's not catching,' says Marjorie, miserable. Is there to be no end to the dreadful things she is responsible for?

But perhaps it is a catching, or at any rate, a transferable ill. A few months later Patrick comes back from college with a full bottle of Grand Marnier he has found in the gutter, and he and Marjorie drink it all between them, and in the morning find themselves entwined together on the floor, sick and hungover, and though Marjorie's mind has little remembrance of what exactly happened, she has the physical knowledge that her body, this morning, is undoubtedly different from what it was the night before, and she, all unbeknownst, handed some kind of season ticket to enter worlds she has so far only heard about.

And as for Patrick, it is certainly true that about this time a kind of natural goodness inside him becomes clouded over; or perhaps it is only that the violent gloom which marked his entry into the world begins to take its toll upon his personality – at any rate he has, thereafter, the gift of bringing disaster not so much upon himself as upon the heads of people less accustomed to it than he. Though Patrick, one might say, has been rendered immune in infancy to Marjorie's disease, others, more fortunate than he, have not. These are the people Patrick seeks out, thereafter, and these the people he in his turns infects and destroys.

The entering of one person into another is seldom without meaning, or without result, breeding at best children and at worst death; at its lowest, disease and humiliation; at its most pedestrian, status and relief; at its most profound, animation, spiritual change and happiness – and no amount of Grand Marnier can undo a moment of it.

All those grey other people scurrying about the streets of our cities – do not under-rate them, or the power they carry, each of them, in the great and convoluted scheme of things.

Patrick under-rates no-one. It is his power.

Grace calls once at Frognal to see Marjorie, finds Patrick installed, and disappears instantly. These days she presents herself as a virgin.

For Grace's Christie feels virginity to be essential in the woman he loves, whilst he does his damnedest to dispose of it.

thirty-eight

Christie is that year's Bachelor Catch. While the winter snow lies impacted month after month, and half Europe starves, and the bombers overhead carry food for Germany instead of bombs, and the gas dwindles to a flicker, and the electric lights waver, and strangers stand close to each other for comfort – Christie shines before Grace like a beacon of hope and promise. He is all clear-cut, up-standing (but only in marriage) masculinity. Christie is Grace's ambition. Not a diploma, not a career, nor the world's recognition, not any more. Just Christie.

She loves him. Oh, indeed she does. Her heart quickens at the sight of him, her bowels dissolve with longing. But she will not, she cannot, succumb to his embraces. He takes her on his boat, well chaperoned (yes, he sails) and up mountains, rather less chaperoned (yes, he climbs). He offers to buy her a flat (yes, he can afford to) but no she will not. No diamonds, thank you, Christie. No wrist watches. No gifts, no bribes, my dearest. Chocolates, yes, oh thank you! And orchids, and invitations to dinner and a taxi ride home, and yes, a kiss, and yes, you may touch my breast (how wicked we are!) and quickly, quickly, goodnight, Christie. My own, my love, my dearest dear. I would die for you but I will not sleep with you.

Christie stops off at Soho on the way home and spends an hour with a tart. How else will he survive?

She loves him. She means to marry him. How else will she survive?

'I can't,' Grace says to him, weeping, wriggling out of his arms on some deserted shore. It is night. The moon shines. The whole world waits. 'I can't. I'm not that kind of girl. If I say no, I know you'll leave me, and then I'll die, but no, no, no. Oh Christie, if you knew how I loved you!'

What a risk she takes. He nearly leaves her, she doesn't know how nearly. Grace disturbs first his nights and then his days, and Christie has enterprises to keep going, and an office, and a staff and a million to be made.

Grace wins the unofficial Slade Prize, not for the most accomplished student, but for the Most Desirable Girl of the Year. Christie stays. He likes success. Grace's eyes are incredible: her skin through the very effort of virtue has the pallor of debauchery. When she walks, sometimes, her knees knock together as if she was a young colt and could hardly control them. It's as if, Christie thinks, you only had to push her and she'd fall down and wait, knees obligingly apart.

But she doesn't, and she won't. Grace wins.

'Grace, will you marry me?'

What a catch, everyone says! This thirty-year-old, tall South African with his land-owning father, his background of parched veldt and black servants, and his riches; and his naïveties about the English social scene, born out of *Cavalcade* and *Mrs Miniver* and *Brief Encounter* and *The Way Ahead*, making a fortune in pre-stressed concrete, lording it over the new lightweight aggregates. You can build high on London clay, these days, as never before. London can become New York. Christie's first to realize it. The safety factors are uncertain. No-one knows quite what they are. Christie tells them, if they ask.

Christie arranges the wedding, the way he arranges anything. He must forego his ambition of a wedding quite like the one in *Father of the Bride*, for the Bride's Mother is dead, and the Bride's Father disaffected in Bournemouth, but Christie does what he can.

The wedding is held in a church in the Sussex village where Christie's English aunt lives. The reception is in a marquee set up in the garden. The sun shines, bells ring, flowers bloom, the virgin bride, beautiful and translucent in white, comes down the aisle. The groom stands beside her; the union is blessed. Was ever there a more charming couple? Cucumber sandwiches, strawberries, champagne. A thunderstorm. Laughter, tears, off to Cornwall and the honeymoon in the Bentley with the old shoes tied behind.

Those little fishermen's cottages, those deserted rocky shores. You could make love on a beach, in those days, and there wouldn't be a soul for miles. (It isn't like that now. The Life Guard would have you up for indecency in five minutes.)

Christie is sated: so is Grace, languid as can be. Tactfully but persistently he inquires about her already ruptured hymen. These things are important.

Horse-riding, she says.

And so it might be, after all.

Then back to St John's Wood and life as a young matron. There's no reason that anyone can see, in those innocent days, for Grace and Christie not to live happily ever after.

Grace even conceives, on her wedding night.

What judgement, what skill, what luck. Playing Grandmother's footsteps with fate. Wanting just enough, never too much.

Good days!

Grace gives birth to a boy in March. Piers. Two years later, Petra is born. They are rather delicate, fragile, whiney children, as if all the strength of preceding generations has gone into the parents and left none over for these afterthoughts. Grace loves them, intemperately.

And Marjorie! Marjorie goes to Grace's wedding. (Patrick is not invited.) She is happy for her friend, and her complexion is clear and spotless. She wears a New Look dress with soft unpadded shoulders, tight waist, and full skirt – and needn't have bothered because at the reception, sheltering from the thunderstorm under an oak-tree, she meets Ben, who does not care in the least what she looks like but likes to listen to what she says.

Within three weeks she has left Frognal and is living in a tiny flat in West Kilburn with Ben. Ben is an architectural student and has been asked to the wedding because his father is a business contact of Christie's. Ben, himself, has many doubts about Christie's business methods, let alone his constructional ones, but keeps them to himself. Ben's family is Zionist. Marjorie wonders whether, having a Jewish father herself, and feeling sympathy with that much suffering race, she should not become a Jew herself? But Ben, who takes his Judaism in a political rather than a religious sense, feels it to be unnecessary. As for marriage, there is lots of time for that. They have a sure sense of a long future together. Besides, if they married, she would lose her grant, finally obtained from a reluctant local authority after many solicitors' letters and injunctions from Helen in Mexico.

Chloe is asked to Grace's wedding, but cannot attend. She has other matters to occupy her mind.

thirty-nine

Chloe offers to cook the children's supper, but Françoise, now quite cheered up, will not hear of it. The most she will allow is that Chloe can help. She bustles about in Chloe's kitchen as if it were her own. Chloe feels ill at ease: as if she were the stranger, not Françoise.

Some people, thinks Chloe, can make themselves at home anywhere. Françoise clatters and sings amongst another woman's pots and pans and thinks nothing of it. It has taken Chloe all of ten years to regard this house as her own. It is as if, having had no proper home as a child, only a room shared with a mother, she has no right to achieve one now. Her adult life is plagued with the notion that she has no real entitlement to anything, to have only what she can snatch when no-one's looking.

And Oliver, of course, stretching out his control to cover the choice of colour of the spare-room wallpaper, the books in the shelves, the newspapers through the letterbox, the food in the cupboard, the greenfly in the garden, the money in her pocket, does not make matters easier. She knows it. All the same, she thinks, it takes two, as always. One to stretch out greedy hands, the other to decline to push them away: out of fear, or idleness, or stupidity or force of habit. All Chloe has to do is go into a Garden Shop, buy a chemical insecticide, put that into the syringe instead of soap and water – and there you are, no greenfly.

But will she? No.

When Chloe first meets Oliver, she is sitting primly on a cushion. She is shy, and not at ease with the others. That is, she looks down her fine patrician nose and appears superior. Chloe does not have a boyfriend, and is naturally anxious that this should be put down to her discriminating nature rather than her lack of capacity to attract. She is raw enough as it is with the humiliation of being pitied, as she is, for having no proper home, no proper family, no proper clothes; not even, she suspects, proper breasts. (The slight ladylike mounds which she soaps, rinses and dries so carefully each morning, seem to her to be sadly inadequate. Not that she has any means of actual comparison, of course – other girls, like her mother, dress and undress, wash and dry themselves, either in privacy or behind towels.) And though she weighs a stone more than she used to – she lives in a students' hostel and has grown plump from too many potatoes and too much misery – the extra weight seems to lie around her hips. Perhaps she is going to turn out pear-shaped, like Marjorie? It is her fear. And now as she sits on her cushion and looks down her nose, her cotton skirt nips her tightly round her waist. It is pretty pink check fabric, which once curtained the Ladies Cloakroom at the Rose and Crown, until faded beyond hope by the afternoon sun.

Oliver, coming late to the party, only there because he could not sleep, disliking his host and by implication his guests, mistakenly believes that Chloe, sitting on her cushion, looking clean and shockable and the kind of girl most likely to annoy him, is in the company of the President of the Dramatic Society, who sits at Chloe's feet and lays his head upon them for no other reason than that he has a headache and wishes to die. When he finally pulls himself together enough to go and look for another drink, Oliver takes his place. He strokes Chloe's ankle. Chloe looks down upon his head, black, curly, silky and riotous. Does she have a premonition, then, how familiar this particular head of hair is to become to her? How she is to watch it, over countless breakfast tables, flourish, fade and thin? Perhaps. Why else does she stay, and listen, and respond, and not obey her impulse simply to get up and walk away, or at the very least move her ankle out of his reach and her future too?

Oliver What makes you think you're so superior?

Chloe is speechless.

Oliver Too good to talk to me, you see.

How black his eyes are: how furious his mouth. He has rolled up his shirt-sleeves. His arms are hairy and sinewy. He moves up and sits next to her on the cushion. She edges over, but still their bodies touch. He smiles.

Oliver Why are you girls so mean with yourselves?

Chloe has the habit of instant guilt. If anyone says 'it's raining', Chloe replies 'I'm sorry'.

Chloe (Now) I'm sorry.
Oliver It's not your fault. It's the way you were brought up. What pretty hands you have. They haven't done much washing-up, I don't suppose. My mother died from taking in washing. She had cancer of the liver. Bleach fumes are carcinogenic, you know.

Chloe, horrified, doesn't know. Oliver moves closer. They are the only pair upright in the room. Someone has blown out all but two candles. His eyes gleam in the darkness. She loses all impulse to move away.

Oliver Mind you, she was only a member of the working classes. You know, those comic characters you meet in novels. One thing's for certain, this lot on the floor will never overthrow the established order of things. Too busy worrying about their sex lives. Will she, won't she, can he, can't he, and if she won't he can, and she will he can't. Who's going to bother with Marx when they're still stuck at Havelock Ellis. Do you know what I'm talking about?

Chloe No.

Oliver I'd better stop talking then. Tell me about yourself.

Chloe There's nothing to tell.

He believes her.

Oliver What cold hands you have. And you're so stiff. Why don't you relax? Shall I take you home?

Mesmerized, Chloe lets him take her back to his attic flat. He makes tea and serves it in tin mugs. It is too late for her to get back into the hostel – she has a late pass but it expires at 1 a.m., when the doors are locked shut, but Chloe does not care, nor wish to burden him with her predicament. She will have to climb back in over the wall, like anyone else.

Oliver tells her about his mother's death, his father's villainy, his lost garden, his two school friends, killed by blast. He curses the government, the war, his race, his religion – he wants nothing of any of it. He cries! Chloe has never seen a man cry before. She didn't know they did. Tears come into her own eyes.

'I wish I could cry for you,' she says, and means it. She throws away her happiness in handfuls, this girl.

Oliver is not in the habit of crying. He feels both ashamed and gratified at so doing. What is she doing to him, this quiet, unsmiling girl? Entering into his grief, accepting it – not attempting to deny it, as do most he meets. In these days he is

157

the last person to believe – as he will later – that the past should remain dead and buried. But then later he has Chloe to bear the burden for him. After, all, he earns the money. The least Chloe can do is cope with his temperament.

But now he trembles as he undresses her and leads her to the bed. She needs no arguments, it seems, or promises. He does not want to make her angry, he does not want to hurt her. He wants to keep her.

Oliver Rudore and Chloe Evans. Love at first sight!

For Chloe does not doubt she loves him. She could spend the rest of her life in his bed, so much does it hurt when she's out of it. Chloe, always so fearful of projecting a future for herself lest some inexorable force, roused from slumber by her daring, picks her up and sets her down again amongst the pots and pans of the Rose and Crown, can now raise her eyes from her text books, and see a vision of a future self, aligned to Oliver Rudore.

Chloe becomes very thin very quickly. She misses meals at the hostel because she is busy cooking Oliver's, concocting marvels on his gas ring. She is short of sleep, since she seldom gets over the hostel wall and into bed before four in the morning, and Sociology tutorials start at nine. (Oliver has no classes before eleven.) In the evenings, when they are not making love, she learns typing from a Teach-Yourself book, the better to type Oliver's essays.

Chloe writes to her mother, not mentioning Oliver at all, but asking whether Gwyneth can provide her with a typewriter. She, who never makes demands! Gwyneth instantly and dutifully supplies one; giving up her Thursday afternoons for three whole months to do so. Mrs Leacock kindly remarking that yes, the Rose and Crown could do with a new machine, and so perhaps Gwyneth would care to buy the old one from her, at a very reasonable price, considering the scarcity of metal, including thirty-year-old Olympias.

As for Oliver, he becomes quite genial. He even acquires some friends, lured partly by the change in him and partly by Chloe's cooking. It is pleasant to see the pair of them together, holding hands whenever they can, thighs touching under the table, not so much lascivious as companionable, and replete.

Oliver's sisters come to visit him, on leave from the telephone exchange. They do everything together: the two-headed, four-breasted monster of his childhood. Look at them now, swaying together into his room, bearing seed-cake and coffee beans, blonde hair curled high in identical curls, wearing the same thin white blouses, with the same buttons bursting apart under the thrust of their ripe breasts. They share the same swooping, raucous laugh, the same mocking geniality: both show off engagement rings, one diamond, one emerald. Chloe likes them. She does not understand Oliver's horror of these bouncing girls. He whispers to her what he never thought to tell anyone – the bath times, when they, the big-girls, bathed him, the baby, and raised his little winkie high, and let it fall, and laughed in the most good-natured way, but laughed. She shakes her head in horror for him.

All the same, confidences or not, Oliver asks Chloe to move her slippers from under the bed, in case they are seen. Chloe is a shiksa and every now and then he feels it.

Chloe faints. Hunger, or pregnancy? Soon she is being sick

in the mornings. Pregnant, of course. Well, Oliver does not like rubbers, neither does Chloe. Besides, she has a kind of half-belief that she cannot get pregnant, that she's not a grown woman but still a child, and has managed to impart this vision of herself to Oliver. A couple of months when she could have got pregnant and didn't reinforce their mutual belief. The third month she is pregnant, and who more surprised than Chloe and Oliver?

That kind of thing only happens to other people. They do nothing, while they try to assimilate the rather indigestible richness of this new experience.

Chloe swells and burgeons and cannot hide her condition from the Lady Bursar when she comes inquiring after Chloe's moral welfare. 'We are in loco parentis, you know.' Chloe next receives a polite letter from the Chancellor's office asking her to leave the university, as it appears she is not benefiting from the course of instruction offered, and the waiting lists are long. There is no point in arguing, since by the next post comes a letter from her local Education Office saying that her grant has been stopped. Clearly, to be an unmarried mother is no easy matter, though in truth to be educated no longer seems important. She can look after Oliver if she does not have to go to lectures.

Although Chloe and Oliver spend two weeks composing a tactful letter to Gwyneth, the latter is still upset when she receives their news. She gets flu and is in bed for a full week. In all the years at the Rose and Crown she has never before been ill. Mrs Leacock stops half her wages.

forty

Procreate and multiply. Harder than you might think for Marjorie, Grace and me. And to think how easily the cows and the bees and the stickleback and the toad and the spider seem to manage! In their various ways, of course; and no doubt the courtship habits of the widow spider are more bizarre than any behaviour pattern displayed by any of us. But of course they have no choice. They merely respond to the stimuli.

Show a red brick to a female stickleback and whoosh, away go her eggs, spurting out to take their chance. She's got no say. It simply happens. And no-one thinks to blame her. No-one says but you should have laid those eggs on a warmer day – poor little things! – and in a patch of the river so full of pike, and so fast-flowing, what were you thinking of! Better they had been never born at all, than subjected to such hardship, you must agree, you wicked, thoughtless mother? Just whoosh, away they went, and no comment.

Whoosh, away Grace went, in such a calm, clear untroubled patch of water too. Private nurses, private hospital, her own gynaecologist, nanny waiting on the sidelines to catch the baby from the monthly nurse.

A son, too, what Christie wanted. And all that money, and all those flowers, to soften the blow.

First babies are all blows, make no mistake about it. Duck when you see one coming. The child-wife becomes a mother. The status-wife becomes a messy cowering helpless thing. Listen to her. Listen to the chorus. Help me, look after me, cosset me, she cries. Me and baby. What precious vulnerable things we are, and yes, I must have a blue ceiling for baby to stare at, you beast. Paint it when you get home from work and can't you get home earlier? LOOK AFTER ME, you bastard! Of course we can't go to the party, what about my milk supply. No, you can't go by yourself.

As for him, he's impossible, more of a baby than the baby itself: pernickety about food, going mad from lack of sleep; he gets drunk, throws tantrums, falls ill, throws baby in the air for fun and fails to catch it when it falls. Oh loving husband, loving father, where are you? And we were going to be so happy, so complete, so different from everyone else! She, the monumental dangerous she, pads about the house, belly and breasts all swollen, desperate, distraught, wondering who this monster is she's married. A baby to cope with, and a madman too!

Tout casse, tout lasse.

When Helen was having Marjorie, look what Dick went and did. And see the trouble that led to!

Tout passe, tout casse.

When Piers was two weeks old, Christie, then working on designs for a Fashion Pavilion for the 1951 Exhibition, made some serious structural errors, found out, and couldn't be bothered calling the plans back for correction.

Well, Christie hadn't slept for a week, had he, and Grace's lovely nipples were inflamed and cracked and when he touched them she screamed, so he fired the monthly nurse, who had clearly been criminally negligent, with five minutes' notice and five months' pay, and then, of course, another couldn't be found for three whole days during which time

Grace sobbed and called for her dead mother and her friends, clustering round the bed, glowered at him as if he were some kind of villain.

Oh, nightmares!

When Inigo was three weeks old Oliver went off on a fishing trip. He couldn't work with a baby in the house, and he had a script to finish. Near the water, he was always more productive.

Two weeks after Petra was born Christie swept Grace off on a holiday to the Bahamas, leaving the baby behind. He needed a rest from babies, he said. While he was away the roof of the half-finished pavilion fell in killing three people – two of them only plebs, builders – but the other one his Chief Assistant. No-one left uncrushed so much as to murmur of criminal negligence; and actually Grace didn't even get to hear about it, she was in a hospital in the Bahamas with a milk ulcer. The operation was clumsily done; she has a scar on her bosom to this day. Christie sued, but won only £2,500 damages and a lot of publicity. Breasts being news and deaths not.

Oh babies! The blows fall hard upon the neonate, a little softer on the multipara; being anticipated, merely hurt the more. A duller pain, perhaps, not quite so piercing.

When Esther was in hospital giving birth to Stephen, Edwin was lifting his potatoes and putting in daffodil bulbs, to please her in the spring. She never saw them, and nor did he, or knew that he had conceded her the victory.

As for Patrick – well! He painted mousy Midge at every stage of her pregnancy with Kevin, and wanted to paint her giving birth, except Midge's father whisked his daughter away in an ambulance just in time – well, not in time, Kevin was born on the hospital steps, even more publicly than if she'd stayed at home – and Patrick was so angry he said let her father visit her. why should I? I'm superstitious about hospitals. And he didn't visit at all. And when Midge was giving birth in St George's, to Kestrel, Patrick was with Grace in the very next labour room, holding her hand as she gave birth to Stanhope. Just as well somebody was there – it was Christmas Eve and the nurses were singing carols in the wards, and the interns had been drinking.

Never conceive in March, Grace would say, afterwards, not if you carry to maturity. Never have a baby at Christmas.

forty-one

Chloe's baby miscarries at five months. Chloe cries and so does Oliver. Something is lost, they both feel it. They have been attacked by outside forces, and something has been taken from them. Yet what pleasure it is to weep together, to be each so identified with the other that loss for one is loss for both, and comfort likewise?

Chloe and Oliver are married in Bristol Register Office in superstitious haste, before worse befalls. It is too late, of course, for the baby, and for Chloe's degree, but not for each other. It also means that Oliver can get a married student's grant, double what he is getting already, and that he and Chloe can live in moderate comfort, while he studies, and she cooks and warms his bed, and, both agree, has the best of the bargain.

Good days. Unmarried students flock to their attic door, to see what marriage is like.

Chloe does not write to tell Gwyneth that she is getting married, only that she has lost the baby. Why not? Perhaps she feels Gwyneth has so little happiness of her own she might be tempted to steal her daughter's by disapproving of the match, or crying, or worse, smiling her small brave smile throughout the ceremony, and raising her eyebrows at the frivolity of this secular occasion; or perhaps it was that Chloe, somehow, hoped to save her mother from the pain of the memory of her own marriage, and widowhood, and the realization that now her life was over, and Chloe's begun.

Either way, whether prompted by nervousness or kindness, Chloe, most unkindly, does not write.

Oliver, likewise, keeps the marriage secret from his family. Why? Well, his sisters were married at about the time of Chloe's miscarriage, in a spectacular double ceremony of joy and lamentation mixed, which costs Oliver's father all his savings in food, ritual, flowers and orchestra, and which Oliver fails to attend, by virtue of tearing an achilles tendon as he boards the train on his way to the wedding. The pain is acute, his paralysis total – how he writhes and groans on the platform; Chloe, seeing him off (not asked herself, of course) is faint with shock and pity – his sisters (he presumes, for they never write) offended, and his father (he assumes) hurt to the quick by the nebbish nature of his atheistical if academic son. Does Oliver wish to compound the hurt (as people will when they discover they have hurt, and never meant to) by keeping his own marriage secret – or was the marriage itself the intended hurt?

gentile girl/woman
(derogatory)

For in Rudore family mythology, shiksas are for laying, not for marrying, and who more shiksa than Chloe, that Christian girl of now scandalous repute?

If you had asked Oliver at the time, he would have looked blank and said 'It is nothing to do with my family whom I marry, or how, or when, or why.'

And he would have said whom, not who, because that was in his nature too.

When Oliver has his degree – and to his dismay he gets a Third Class Honours degree and not the First he has predicted for himself – he and Chloe move to London. They live in a bed-sitting room in Battersea, beneath the towers of the Power Station, which sends out a cloud of black smoke to cloak the air above them. For this was in the days before London became the clean and almost sparkling place it is now, and fogs and smogs harassed the life and lung of its inhabitants.

Chloe, without any academic qualifications to speak of after fifteen years continuous study, feels herself lucky to get a job as a counter assistant in the British Home Stores selling twin-sets – those short-sleeved round-necked jumpers each partnered by a long-sleeved cardigan in the same (and usually pastel) shade. Sometimes she is moved to the jewelry section, where the strings of mock pearls, which complete the effect of the twin-sets, are sold. She enjoys her work – folding, smoothing, measuring, handling – her every movement neat, precise, feminine and controlled. Her capacity for dedication is immense. She is very soon offered promotion to assistant manager, but declines. To accept would mean an extra half-hour's work a day, and arriving home later than Oliver. She feels she ought to be back before her husband, to have the room warmed and the tea ready. The fogs and smogs make him cough.

It is to Chloe such an astonishing and unlikely pleasure thus to have the legal and permanent enjoyment of a man that she becomes almost religious, for fear of God's revenge. She will call in at the Catholic Church on her way home to light candles and placate Him.

And still she does not tell Gwyneth she is married. She writes, but does not visit.

Oliver works variously as a supply teacher, as assistant floor manager for BBC radio and as Welsh Rarebit maker at Lyons and so on, but his views are (according to his employers) arrogant and impossible, and he is fired from positions whence no-one has been fired before – a matter for some pride to both Chloe and him.

What an original person Oliver is – so brave, honest and full of integrity. Ah, she loves him! Oliver hates the rich, the powerful, the smug, the beautiful, and the successful. Oliver equates virtue with failure, and integrity with poverty. Oliver sleeps badly; he wakes shrieking from nightmares; he suffers atrociously from migraines, indigestion, bronchitis, hangovers and depression. Well, she knew all that.

Chloe shares Oliver's distresses gladly. She lives through his depressions, soothes his migraines, appreciates his writings, nurses his indigestion, endures his rages – knowing them to be with himself and not with her, however loud he shouts and however many plates he throws, and however many tears she, in the end, is forced to shed. And knowing that, come nightfall, and the wearing thin of his anger, he will look surprised, and clasp her to him, loving her as much as he loves himself – and what more than this can any woman ask of any man? These too, it seems, are happy times. And the light from this happiness casts a glow both before and after in both their lives.

This was the fore-vision, no doubt, which comforted the child Chloe as she lay fearful in her hard bed: and gave the young Oliver the will to plant and replant his garden, though the soot fell, and the dogs and the cats shat, and his sisters planted their great erasing feet amongst his tender seedlings. And this is the happiness which neither Oliver nor Chloe can now forget, as they circle each other, in and out of the events of their lives; the children, her friends, Patrick Bates; for how many more confusions, it turns out, have already been planted in her young life than in his, on that first night they met, which were later to flower, and proliferate and grow rank.

One day, of course, they are obliged to go to visit Gwyneth. She looks up from the tankards behind the bar of the Rose and Crown at the two young people facing her, and for a moment, almost wilfully, does not recognize her daughter.

Chloe Mother.
Gwyneth (Presently) Oh, it's you, Chloe.
Chloe Mother, I have something to tell you.
Gwyneth You're married, I know. Marjorie came down to see me and told me.

Female friends. Ah, female friends.

Chloe (Indignant) Then why didn't you write to me—

Gwyneth just stares at her.

Chloe (Panicky) Mother, don't be like this.

Gwyneth looks older, and tireder, and sadder. Chloe looks as lovely as she ever will. The abortive pregnancy has left her trembling on an uncertain brink somewhere between the girl and the woman: she has the best of both worlds. Gwyneth goes off to clear the tables.

Oliver It's my fault, Mrs Evans.
Gwyneth (When she returns) You look just like her father, you know that, don't you. I hope your lungs are good, that's all. Keep the sheets well aired, Chloe.

It is forgiveness, acceptance, and reconciliation. She and Chloe, who lived so close and who so seldom touch each other, actually embrace, and cry a few tears. Mrs Leacock allows her to give the young couple a free supper in the Nookery, and even to sit with them while they eat it. Well, Sunday evenings are slack.

Chloe assumes that the next step is for Oliver to introduce her to his family. She says as much to him as they lie awake one night in their Battersea room. Oliver is racked with coughs. The fog closes in upon the windows, seeping through cracks, and the un-lined cotton curtains do nothing to keep it out.

Oliver is earning fifteen pounds a week, which is wealth beyond dreaming, but will spend not a penny more than he can help. He works for the Rank Film Organization, where he started at eight pounds a week, and in spite of his noisy hatred of the commercial film industry, and his public castigation of it daily in the canteen as the whore of Cinema, and his drunken afternoons, he is not fired. Rather, his employers, seeing this behaviour as the sign of talent, insist on promoting him. He is given one film to write, then another. He has a gift for it. B-features, seedy thrillers; Oliver is totally involved as he writes them, giving them an internal validity no-one else quite manages – and totally horrified at himself when he has finished.

Chloe Don't you think we should go and see your family?
Oliver I haven't got a family. I only have a father. My sisters have passed into their husband's care, thank God, and I hope they're equal to it. The uncles and aunts are on their way to Bishops Avenue via Golders Green and Stamford Hill. (This being the route British Jewry takes from East End poverty to North London prosperity.) I have less of a family than you do, Chloe.
Chloe It's not a competition, Oliver.

This is not the sort of thing she should say, or usually does. But having offered Oliver his in-laws, she feels the least he can do is offer her the same. Or is he ashamed of her? Married life, to Chloe, is beginning to seem more complicated than she had at first supposed. Unless, of course, she can continue for ever to subjugate her own interests in the way she so far has. Oliver turns his back on her and tries to go to sleep. She will not let him.

Chloe And Oliver, please darling, it's ridiculous living the way we do now you're earning so much money. All my wages go on the rent, which is two pounds two shillings, and food, which is three pounds however hard I try, and your fares, which are six shillings every week, and that leaves me with three shillings a week for everything else.

Oliver It was your idea to save.

Chloe Yes, but not *all* your salary.

Oliver Are you saying I'm mean?

Chloe Of course I'm not, darling. We're not quarrelling, are we? We never quarrel. It's just I darn and I darn but my knickers are in rags, and your socks must be dreadfully uncomfortable and the sheets have been sides to middle twice – can't you feel it – and the egg slicer has worn so thin it bends when you pick up an egg and it falls off. I lost two last week that way and it's such a waste. We bought it at a jumble sale anyway. If I could just have three shillings I could get lining material for the curtains and then you'd sleep better. If it's not the fog coming through, it's the lamplight from the street. You never used to be like this, Oliver.

Oliver For God's sake, Chloe, stop nagging. I've got to get up at eight tomorrow in order to get half way across London so I can prostitute my soul from nine-thirty to five-thirty in order to keep you. If I wasn't married I wouldn't dream of doing it, I can tell you.

Chloe is tearful, and silenced, for a while.

Chloe (Presently) And you're always so tired when you come home, and if you stop work at five-thirty why are you never back 'til eight, and you're bad-tempered and I'm fed up and miserable and I wish I'd never married you.
Oliver It's mutual.

Chloe is horrified. She weeps such pitiful tears that Oliver is alarmed and comforts her, and they don't get to sleep until four in the morning, and the next day Oliver has a temperature and has to stay at home.

So Chloe curbs her tongue and her needs, and goes on polishing, patching, darning, smiling and mashing turnips at twopence a pound, until one Friday evening Oliver comes home with a bottle of whisky and drinks it in surly silence, out of his tooth-mug, staring into the gas fire with its four broken radiants.

Chloe knows betters by now than to ask him what the matter is. She goes to bed, in her British Home Stores nightie, reduced ten per cent for staff, and tries to sleep.

At two o'clock Oliver rouses her, and she dresses, and they walk to Chelsea and from there take a taxi (madness!) to an address off Hackney Road. Chloe is being taken at last to meet old Mr Rudore.

'But it's the middle of the night,' says Chloe.

'He never sleeps a wink,' says Oliver, 'or that's what he's been telling me all my life. So night or day, what's the difference?'

Mr Rudore, poor shuffling old soul, is roused from deep slumber as he lies in his brass bed beneath his feather quilt in the back bedroom of his two-up, two-down house. Alley cats yowl and prowl about his dustbins.

Mr Rudore, though sleepy, does not seem disconcerted by the hour of his prodigal's return; rather there is a look of pleased animation in his glittery old eye, and gratification at the renewal of a temporarily lost source of entertainment and mirth.

He makes Chloe tea and toast, and shows her photographs of family holidays, taking particular pleasure in a Bournemouth snap of Oliver, naked on a beach, at the age of five, with bucket, spade and starfish.

Oliver I'm sorry we came so late.
Oliver's Father So it's the middle of the night. So she's a lovely girl. So you should want to let your father know.
Oliver We've been married three months.
Oliver's Father So that's well and truly married.
Oliver She's a goy. A shiksa.
Oliver's Father So long as she stops her husband drinking.

It seems that Oliver's father can hardly contain his mirth.

Oliver I'm sorry I missed the girls' wedding.
Oliver's Father Weren't you there? I could have sworn I saw you there, my boy.
Oliver No. I hurt my ankle. I've never been in such pain in all my life. I sent a telegram.
Oliver's Father The telegrams there were! By the hundred! Their poor mother, that she shouldn't live to see it.

Oliver can't win. Mr Rudore settles Chloe down and hour

after hour, through that long night, details to her an account of his still raging litigation with Maison Furs, the establishment which sold his wife a fur coat when they could see she was dying. Chloe struggles with sleep. She has to be at work the next morning, unlike Oliver or Oliver's father. Oliver fidgets.

Oliver (Interrupting) Father, about money. How are you managing?

Oliver's Father Quiet, boy. The next week, Chloe, the very next week, they had the nerve to send this bill, here it is – now where is it? If I've lost it that's got me finished – ah, here it is. See the date? The 25th. And those initials scratched out. They changed typists, that's a sign of guilty conscience, if ever I saw one—

Oliver Father, I can let you have two pounds a week, if that will help. I'm doing quite well in the film industry.

Oliver's Father Quiet, boy! If you ask my opinion, Chloe, that typist couldn't bring her sweet fingers to type anything so grasping and heartless—

Oliver Three pounds a week, father.

There is silence.

Oliver But you are not to use it for lawyer's fees. And you are not to sue Dr Richman for negligence. He did everything he could for mother; if anything killed her it was overwork, and you know it.

He does not say he lays his mother's death at his father's door, but of course he does. It was his father's meanness and stubbornness, he is convinced, which made his mother's life a misery and so he often tells Chloe. Oliver's father weighs £150 a year in Oliver's hand against a possible £1,500 in Dr Richman's bush, and plumps for Oliver.

He even seems prepared to take Oliver a little more seriously, and as the dawn breaks and Oliver and Chloe take their leave he actually says—

Oliver's Father You have broken this poor old man's heart, my boy. Marrying out!

And he screws an aye-aye-aye wail out of some almost forgotten racial memory.

Oliver, satisfied, prods Chloe awake again and they walk all the way home through the beauties of the dawn. Chloe gets blisters on her feet. She is wearing her slippers and the soles have worn through. She is very tired at work the next day.

Oliver's meanness slips off him, as if someone had removed a strait jacket. His whole spirit seems to stretch and grow. Next time he is asked to write a film he holds out for payment on freelance terms, and gets it. He uses the money to put down a deposit on a house in Fulham, and they move into it. As if in gratitude, Chloe becomes pregnant again: stays in bed most of her pregnancy, and is delivered safely of Inigo, Oliver's son.

forty-two

Will Inigo, now eighteen have fish-fingers with the younger children, or wait for the *boeuf-en-daube*? Although at ease in adult company and, it sometimes seems, both more sophisticated and more righteous than his elders, so that they feel obliged to temper their conversation in his presence, hearing it anew through his critical yet innocent eyes, he enjoys the company of his brother and sisters, both fleshly (Imogen) and spiritual (Kevin, Kestrel and Stanhope).

It is a belief in many rural communities, and of practical consent in dog-breeding circles, that a female will not breed true once she's been had by a male of the wrong pedigree. Thus the Alsatian bitch that gets off one night with a Labrador is a write off: and a cow will be mated with two bulls in quick succession, the first for milk, the second for meat. Does Inigo, Oliver's child, have something of Patrick in him? Impossible to believe, yet he and Stanhope are so similar in looks – if not in build – it is hard not to imagine they are brothers: and Inigo and Imogen seem to share Patrick's looks, not Chloe's. Rows of hard blue eyes survey Chloe across the table: it is the triumph of crude vitality over gentility.

And do not think that Chloe thought of Patrick more than once or twice, while she gestated Inigo. She did not. She knew he was living in Marjorie's house, no more than that, and had long ago confessed to Oliver the details of her encounter with Patrick beneath and on top of her mother's bed. She would have told the story in the most general of terms; it was Oliver who insisted on the detail. It seemed to fascinate him.

Now Françoise, leaving Chloe peeling potatoes for the chips, goes to find Inigo to ask him whether he will join the children for supper, or stay up late, perhaps too late for his health and energy, and eat with the adults.

Françoise has a degree in Psychology. She is twenty-eight. She is the only daughter of the best restaurateur of Rheims. Picture her standing, one morning, amongst the unswept litter of Victoria Station, off the boat-train, with only one suitcase. She has left home in pique and panic, her fiancé of eight years' standing having abandoned her on the eve of their wedding, for Françoise's best friend.

How can she stay in Rheims, and face the pity of friends and family? But where, now she is in London, can she go?

It is at such desperate moments in our lives, of course, as Grace frequently points out to Chloe, that help of one sort or another materializes. The day a husband slams out of the door, a fresh suitor, hitherto undreamt of, appears. The dog is run over: that very day a stray parrot flies in through the window. By the same post the mortgage is foreclosed and an uncle leaves you a villa in Spain. Look warily at these sideways gifts from fate, Grace advises. They are usually loaded. The suitor brings pregnancy, the parrot psittacosis, the villa aged relatives. By the same wisdom, Françoise, standing lost and helpless on Victoria Station, with no past and no future, does not despair, and is right not to.

For on the platform Françoise is approached by Thérèse, a French girl of the kind she, Françoise, most despises, small, fair, timid, virtuous and Catholic, who asks Françoise to mind her bag, and at the very sound of the French tongue collapses into tears. Thérèse is returning to her *chère maman*, after three weeks' disastrous stay as an au pair in an alarming household in the heart of the English countryside, where the children did not belong to the parents, there was no religion, washing-machine or vacuum cleaner, dinner was frequently at midnight, she was required to work long hours for little pay; the master of the house, who they said was a creative genius and in the film industry but in fact was writing a very important book, so there weren't any film stars, made suggestive remarks and clearly wished to seduce her, and the lady of the house, having just had her own novel refused by her publishers, was bad-tempered and unjust. Thérèse had packed and left the night before when required to make bread like a peasant. Life is very sad, is it not? Thérèse's mother had sent her off to this English country house with a frilly apron with which to open the door to milords, but no milords had arrived.

Françoise, who has a great respect for literature in all its forms, extracts the address of the household from Thérèse, and makes her way to Chloe's door.

It is true enough that Chloe at this time is more short-tempered than usual. She has, over some eight years, and in all secrecy and diffidence, managed to complete a novel. She sends it, unsolicited, to a publishing house, who, to her surprise, accept it with moderate enthusiasm. Oliver has not read the manuscript, nor does he do so until it is in the printing presses.

Well, Oliver has been very busy and none too happy. His latest film, written at great emotional and financial cost to himself, and a departure from his normal big-budget top-star cops-and-robbers commercial successes, being concerned with the fragile sensibilities of a man sexually betrayed by his wife (himself and Chloe, some said), has finally been made and screened, and although not slammed by the critics, has been ignored and failed to get distribution either at home or abroad.

So if he has not read his wife's manuscript until this stage it is hardly surprising. When he does read it, he calls for its immediate withdrawal. The publishers demur. Oliver issues an injunction – he has taken over his father's passion for solicitors – and succeeds in getting publication stopped, though at considerable cost to himself. Thus he addresses Chloe, in the mildest terms, for someone so tried by the folly of a wife:

Oliver Chloe, my dearest dear, what were you trying to do to us? To thus air our domestic grievances to the world? All you could do is harm the children, yourself, me. No artistic endeavour in the world is worth that, surely. It is a great achievement of yours, Chloe, you've had it accepted, and we both acknowledge its worth, while not pretending it's any great work of art. Isn't that enough? My clever literary Chloe! But you know how dangerous this autobiographical stuff is. No-one, honestly, is interested.
Chloe Oliver, not by any stretch of the imagination is that novel about us. It's about twin sisters.
Oliver Yes, my dear, and you based it on my sisters, did you not?
Chloe Your sisters aren't twins.

But Oliver is right and she knows it and her resistance crumbles. She has used his sisters, those lively Jewish matrons, whom she so liked and he so feared, and tapped the sources of their energy and jollity, without permission, and feels like a thief in consequence. All the same, she is unusually cross, for a time, with Imogen.

And worse, as a result of her libellous folly, and the increase of Oliver's overdraft – already burdened by his venture into filmic self-examination – by the £1,500 he is obliged to pay her publishers in recompense, Chloe finds herself morally responsible for Oliver's financial anxieties.

Oliver, as Grace says, has money disturbances as other people have eating disturbances.

It is part of the pattern of Oliver's life, ever since he resigned himself to supporting his father, that he should always be in debt, always endeavouring to earn more rather than spend less – though he demands prudence and parsimony from his family; and if, as frequently happens, so many tens of thousands of pounds should tumble through his letter-box all at once as would make any more ordinary person free from anxiety for the rest of his life – Oliver will take to gambling and dispose of his good fortune that way, and feel quite convinced, too, that in some mysterious way it is Chloe who has driven him to it.

Now, for once, Chloe feels actively responsible for his sleepless, agitating nights. She prepares to take a job in a rather shoddy department store in Cambridge as a trainee buyer. Oliver, on hearing what the salary is to be, tells her that she is wasting her time and her life, and her family's happiness and future, but for once Chloe persists. She employs Thérèse, underpays and overworks her on Oliver's instructions, and is irritated by her long-suffering face. She, Chloe, at least suffers cheerfully. Did not Esther Songford once tell her so to do? She nags and snaps at poor Thérèse.

And if Thérèse, running away from her torment, encounters Françoise on Victoria Station so that now she stands on Chloe's doorstep, is this not exactly what Chloe deserves? Though

Thérèse, to be fair, would bring out the bully in anyone.

Thus Chloe describes her household to Françoise, at that initial interview:

Chloe My husband is a writer. He needs peace and quiet and a tidy house if he's to function properly. His digestion is delicate, and he cannot eat eggs, they give him stomach cramps. He will not eat carbohydrates for he is watching his weight, and we steer clear as much as possible of animal fats for fear of cholesterol in his blood-stream. Within these limits, he likes to eat very well. He has a light continental breakfast in bed – just coffee and bread and butter, but the bread must be fresh, which means we make our own. I'll continue to do that in the meantime – I let the dough rise overnight and then pop the loaves in the oven an hour before his breakfast. As for coffee, it must be made with freshly ground beans – he cannot bear the taste of instant coffee. It seems to get into his lungs. We have some trouble getting good quality beans, but now I'm going into Cambridge to work I can of course pick some up in my lunch-hour. But do remind me! Don't let me forget, it makes such a bad start to the day. Inigo is eighteen and is in his last year at the Comprehensive. Imogen is eight and goes to primary school just down the road. She comes home for lunch. Three other children stay at half-term and holidays – Kevin and Kestrel, fourteen and twelve, and Stanhope, also twelve. They share a birthday – Christmas Eve. We haven't much domestic machinery, I'm afraid, we like to live naturally. But I'll help with the washing. You know what boys are. Fortunately everyone's quite healthy except for Oliver's migraines. And he suffers dreadfully from insomnia. His nights are a battle against it, and when he sleeps, he has nightmares. We have separate rooms. We have to. I snore, I'm afraid. I don't throw off colds easily and I get stuffed up – and, well... I need someone to run the household while I'm at work. Feed, clothe, care for everyone. Not so much an au pair, or a household help, as a replacement.

Françoise You want someone to replace you?

Françoise's brown eyes are bright and somehow shuttered. She has hairy moles upon her chin, strong fat forearms and short legs. She looks stupid, but she is not.

'Yes,' says Chloe, 'I want someone to replace me.'

And so she does. At this point in her marriage she would gladly leave Oliver.

For Oliver finds fault with Chloe all the time. If she rises from the table she is restless. If she sits at it she is lazy. If she talks she is yacketing. If she is silent she is sulky. Chloe cannot bear to lie in the same bed with Oliver. She suffocates. Oliver says Chloe's snores keep him awake: his wife has enlisted on the Enemy Insomnia's side. Chloe moves to another bedroom. Chloe has no weapons left.

The children's eyes are anxious. They watch their parents carefully. Imogen sulks. Inigo's face gets spotty.

And how can Chloe leave? Where can Chloe go? Oliver might make himself responsible for Inigo, but there would still be Imogen, Kevin, Kestrel and Stanhope to provide for, and without Oliver's money, how could Chloe do it? Is there a divorce court in all the land which would agree with her that Oliver was unkind? She doubts it. Courts of Law are staffed by men. And perhaps the law would be right, and Oliver was not unkind, and it was she herself who was impossible, alternately restless, lazy, yackety, sulky, and frigid.

She who once lay so close to Oliver, slept soundly with her legs thrust between his; or half-asleep, embracing, knew herself to be exalted from her daytime body into that other night-time self, into that grand compulsive being which nightly rides the surging horses of the universe – she, Chloe, frigid! Her daytime self in full possession even when asleep – mean, aggrieved, resentful, out of tune with the rhythms of the earth; spiteful too – killing the kitchen pot plants with a glance.

It might be parasites which do the damage, of course, but Oliver says they die because Chloe has failed to water them.

Yes. Certainly Françoise can replace her. Certainly!

forty-three

One morning, when Françoise has been with her for six months, Chloe stands in her kitchen drinking a cup of coffee before running to catch the bus to take the train to get to work in Cambridge. It is term time. Inigo has left for his school. Françoise has taken Imogen along to hers. Françoise now works there on Tuesday mornings as a speech therapist, an arrangement which suits Françoise very well. It would have suited Chloe well, too, had she thought to apply for the job.

Oliver, in an evil mood (she knows by the forward curve of his shoulders), comes into the kitchen, and thus the conversation goes:

Oliver Chloe, I have something to tell you.

Chloe Could you tell me this evening? I don't want to be late for work.

Oliver This is rather vital, actually, to all our interests. But since it concerns people and their happiness and not pay-packets, I can understand you wouldn't think it very important. Off you go, my dear. Don't miss your bus whatever you do. Or there'll be a shortage of maroon crimplene in Cambridge tomorrow! Off you go to your chosen profession, Chloe.

Chloe sits down and takes off her gloves.

Chloe I'll take the next bus.

Oliver Thank you. I'm touched at your concern for your family. You must be the only woman left in the country who wears gloves.

Chloe I'm sorry if they irritate you. I only wear them because it's cold in the mornings and the bus isn't heated. If you'd let me take the car I wouldn't have to wear gloves.

Oliver Chloe, last time you drove the car you ruined the exhaust. If you haven't the sense to realize you can drive forward over a ditch but not backwards, you're scarcely fit to be driving. Anything might happen.

Chloe It wasn't a ditch, it was a bump in someone's drive. It could have happened to anyone.

Oliver I'm not criticizing or scolding, merely saying when you drive I'm worried stiff, and then I can't write, and if I don't finish this novel soon God knows where the next penny will come from.

Chloe From films, I suppose.

Oliver I'm not going back to writing that crap.

Chloe Are you worried for the car, or me?

Oliver For you. You're in a bad mood, Chloe. Perhaps you'd better get off to your office, after all.

Chloe I'm sorry. I shouldn't have said that. It was provocative.

Oliver (*Magnanimous*) That's all right. I'm irritable myself. I'm not used to worrying about money. There've been so many expenses lately, what with your publishers to pay off.

Chloe Oliver, they are still prepared to publish, amazingly enough; don't you think it would be possible just to show the manuscript to your sisters and see if they recognized themselves?

Oliver Thank you. I don't want to be sued by my own family. My early life was made miserable enough by litigation. I couldn't stomach any more of it.

Chloe has gone too far. And she has missed her bus. Home and office will both be a source of misery for the next few days.

Oliver I came into the kitchen because I had something important to say and I have been deflected yet again into rancour and argument. I don't want to argue with you, Chloe. It tears me to bits. I want to talk calmly and rationally about Françoise.

Chloe Oh yes. Françoise. I know about that.

Oliver How?

Chloe I make the beds.

Oliver I pay Françoise to make the beds.

Chloe She has quite enough to do. And actually, I pay her.

Oliver She has taken over your work; it is perfectly proper that you should share your pay-packet with her.

Chloe I'm not complaining.

185

Oliver I am. It leaves you hardly anything to contribute towards the expenses. Running this house is turning into a nightmare. The children are monstrously extravagant – no-one makes the slightest effort to control them. I find lights left on all night – even radios. And of course the holidays are coming up and the bastard tribe will be arriving—

Chloe (*Ferocious*) None of them are bastards.

Oliver I was joking, Chloe. See how you are spoiling for trouble? Things are too bad: the strain is intolerable. How can I write if I don't have domestic peace?

Chloe If we slept together again – I mean, just share a room.

Oliver You snore. It drives me mad.

Chloe Or at least—

Oliver No.

Chloe It's ever since Imogen was born.

Oliver You're obsessed. That was eight years ago. I've accepted the child as my own. What more do you expect?

Chloe But you haven't accepted me back.

Oliver What nonsense you talk. You had a perfect right to sleep with Patrick Bates if that was what you wanted to do. We should all be free to follow our sexual inclinations.

Chloe Like Françoise, you mean.

Oliver Yes.

Chloe (*In tears*) Imogen spoilt everything, didn't she.

And so she did, the pretty little thing, with her long legs and her blue eyes, and her reddish hair and her cleft chin, and her everlasting chatter. Wrenching Oliver and Chloe apart, like a surgeon's knife parting Siamese twins, obliging them henceforth to live their separate lives. It seemed there was a hole torn in Oliver's side, from which the living energy flowed.

Buzz-buzz, goes Patrick through Oliver's life, another buzz-bomb; wham-bam it falls, and there's ruin and destruction, nothing left of anyone's efforts. Broken things are broken: patch and mend as you like, make the damage unnoticeable to strangers, yet you who saw it broken know it's not the same.

Oliver looks at Imogen and goes through the motions of fatherhood, and his riven side hurts as if a sword had been driven into it.

Oliver goes to the doctor again and again about the pain in his side but the doctor finds no physical cause for it.

('It will be stigmata next,' says Grace to Chloe. And Chloe, next time she sees Marjorie, says that Grace is impossible to communicate with, these days, so clever-clever she's become. 'All words and no feeling,' complains Chloe to Marjorie, her friend, of Grace, her other friend.)

'Imogen spoilt nothing,' says Oliver now. 'I'll see Françoise gets back to her room by morning. We mustn't confuse the children. And you must remember I love you very much. And that Françoise helps me sleep.'

'Don't you find her rather hairy?' asks Chloe.

'It's a sign of passion,' says Oliver, and Chloe does not pursue the matter further, for fear of a pain which seems threatening to constrict her chest, but which, if she is careful, will never quite emerge to consciousness.

'I've missed my bus,' Chloe says, miserably.

'I'll drive you,' says Oliver, generously, and does, and on the way in to Cambridge tries to explain some of his antagonism to her going out to work. He needs Chloe at home, he says. He only feels secure if she's at home. And now he is getting on well with his novel, he really needs to have her at hand during the day to read aloud to, so he can properly balance the sentences. No, of course Françoise won't do. She is foreign. Besides, he doesn't respect her judgement or her creativity, as he does Chloe's. It is Chloe he needs, she mustn't think otherwise. She is his wife. He has all his emotions invested in her, he explains, and his past, and his present, and his future. It is just in this one very small and insignificant sexual area that he needs another younger person who doesn't snore and who responds properly and naturally and Françoise fits the bill very well, besides taking the domestic load off Chloe. Perhaps Chloe could ask the Head Buyer for three months' leave of absence, just during the middle period of his novel? Which is now. If her employers value her services, they'll be happy enough to oblige.

Chloe asks. Chloe loses her job.

'You weren't cut out for it,' says Oliver, 'or you would have made more impact. They'd have kept you on at any cost, just so long as they could make a profit out of you. You're well out of it: you were miserable and exhausted and bad-tempered all the time. You were beginning to get chilblains.'

Chloe recovers her temper and Oliver from his displeasure, and the household falls into a placid rhythm. The children breathe again and flourish.

Françoise goes to bed at midnight, lies awake for an hour, and then moves from her own bed to Oliver's at precisely one in the morning, and goes back to her own bed at two, having prepared Oliver a hot cup of chocolate to help him sleep. She gets up at eight to help Chloe with the children's breakfast. Chloe gets up at seven-thirty to put the bread in the oven for Oliver's nine o'clock breakfast. It needs half an hour to bake and a full hour to cool. Hot bread, as everyone knows, is indigestible.

Chloe sits in Oliver's room between midday and two o'clock (Imogen, not over-fond of Françoise, has chosen to eat school dinners, cabbage and all), and waits for Oliver to read to her. Occasionally there is something to be heard; usually there is silence. Oliver will type busily from ten to eleven, read over and think about what he has written from eleven to twelve, and then, as like as not, scribble everything out. Presently he says he thinks perhaps Chloe's presence inhibits his creative flow, and thereafter she sits in the living room waiting for his summons. After a time the summonses cease coming, and one spring morning she takes it on herself to go to London for the day, and talk to her friends. Grace and Marjorie.

Both of whom, come to think of it, have their own troubles. If they have little time or energy left for Chloe, beyond a cursory, ill-considered and possibly even malevolent 'divorce him! Leave him! throw her out!' is that surprising; or more than she deserves? All the same, she is hurt.

forty-four

Marjorie, Grace and me.

Marjorie is well acquainted with death. Her sad brown eyes seem created for its contemplation, her sturdy feet for the stirring of a dead body on the floor. Patrick Bates once said she smelt of death, and that is why of all the women in the world, having slept with her once he never would again. Her skin was dry even in adolescence – it flaked away as if it was dying, not growing.

As a child Marjorie would bravely pick up dead birds and bury them – maggots and all. The rest of us looked the other way.

Being so accustomed to death, it seems that she has trouble facing life. She prefers the world on the page, or pictures flickering on the screen. The media world is full of such refugees from reality.

Marjority tried once. Yes she did. Living with her Ben, carrying his six months' child. Two days after Ben died Marjorie started to bleed, just gently, and feel generally uncomfortable, so she called the doctor. He came at once, to her surprise, and she lay on the bed while he talked and chatted and kept her cheerful. Not that she was uncheerful.

'If I keep it, that's good,' she says. 'If I lose it, that's good too.'

He was a small fine-boned man, like an elf. She liked him. He'd seen many people die.

He told her what her chances were of keeping the baby and not miscarrying. Fifty-fifty, don't despair, he said, and she didn't.

But through the evening the chances worsened, the odds shortened.

A pain. Yes a contraction. Gone again, but forty-sixty, I'm afraid. But you never know! Think happy thoughts, girl. He calls the ambulance, nonetheless.

A sudden flow of blood, stopping soon. Thirty-seventy. Pregnancy suits her. Her skin stops flaking, her complexion clears, she feels placid and content. Even her hair grows silky and falls in waves about her face. She hasn't told her mother. She didn't want her mother, for once, to turn up and change everything.

A pain, this time the face distorting. Marjorie lies more flatly on the bed. Twenty-eighty, he thinks. Poor little baby, breaking free; or else cast out by a host too shocked to shelter it, who's to say? Too small, at any rate, to survive. No ambulance, as yet. It has lost its way.

More blood, more groans, the legs parting.

Ten-ninety.
Five-ninety five.
One-ninety nine.
Nil-one hundred.

Good-bye baby. Here you come.
Life does not continue.
Grace gets in first, of course. Grace murders. Grace has abortions. Like having a tooth out, she says. She looks forward to it. All that drama, she says, and distracted men, and the anaesthetics are lovely, and you wake up with no sense of time passed. What luxury! Marjorie says that if Grace had done what her father wanted her to, and looked after the infant Stephen, her baby brother, she might not afterwards have disposed of foetuses with such abandon. I, Chloe, think it is due more to the way Christie battered the maternal instinct out

of her, than anything else. For Grace did have such an instinct once – she wailed like an animal for her stolen children.

I heard her. It is the reason I look after Stanhope for her, and the reason Oliver allows me to. We understand why poor Grace can't. We witnessed it.

I have never seen a dead person, only coffins, but I have imagined the body within and taken responsibility for it. I would have a dozen children if I could; if Oliver and common-sense allowed. The answer to death is life, and more life, which is why the world is getting so overcrowded. Or so they say.

Leave Oliver, Marjorie says. Divorce him, Grace says. Save yourself, they both say. If only they seemed more saved themselves.

forty-five

Inigo says he will stay up for the *boeuf-en-daube*, although he has school tomorrow. He is in his last year there. If he gets his A-levels he will go to York University. Inigo is too old to be told how to behave, when to eat, how to dress, how to speak, how to get on in the world – anything, in fact. He comes and goes as he pleases. He is a well-built dramatic looking boy of eighteen, with his father's hook-nose and upstanding black hair – which, being uncut, forms a wide curly halo round his head – and hard blue eyes. He plays rugger.

Inigo seems nothing to do with Chloe any more. Inigo is his father's child, and she just a servicing machine. She is irritated with him. He seems to admire Oliver for having got

Françoise to bed – Oliver tells Inigo, too, as well as his mother, believing as he does in sexual frankness with the young, and she suspects them of having oh-you-dog snicker-snicker sessions when they listen to records or go fishing together.

Chloe is hurt. Was this what she raised Inigo for? Trained him in understanding, forgiveness, patience, love: raised him with open, liberal consideration and care? And see, he is as prurient and predatory on the female sex as any young man of her own generation! Inigo is not to be her champion, either.

Kevin is fourteen. He is a thin wiry child with his father's coarse red hair, and blue eyes, and the same cleft chin – but he is wiry as his father is stocky. He is always hungry. He piles food on to his plate, pulls it towards him, crooks his left arm round it to protect it from scavengers whilst he bolts it down with his right. He was hungry for his first three years. It seems that no amount of food will ever make up for it. He goes to the Masonic boarding-school, now in recess for the Easter holidays. His hair is cropped short and he has a pasty look, and his vowels do not have Inigo's ringing purity. He collects anything – stamps, wild flowers of England, car registration numbers. His room is awash with notebooks and cardboard files. He plods doggedly through school, and work, and holidays with Chloe, and never inquires after his father.

He opts for fish-fingers now. So does Kestrel.

Kestrel, his sister, is twelve. Her birthday is on Christmas Eve. She goes to the same school as her brother – girl's division. She is determined not to grow up. She wears ankle socks and sandals and would wear her school-uniform throughout the holidays if Chloe didn't wrench it from her. She has her hair short and carries her homework wherever she goes, like a weapon. She loves school and is Form Prefect and, Chloe thinks, can hardly be popular. Kestrel likes to tell everyone what to do, and how, and when, and has spots on her chin which she covers with plasters. She has her mother Midge's mousy colouring and round innocent face, but hard blue eyes and Patrick's chin.

Stanhope will have fish-fingers too. *Boeuf-en-daube* sounds foreign. His birthday, also, is on Christmas Eve. He and Kestrel were born on the same day, in St George's hospital at Hyde Park Corner. Kestrel's mother Midge had booked in properly. But Stanhope's mother, Grace, was taken there from Selfridges, where she'd tapped a lady at one of the perfumery counters on the shoulder and said 'excuse me, I'm having a baby'.

Stanhope looks bewildered and brave. He goes to a rather small public school.

Stanhope is not unlike Kevin, whom he admires, but has a more delicate and refined cast of countenance. Clearly unsuited to competitive sports, Stanhope talks of nothing else. He runs himself ragged on cross-country runs. Last term he was picked up collapsed three-quarters of the way round the course. He was leading. The school let Grace know but she forgot to pass the message on to Chloe and no-one came to visit him in the school san. No-one.

On Grace's instructions, Chloe is obliged to maintain the myth that Stanhope is the son of an airline captain who crashed the day after his birth. 'He'll like that,' says Grace, 'anything is better than having Patrick Bates for a father.' When Chloe remonstrates at the impracticality of such a story, Grace becomes quite offended. 'I *am* the child's mother,' she says.

One day, when Stanhope seems strong enough, Chloe means to tell him the truth. But every holiday he appears more fragile, more delicate, more emotional, and not tougher at all.

Imogen is Chloe's darling. She is an artful prattler. Imogen loves Oliver with an all-pervasive love. He melts before it, even as he resents her.

How can Chloe leave? How can she carve through these patterns of dependency and hope, in the interests of something so impractical and elusive as personal happiness?

Françoise cooks twenty-four fish-fingers. She has to. Oliver has found the two packets in the tiny ice compartment where he keeps the champagne, and such is his dislike of packaged foods that naturally he removes them, and puts them on top of the refrigerator, where they soon thaw and turn soggy, and if not cooked quickly will be wasted.

Chloe has turned four pounds of potatoes into chips. There is no chip basket because Oliver despises chips, but Françoise manages very well with the egg slicer and a deep frying pan.

Chloe opens two cans of peas.

Françoise and Chloe sit at either end of the table, the children sit in between. There is laughter and frivolity. Stanhope finds the secret bottle of tomato sauce. Oliver will not emerge till midnight.

They are all remarkably happy.

forty-six

'The new ways are so much better,' says Françoise, as the two women wash up.

The children watch *Star Trek* in the living room. The set is small and portable. Oliver feels that to own a small screen is less of a concession to the vulgarities of the media than to rent a large one. The children do not seem to mind. The fuzzier the image on the screen, the more attentively they stare.

'Are they?' asks Chloe, really wanting to know. 'Are you sure?'

'I could not endure to live like my mother.'

'Aren't you?' inquires Chloe, but she is brooding. Her mood has changed. Why did Oliver ask Françoise to listen to his work today, having had none to offer for weeks? It is as if Oliver has merely been waiting for Chloe to leave the house in order to humiliate her. And not just waited, come to that – but used boredom to drive her out. But Oliver is not like that. Surely. Not when it comes to his work.

'No indeed I am not like my mother,' says Françoise, incensed.

'You're washing up.'

'That is altogether different. I do it under different circumstances.'

Françoise is quite panicky.

'*Mon Dieu*,' she goes on, 'I fought at the barricades in 1968. I was arrested by the police. I was beaten as if I was a man. I was freed. I locked myself in a lecture hall; myself and my comrades starved. Only at the very end did I capitulate. I could not be expelled, after all. I had to have my degree.'

'What for?'

'For *my* freedom. I did what I could for France. I suffered for France. My freedom meant something too.'

'And this is freedom?'

Françoise polishes a glass so hard Chloe is afraid it will break.

'Careful,' says Chloe.

'I am sorry,' says Françoise. 'I think I am rather tired. I am not getting much sleep.'

'I am,' says Chloe.

There is silence. Françoise strains off the chip fat into a pottery bowl. Chloe sets the yeast to prove for Oliver's morning rolls.

'I am not doing this for long,' Françoise says. 'You understand? Presently I will do work appropriate to my education. My friend who married my fiancé did not receive academic qualifications – she was trained as a confectioner. Instead of making a free and open liaison with my fiancé as I had planned, I succumbed to my parents' wishes and a ceremonious wedding was arranged. My friend the confectioner visited for the festivities and on the eve of the wedding she and my fiancé eloped. The humiliation was extreme. My friend earned more money as a confectioner than I did at the education office, and was more pretty than I. She too has facial hair but hers, being fair, is less apparent. Nevertheless, to be rejected for someone so inferior was most painful. I wished to come to England, for this is the land where the relationship between the sexes is free and decent and honest. Where else in Europe could we three live thus and be happy?'

'Where indeed?' says Chloe.

'If only my mother had been more like you, and taken in my father's mistresses and made them welcome. They were my friends in any case and told me all there was to know. There should be no sexual secrecy.'

Why does Oliver want to sleep with this girl, wonders Chloe? She is both ridiculous and humourless. Or is that perhaps why?

Inigo comes in, holding a grubby white sports shirt.

'Do you see this?' he says, distressed. 'It's my football shirt. It hasn't been washed. I need it tomorrow.'

'I'll do it,' says Françoise, with alacrity. 'If I wring it well and leave it in front of the Aga, it should be dry.'

Inigo pinches Françoise's bottom by way of showing his gratitude. She squeals and jumps and laughs and blushes. Bachelor of Psychology as she is.

Chloe leaves them and joins the children, and watches the Captain and Mr Spock put paid to the monstrous inhabitants of space, which so often invade their spaceship in the form of blank and beautiful young women.

Kevin, Kestrel and Stanhope move to make room for Chloe on the sofa. It is done silently and sightlessly. No-one takes their eyes from the screen. Imogen, all eight years of her, creeps from the floor on to her lap. Chloe is incorporated and enclosed. It is a comfort. The woman has to do with the children, she thinks. Anything else is an optional extra, a luxury, a bonus from fate.

Fate! Let us not think that we can too easily get the better of it, change the pattern of our lives. The Fata Morgana are tricky ladies, and obstinate too. The wisest of us know how to deal with them – to wish for things sideways, out of the corners of our minds, facing neither our hopes nor our fears too squarely. Conceive of defeat, and it is already upon you – yet to avoid it, it must be conceived of. Yet gently, gently, sideways. Wish too hard, too strong, hope too fiercely – someday I shall conceive, someday marry, someday be forgiven, someday walk again – and fate turns against you with an implacable obduracy. You can almost feel it sneer and turn its back on you. The worst does happen, goes on happening, and yes, this is you, you of all people, trudging into old age childless, or crippled, or with the weight of dead men hanging round your neck, worst fears realized, best hopes dashed.

So don't wish too hard, don't pray, don't go on your knees or the sightless eyes will focus on your bowed head. Rather step close behind, unseen, keeping pace, like a child playing Grandmother's footsteps. If you have a whitlow in your finger, expect it to be worse next morning, not better. Or you'll be one finger less next week. Oh, careful! Be careful.

Inigo has a fever. He is six. Chloe hears him coughing in the night. She goes to see. It is three in the morning; she is very tired. She takes his temperature. 105°F. Chloe goes back to bed. Chloe dreams that in the morning she finds Inigo dead. And when dawn comes and the proper time for getting up, why up she gets from her uneasy sleep, and what does she find? Inigo well, his temperature normal. What happened in the night? Did angel wings flutter, did some more heavenly, less monstrous mother come down to nurse and succour him?

Four angels round my bed
One at foot and one at head,
One to guard me while I pray,
And one to bear my soul away.

Inigo's little friend Michael O'Brien taught him that. Perhaps it saved him? Something did, and it wasn't Chloe. Inigo sings it to himself at night, as other six-year-olds sing themselves to sleep with rude exciting songs about bosoms and bums.

What's the time?
Half past nine!
Hang your knickers on the line.
When a copper comes along,
Take his off
And put yours on.

Inigo is nine. Inigo has toppled off the garage, face first. He lies where he falls. His friends stare, turn him over. Some run home in panic, others to fetch Chloe. Chloe comes running, face whiter than Inigo's; the brain flutters, trembles, registers finality. What scene is this, to be forever graven on the mind? A child limp upon the ground, two hundred yards away. Your child? Yes, your child. Wish this upon some other mother? Why doesn't he get up? Is it a joke? Or is it death? And still the distance isn't covered, and the legs move heavier and slower than in a dream. All those dreams, leading up to this? No.

Inigo's alive. He breathes. He moans. His face is dirty with mud and blood; a pulpy, bloodless wound on his temple. What's beneath that? Does it always look worse than it is, or is it always worse than it looks, which? Now what? Neighbours gather. The slow-motion dance goes on. Doctor? No, don't move him. Ambulance? No they take too long. Someone fetches a car. 'Wait, wait,' says Chloe, 'let me clean him up a bit.' They wait. Someone fetches a flannel. Chloe wipes the face. All mothers do this, in emergencies, as cats lick kittens. First lick the handkerchief, wipe the face, the hands, compose, establish order and cleanliness, the everyday standard of things. Then you can think.

'Don't do that,' someone says. 'The worse they look the quicker they act, in hospital.' But no-one doubts from the now shuddering body and the grey and mottled face of Inigo, that they'll act quickly when they see him. Chloe sits in the back of the car, they place Inigo on her lap, push in her handbag after her. Inigo is in a coma now. Is that a coma? One mile to the hospital.

Inigo's all right. Three fractures to the skull, none depressed, no brain damage, superficial face lacerations, and two dented knees. They nearly lost him, from shock, some six or seven times during those first two hours. After that all's well.

Inigo is in hospital for three weeks. Chloe loses nine pounds in weight. All to the good; Oliver says she's getting fat.

Oh my friends, my female friends, how wise you are to have no children or to throw them off. Better abort them, sterilize yourselves, or have your wombs cut out. Give birth, and you give others the power to destroy you, to multiply your hurts a thousand times, to make you suffer with them.

It is nothing to be Inigo, lying there semi-comatose as the car jerks and stops. (The Samaritan is a bad driver, goes the wrong way round the roundabouts, loses the way. Yes, they should have called an ambulance.) Nothing to be Inigo, dreadful to be Chloe, suffering for herself and him.

And never have parents, either. Flee the country, emigrate, seek out the antipodes, so you do not have to go to Sunday tea and witness the fall of what was once so strong and competent. Be like Patrick Bates. Seal yourself off.

Blessed are the orphans, and the barren of body and mind.

In the kitchen Inigo laughs and Françoise squeals. *Star Trek* finishes. *Panorama* begins. They switch to *High Chapparal*.

forty-seven

Chloe sits on the sofa amongst her children, and wonders, listening to serpent voices in her ears.

Does Oliver mean to make Françoise pregnant? Is this his plan? He has fathered only the one child, perhaps he feels it is not enough? Perhaps his urge to create, which has made him both so rich, so poor, and so absurd, now spills over again in sorry imitation of Patrick?

Is this why he has chosen Françoise, and ignored the dozens of pretty, lively girls who in the past have lain down hopefully in his path? Because Françoise has broad thighs and a generally relaxed and fertile air? Whilst she, Chloe, thin and nervous, has miscarried time and time again, before and after

Inigo, and until Imogen, relinquishing the children of his loins into nothingness again, as if from spite? Perhaps Oliver felt not grief with her, but resentment, against her?

Does Oliver want revenge? Is that it? Has he waited until now, knowing that it's too late for Chloe, and her life bound inseparably with his, but his not necessarily to hers? Now, when she can no longer drum competitors out of the thin air and escalate the conflict. Too late for her to wage wars of attrition; not for him. Knowing that she's older, tireder, nearer defeat; that if he hands her a baby and says there you are, bring it up, I'll have your next twenty years, thank you very much; why then she'll nod, and acquiesce, and bake another loaf.

These are night fears, Chloe thinks. They have no place while television puts off darkness, casting its worldly shadows all about. These are notions put into her head by her friends, her female friends.

Oliver has no reason to be resentful.

For it was Oliver who sought Patrick out; Oliver who became Patrick's friend, his fan, his confidant, his drinking and gambling partner – his pimp. God help us – in the years when Patrick painted portraits and was hailed (by some) as a second Goya, and stars of stage, screen, commerce and politics came knocking, one or two, on the rather ordinary door of his Acton semidetached (how camp); and later (how trendy) in droves to the penthouse he shared with Grace; and later still, trickling in after Midge's suicide, to the barred basement where he now lives. It was Oliver, in this middle period, who insisted that Patrick paint Chloe – made her go and sit in front of him, all but naked, day after day. What did he *think* would happen?

That was in the early sixties, when England, as it were, discovered that God was dead, and that sex and youth was lovely, and age and experience sad, and that images mattered more than reality.

A topless dress and a miniskirt – a flurry of excitement, and what? Why, Imogen, and a race of children shaking their heads over the future, concerned lest Concorde make the atmosphere fly off the earth and discussing how best to cope with the 2.25 children each they are determined not to exceed.

Good days, those, for Patrick – not yet so crippled by meanness that he couldn't bear to buy paints in order to paint. Not yet abandoned by Grace; not yet dancing on Midge's grave.

A good time for Oliver. Four Hollywood epics under his belt: flying to and fro from the States, sometimes with Chloe, Inigo and nursemaid, sometimes not. A large Hampstead home; smart worldly friends with long un-English names. Clinging to Chloe at night, laughing with her at the strangeness of fate: which gave what they wanted: namely, critical acclaim for him, and children for her.

Good days, all the same, before discontent crept in, and drink, and all-night poker sessions; and parties so hard, fast and far-away that marital fidelity appeared ridiculous: and the friendship with Patrick, in which the two of them reeled about London, and in and out of pubs, clubs and the houses of friends – who were all too happy, whatever the hour of night, to receive so notable an eccentric pair.

Then back, in Patrick's case, to Midge, breakfast, and work. And in Oliver's to Chloe, vomiting and hangover, and the gradual disenchantment, the realization that though Patrick had the disease itself, that genuine hotline to Apollo, Oliver could only ever have the symptoms, operate on a rather blurred and feeble extension, and that no amount of rubbing up against Patrick would make the slightest difference.

Not such good days for Chloe.

Poor Chloe, lying half awake all night on her soft bed, feeling only the soft weight of the very best bed-clothes on top of her, waiting for the sound of Oliver's car returning, jerking into wakefulness at the least noise – a taxi outside, or the cat, or the maid – pregnant, perhaps? – on her way to the bathroom for the second time, never Oliver. Where has he gone? Whose bed is he in? Slumped drunk and senseless in some whorehouse, or in the arms of some smart young person they both know well? Where perhaps he was the night before, and before that? How can I preserve my dignity before my friends, how can I smile and look serene at the parties you take me to, knowing what I know, and what they know? That you prefer anything in the world to me?

'Hogamous, higamous,'

Oliver sighs to her over the breakfast table, seeing her puffy red eyes.

'Men are polygamous.
Higamous, hogamous
Women monogamous.'

'All this clobber,' he'll say, looking round the tasteful antique furniture she collects and cherishes, 'what do you want it for? You're becoming very worldly, Chloe. Bourgeois to a degree. Possessions and people. People and possessions. You shouldn't seek to *own* them, Chloe. You can't.'

'This jealousy of yours,' he'll say, 'is pathological. It's the sign of an immature personality.'

'I don't understand why you worry,' he'll say. 'These other women mean nothing. You're my wife.'

'For God's sake,' he says, irritated, 'go out and have a good time yourself. I don't mind.'

He lies in his teeth, but she doesn't know this. She only wants Oliver. It irks him (he says) and cramps his style. He who only wants her to be happy, but whose creativity (he says) demands its nightly dinner of fresh young female flesh.

Gradually the pain abates, or at any rate runs underground. Chloe gets involved with Inigo's school: she helps in the library every Tuesday and escorts learners to the swimming pool on Fridays. She helps at the local birth control clinic and herself attends the fertility sessions, in the hope of increasing her own.

Oh, Oliver! He brings home clap and gives it to Chloe. They are both soon and simply cured. His money buys the most discreet and mirthful doctors; Oliver himself is more shaken than Chloe, and her patience is rewarded: he becomes bored with his nocturnal wanderings and stays home and watches television instead.

Not such good days for Midge, either. Patrick out all night and shut up in his studio working all day, and forgetting to buy the family's food – which he is prone to do at the best of the times, for he himself will go for days without eating, if he is absorbed in a painting, and if he can, why cannot they? Are they not his flesh and blood, Midge and baby Kevin? Patrick does not give Midge money (she is a bad housekeeper, he feels, and squanders enormous sums, given half a chance, on rent and nappies and washing materials) but sees to his family's needs himself.

What does Patrick spend his money on? His friends wonder, looking at Midge's thin face, and her quiet, scraggy baby, and the shabby furniture – all of it acquired or given, none bought. All Midge knows is that he will give a beggar in the street ten pounds and think nothing of it, but that if she presses him for extra he is angry with her for days and will not speak to her. She would rather have his company than his alms. Still, she worries about Kevin's lassitude, and the struggle between her desire to please Patrick and her desire to feed her baby gives her an ulcer.

She goes into hospital for a month, and Kevin goes to his grandparents, who soon fatten him up. Grace sleeps with Patrick in the studio while she's away: and insists on remaining in the room while he paints his other lady clients. Midge wouldn't dream of behaving in such a way.

Quite nice days for Grace, really. Now divorced from Christie, indifferent to the fate of Piers and Petra (rock in two languages), living it up with Patrick, persecuting Christie's second wife Geraldine, heavy breathing down her telephone night after night, painting 'mass murderer' in gloss paint on her mini, writing to Geraldine's employers, clients, family and friends that Geraldine is variously an ex-convict, ex-whore, bigamously married, a man in drag; until obliged by the law to desist.

'Geraldine hasn't done you any harm,' says Chloe to Grace. 'It's none of it her fault. I wish you'd stop it.'

'I don't care whose fault it is,' says Grace. 'It makes me feel better. Bad behaviour is very animating, Chloe. You should try it yourself some time. One could get hooked on it.'

Grace is in fact quite sorry for Geraldine, and frequently rings her up in office hours to tell her so, explaining that Christie doesn't love Geraldine, that she's not anywhere smart enough for Christie to love, and that he has married her only to get custody of Piers and Petra.

Geraldine is a child-care officer, and a pleasant if humourless soul. She is in her turn sorry for Grace, thinking her mad, and telling her so when provoked sufficiently.

Grace is of course right about Christie's motives in marrying Geraldine. She has been right about Christie longer than anyone. As Marjorie says, it is a pity that Grace who is, as it turns out, of all of them the one most capable of moral action – for did she not leave Christie on the grounds of moral principle, rather than on the promptings of personal female desperation? – should thus hide the light of her essential rectitude beneath a bushel so dreadfully overflowing with nonsensical bad behaviour?

Pleasant days for Marjorie, too, believe it or not. Marjorie is working her way up through the ranks of the BBC. With her Double First and short-hand typing to back her, she becomes first a secretary, then a research assistant, then is promoted to Personal Assistant to a Hungarian drama director by name

Marco, who talks ceaselessly in praise of his own talents – which indeed are considerable.

Thus Grace and Chloe discuss their friend, at the time:

Grace She's in love with him. She must be, to put up with him.
Chloe She's paid to put up with him. Besides, she's learning a great deal from Marco. She says so.
Grace That means he's getting her to do all the work. Camera scripts and so on. While he sits on his arse. I expect she sleeps with him after tapings to relieve the tension: they all do, you know, those PAs. It's their function.
Chloe Majorie isn't easily taken in. She's much too clever.
Grace Clever never got a woman anywhere. Look at me. No, Majorie's become a BBC camp-follower, that's all. It's a dreadful fate. Those PAs never marry. It's their own fault. They do all the work and are shocked if they get any credit. They give it away in handfuls to whoever they're in love with, producer or director. They sublimate by becoming dedicated to the media, like nuns.
Chloe How can you be a camp-follower and a nun at the same time?
Grace You are so literal, Chloe. You must drive Oliver mad. I suppose this Marco of hers is married?
Chloe I believe so.
Grace (*Triumphant*) There you are, you see. He'll use her to do his camera scripts and send flowers to his wife when he's away in the Bahamas doing a thirty-second insert for some boring play, which he could just as well have done in Margate, and Marjorie will wait for him for ever. Serve her right for having no principle and going with married men.

Grace is just off to sleep with Patrick. Midge is due out of hospital the next day. Chloe murmurs a protest but Grace ignores it.

Grace is as wrong about Marjorie as she is right about Christie. Marjorie escapes the category that waits for her like a Venus flytrap, becomes first a director in her own right, and then a producer. She must put up with the obloquy which follows successful women in offices – the criticism of looks, dress and manners – and withstand the implication that by virtue of having attained a position which many grown and earning men would dearly like to reach, she must somehow be lacking in essential female grace. It is all nothing new to her: it is, in effect, merely the old vision of herself, repeated, which her mother so frequently held out to her.

Pleasant days. An ill wind, Marjorie sometimes thinks, toughening up her poor cold heart. If she'd had the baby, would she have come so far? If Ben had lived, would she have wanted to?

forty-eight

Left-over days for Gwyneth, with Chloe gone.

Chloe goes to Ulden to visit her mother. She takes Inigo, aged eight. Oliver has bought Gwyneth the cottage next to the Rose and Crown, and now Gwyneth sleeps there and spends her day off cleaning its floors, and is not noticeably grateful for the change in her circumstances.

On this particular Sunday, the Leacocks are off to Italy on holiday. Gwyneth has, for once, been left formally in charge, and not just unofficially. The Rose and Crown flourishes: it has twenty beds, ten bathrooms, not enough fire escapes and a restaurant with a good wine list and a Spanish chef and Portuguese waiters. The public bar has been swept away, along with good cheap local beer, and the spirit of the Cosy Nook extends throughout the premises; somewhat plushed up, of course, with rosy mock Victoriana replacing the faded maroon original.

Gwyneth earns four pounds a week plus meals. A five hundred per cent increase on her original salary, as Mrs Leacock emphasizes. Gwyneth rises these days at seven and goes to bed at twelve. The girls who work under her earn double what she does, but Gwyneth seems to take a pride in the lowness of her wage.

'Only four pounds a week,' she says, with awe. 'They wouldn't get anyone for that now.'

Although she is always pleased to see Chloe, and delights in Inigo, she seems uninterested in Chloe's London life. Chloe is half relieved, half hurt. It was as if, with her marriage, she has become a stranger to her mother.

And indeed – living with, getting pregnant by, and marrying Oliver, without her mother's knowledge, let alone permission, were not deeds calculated to increase the bond between them. Rather it was to loosen it – with that destructive instinct for self-determination which the loving daughters of loving mothers sometimes so alarmingly exhibit. And loosen it, it did.

Gwyneth has understood and forgiven. But she keeps her daughter at a distance now.

'The girls are so slip-shod,' she complains to Chloe. 'They have no standards. You have to watch them all the time,' and although it's her day off she takes Chloe to lunch in the restaurant, instead of cooking for her in the cottage, so that she can keep an eye on the staff, the food, and the guests.

Gwyneth makes excuses.

'I do hardly any cooking in the cottage,' she says. 'I can never get used to cooking food for myself. All that work and only me to appreciate it. Besides, if I eat by myself I get indigestion. It's the quietness, it worries me. I like a bit of clatter and a shout or two, and even an argy-bargy, so long as it doesn't turn nasty!'

The waiter brings Inigo a mountain of chips, especially prepared for him in the kitchen. He's pleased by this special attention and smiles benignly at his mother and grandmother. He is a beautiful, clear-eyed child. Chloe feels such a pure clarity of love for Inigo, at this age, that it pierces her with almost more pain than any Oliver has ever caused her. Chloe picks at gammon and pineapple. She does not have much appetite, these days.

Chloe When you retire, mother, you'll have to be a little more on your own. Do try and get used to the cottage.
Gwyneth (Horrified) I mean to work until I drop.
Chloe But why? You don't have to work any more. And if you're getting varicose veins—
Gwyneth Only little ones—

Chloe And if your insides are giving trouble—

Gwyneth has complained to Chloe that occasionally, though past the menopause, she bleeds a little from time to time.

Gwyneth If I forget about it it will go away.

She asks after Marjorie. Gwyneth has seen her name on the television screen – albeit low down on the credits – and is pleased to know she is doing well.

Gwyneth Such a bright girl. So were you all, bright as buttons

She asks with some temerity after Grace. Tales of Grace are often cataclysmic.

Chloe Grace? Litigating.
Gwyneth That should keep her out of trouble for a while. And little Stanhope? What a name to call a baby!
Chloe He's with me most of the time. Well, with the au pair.
Gwyneth I expect it's for the best, though it's hard on you. She never sounded the best of mothers, to me. Leaving the poor little thing alone like that.

Grace goes out drinking, one night, leaving the sleeping two-year-old Stanhope locked in the flat. He wakes, is terrified, dials telephone numbers at random, gets through to the Continental Exchange, who keep him soothed and reassured while the call is traced and help summoned. When Grace comes home at three with a Nigerian in national dress there are the police, the NSPCC and a Children's Department official waiting for her.

Poor Grace. Everyone gets to hear about it. Even Gwyneth, tucked away in Ulden.

Poorer Stanhope.

Grace consents to let Chloe have Stanhope. She has never cared for him. It was Chloe who talked Grace out of having an abortion so it seems only fair that Chloe should put up with the consequences.

Gwyneth Poor Grace. Poor little Grace. She always seemed to have so much and really it was nothing.

She puts her hand on Chloe's arm and strokes it, with a brief return of the passionate, protective love she once had for her child.

Gwyneth I'm glad things are all right for you. I did my best for you but it wasn't much. I don't deserve what you've turned out to be. And Oliver doesn't mind about you having Stanhope?
Chloe No. He has a great respect for Patrick Bates.
Gwyneth (With unaccustomed asperity) I can't think why. I must say I could never see his charm. It was a bad day when he was posted here. I wish he'd been sent to Aberdeen. Upsetting all you girls the way he did. And that poor wife of his, I don't know why she puts up with it.
Chloe He's very creative.

Inigo has been taken off by a waiter to inspect the ice-cream stores. At the table next to theirs four grey-suited men with competent, choleric faces grow impatient because their steaks take so long to arrive.

Gwyneth excuses herself, and vanishes into the kitchen. Gwyneth's rump is broad and solid, her waist vanished into stolid flesh. If she was ill, thinks Chloe, surely she'd be thin? The steak appears at the next table: the four men eat. Gwyneth returns, satisfied.

Gwyneth Creative! What kind of excuse is that? Your father was creative, and he did what he had to for his family. He knew real life came first. The other is make believe.
Chloe (Flatly) Father died. If he'd gone on painting pictures and not the outside of houses, he might still be alive.
Gwyneth It was the choice he made, and the right choice. You've got to live by ought, not want.
Chloe No. People should do what they want. If they don't it just means trouble for everyone.

It is the nearest they have ever come to an argument. Gwyneth's mouth tightens. Chloe moistens her lips. She feels an unaccountable rage with her mother. The four men at the next table are in discussion with the waiter, who presently sidles up to Gwyneth.

Waiter That's the new management. Sneaky bastards, the Leacocks. They've gone and sold the place. I don't suppose they told you either.

215

Gwyneth turns pale. She looks as Chloe remembers her looking twenty-five years earlier, when she came home a widow from the Sanatorium, having left the house a wife.

And that is what the Leacocks have done. Sold the Rose and Crown as a going concern to a big chain of hotels. And why not? It's what the Leacocks always meant to do: and he is sixty and she is fifty-five, and Gwyneth should have seen it coming. And if they did not confide in her – well, why should they? Gwyneth is only an employee.

So Gwyneth tells herself, as once she told herself that there was no good reason why Chloe, a grown woman now, should ask her to her wedding. And telling herself often enough, convinces herself, and when the Leacocks return from holiday, Gwyneth smiles at them, and when they leave for Wales, within the month, giving her a lampshade as a farewell present, she waves good-bye and promises to write, and only when the following week the new management replace her with a younger woman from another hotel, and she finds herself unemployed, she wonders briefly why the Leacocks have not seen fit to safeguard her position. Twenty years!

Gwyneth sits in her little cottage and thinks of nothing in particular for a long time, and next time Chloe goes to visit her, she complains of stomach pains and Chloe tries to get her to go to the doctor but she won't.

'It's the change in diet,' she says, 'it's nothing. I'm very happy here and all sorts of people pop in to see me, you mustn't worry about me, Chloe. And I had such a nice postcard from the Leacocks – they've bought a little house in Malta.'

'Those monsters,' says Chloe.

'You mustn't say that about them,' says Gwyneth. 'They've always been very good to me.'

'They've exploited you for years,' shouts Chloe. 'They've conned you and laughed at you, and you asked for it. You've stood around all your life waiting to be trampled on. Can't you even be angry? Can't you hate them? Where's your spirit?'

She stamps and storms at her mystified mother. It is the worst of her times. Oliver has been out with Patrick for the last two nights. Out prowling like any tomcat, bent on nocturnal mysteries. If I love him, Chloe tells herself, I'll let him do what he wants, and a jealous wife is an abomination; and listening to herself, believes herself. Not for nothing is she her mother's daughter. When Oliver comes home she'll smile and make a pot of coffee and tell him who's phoned and who she's seen.

It drives him mad. His trousers are stained with semen; he hasn't even bothered to take them off, then, or else he's been too drunk. Chloe washes them, patiently, with purest, gentlest soap flakes. He's trying to provoke her. She will not let herself be provoked. Even going to the doctor for treatment for VD she does not permit herself anger, only distress.

Oliver gives up the effort; he stays home, says hard things about Patrick, doesn't drink, writes another script. Is this victory, or just postponed defeat? Chloe thinks it's victory. Oliver stares at her with sombre, furious eyes, and says nothing, and at night drives himself and her into the most elaborate and curious of positions, and still she merely smiles, and obliges, and if in the morning she's bruised and bitten, isn't that love and didn't she enjoy it?

In the meantime she has pushed and prodded her mother to the doctor's. What you want, mother, is a hysterectomy, says Chloe. Get your womb taken out, removed, cut away. Then you'll be a person, not a woman, and perhaps you'll get your spirit back from those sad depths to which it has so pitifully sunk.

'Cancer,' says the doctor, investigating, and lo, there it is, everywhere.

'In my young days,' says Gwyneth's friend Marion, who keeps the sweet shop, 'that word was never spoken, and it was better that way. It's talking about it makes it happen.'

forty-nine

The children are in bed. But only Kevin sleeps. Sleep obliterates Kevin's day as his head touches the pillow, as a lake might obliterate a candle. The other children lie awake. Stanhope learns League Tables – he hopes one day to win a Brainchild Quiz and impress his mother. Kestrel lies wide-eyed in the dark and tenses and relaxes her calf muscles to strengthen them for a hockey victory. Imogen, precocious, reads the Bible, as once her mother did.

'Remember now thy creator in the days of thy youth,
When the evil days come not—'

And they don't. So much Chloe has achieved.

Inigo waits up for midnight dinner. At eighteen his life has already fallen into a kind of quiescence. He has the patience and dignity of an old man. Sixteen was riotous with sexual activity, as he was obliged and blown by a whole tribe of lost girls, aged thirteen, fourteen, fifteen, who had hysterics in lessons, and collapsed at games – dizzy with sleepers, bombers, pot and acid – grasping at sexual straws in a sea of parental anxiety and distress. Now a couple of years later, the girls have grown respectable. They work for their exams, polish their shoes, wear no eye make-up, return to a state of near virginity and instead of passing into other worlds at parties, would waltz and fox-trot if only they could.

Inigo thinks he will go into politics, and bring about the Socialist revolution his parents so patently failed to achieve. Kropotkin and Engels are his heroes. Marx and Lenin he considers rather trashy modern stuff. And Chairman Mao a mere poet.

So much Chloe has achieved.

The *boeuf-en-daube* is cooked. The rice is drained, the salad tossed. Françoise has laid the table, and arranged a posy of spring flowers as a centre-piece. She has picked crocuses. Chloe has never known anyone to pick crocuses before. She had thought them inseparable from the earth in which they grew, but it seems she was mistaken.

Inigo goes to fetch Oliver. When Oliver is in an uncertain temper, Inigo is commonly sent to fetch him. Oliver is proud of Inigo, flesh of his flesh, love of his love, so socially and sexually competent, and president of the school astronomical society as well. No bar-mitzvahs, no chicken soup, no aie-aieing for him. Presently he'll go to Oxford, and won't have to go on a scholarship.

So much Oliver has achieved.

Oliver has had a bad day. He sits and broods and considers his ill-fortune. Thus:

1. A letter from his father demands that the roof over his poor old head be mended. It is leaking. The Rudore family house has long since been condemned, and stands alone and crumbling in a sea of builder's mud while Mr Rudore's solicitors (at Oliver's expense) fight the compulsory purchase order.

2. Two telephone calls from Oliver's sisters, now cheerful, fertile ladies living next door to each other in the Bishops Avenue – that mecca of all desire – with expensively coiffeured hair, crimson nails, chauffeurs and charge accounts, suggest to him that since their husbands have that week given away all their wealth to an Israel Defence Fund, the least that he, Oliver, can do to compensate (for what they regard as anti-Zionism and he as natural common sense) is not just mend but renew his father's roof. What's more, they say, they have been together to see Oliver's latest little film – showing, without his knowledge, at an Art Cinema in Golders Green – and have found it quite brilliantly funny. Oliver can't remember there being a single laugh line in it.

3. Chloe has been to London to see her friends. His indifference is faked – anxiety knots his stomach. Is she disloyal? Do they talk about him? Do they laugh? Oliver lives in terror of being laughed at. When he leaves a script-conference it is his habit to lean against the closed door to make sure they're not laughing at him. Quite often, of course, they are.

4. Oliver has succeeded in reading his last completed chapter to Françoise, having contrived Chloe's absence without upsetting her –

but instead of it bringing gratification and reassurance, as he had hoped, and a literary response as obliging as her sexual one, she has been rancorous and hard to please, and even criticized his grammar. He had thought for a while that Françoise, with her stocky limbs, solid peasant frame and slow smile, was the personification of primitive female wisdom; and, rightly, that her instinctive perceptions would turn out to be only thinly overlaid with academic sophistications: but essential wisdom has turned out to be stupidity, and innocence limitation, and honesty intransigence. Françoise hears only the construction of his sentences, and is deaf to their meaning and the intertwining patterns they make; and does not even possess that natural and kindly grace which at least Chloe, for all her faults, deigns to offer him – that of keeping quiet about what she does not like.

Now he dreads the night, and the punctual returning of Françoise to his bed. A bad day for Oliver.

No doubt he will find ways of recovering from it.

'You never go to parties these days,' he accuses Inigo, when his son comes to tell him that dinner is ready. 'You're always here.'

'Parties are a waste of time,' says Inigo.

'What isn't?' inquires his father, with the cynicism required of age, and Inigo smiles politely.

'You think I'm a decadent old has-been,' says Oliver, hopefully.

'I think you're a very respectable and responsible person,' says Inigo, sincerely. He's not laughing at his father, is he?

'The roof is mended,' Inigo goes on, 'the bills are paid, the household is stable, though not totally orthodox, everyone appears placid. What else can one ask of parents?'

'I'm glad you can accept Françoise,' says Oliver, spoiling for the trouble Inigo is so reluctant to provide.

'I'm glad *you* can,' says Inigo. 'I imagine a young woman must be quite tiring for someone of your age.'

'Not at all,' says Oliver. 'I suppose you have three women at one time?'

'I have,' says Inigo, 'but I don't think anyone enjoyed it. It was the girls' idea, not mine. Girls seem to have a great need to be debased, don't you think? One doesn't wish to be party to that kind of thing.'

Yes, Inigo is laughing at Oliver.

Oliver sits at the head of the table, and Chloe sits at the foot to serve the food. Inigo and Françoise face each other. Oliver's shoulders are hunched forward. His neck muscles twitch. How are we to get through dinner, wonders Chloe? I must hold my tongue and speak only pleasantries, and remember that for Inigo's sake – and indeed, for Françoise's – I must appear to be cheerful, sane, and in control of my destiny.

And thus the conversation goes:

Oliver Good day in London, Chloe?
Chloe Yes thank you.
Oliver What it is to be born a woman! Free to roam the streets and buy hats while husbands work their fingers to the bone.
Chloe I didn't do any shopping, actually. I'm sorry if you missed me.
Oliver I was only joking, Chloe. You're so serious, aren't you! And

I didn't miss you. I read to Françoise instead. She's a very good critic, within limits. Aren't you, Françoise?

Françoise I say what I think. That is all I can do.

Oliver Few people have the courage, you'd be surprised. We'll send you off to evening classes, shall we, just to sharpen up your English. Then you won't have to bother any more, Chloe.

Chloe It isn't any bother, Oliver, you know it isn't. If I can help I'm only too glad.

Oliver You're all right on screenplays, Chloe. In fact, very good. They have a commercial basis which you understand. But novels are different. Françoise has a more literary approach. She does have a degree, after all.

Inigo Mother went to college, didn't you, mother. What happened? Why didn't you get your degree?

Chloe doesn't reply. She finds her voice doesn't work, and there are tears in her eyes.

Oliver Go on, Chloe. Answer the boy's question.

Inigo Tell you what. I don't think I'm going to enjoy this meal. I recognize the symptoms. I'll take my dinner and eat in front of the telly, if no-one minds.

Oliver There's nothing on.

Inigo That's what's so soothing. Smashing grub, Françoise.

He takes his plate and goes.

Oliver I wish you wouldn't upset the boy, Chloe. It's so pointless.

Chloe I didn't mean to.

223

Oliver There's no reason to sound so flat and depressed. You'll turn into your mother if you're not careful. Are you jealous? Is that what it is? Jealous of Françoise?

Chloe Of course not.

Oliver I am afraid you are. Very well, I can't have you upset. If you don't want me to read to Françoise, I won't. God knows what I'll do instead. So. Who did you see in London? Marjorie and Grace, I suppose.

Chloe Yes. I told you.

Oliver And what was their advice?

Chloe What do you mean, their advice?

Oliver I'll tell you if you like. Marjorie said throw Françoise out and Grace said divorce Oliver for all the alimony you can get.

Françoise Please, I cannot follow. Oliver, you are talking in such a soft voice it is difficult to hear and I think you are saying important things.

Oliver No. You are mistaken. I'm discussing gossip and chit-chat and mischief, and I will speak as I please.

Françoise I am sorry.

Oliver Well, Chloe?

Chloe I didn't ask for advice. I didn't mention us at all. They offered it.

Oliver Interfering bitches. Of course if you want to end up like either of them, take the advice they offer. Why not? You could end up living with them. Three dykes together.

Françoise Perhaps you would like to be alone. Perhaps I should join Inigo.

Oliver Stay where you are, Françoise. There, Chloe, now you're upsetting poor Françoise too. You are a bitch.

Chloe I'm not. You're upsetting her. This is ridiculous.

Oliver I'll tell you why you can't in fact take your friends' advice, and why you are so tearful and upset. You can't throw Françoise out, much as you'd like to, because this is my house, my property, I have whom I please here and you have no say. You can't divorce me because you have condoned her stay here, and you know it and your friends know it, and I have committed no matrimonial offence. Besides, who would look after the children?

Chloe hasn't eaten a morsel of her food. It congeals on her plate. She tells herself that Oliver does not mean what he is saying, and that tomorrow he will be friendliness and sweetness itself. After such outbursts he usually is. So long as she can hold her tongue all will yet be well.

Chloe I don't take any notice of what they say, Oliver. You know I don't.

Oliver Then why bother to go all the way to London to see them? If you must gad about why didn't you go to a matinee and keep up on your culture like all the other middle-aged mums?

Chloe You didn't seem to mind me going this morning, Oliver.

No, she should not have said that.

Oliver I'm not your keeper. You do what you want and go where you want. So long as I'm not expected to look after the children. What really upsets me is you coming back from London. Why didn't you stay away?

Chloe Please. Oliver.

Oliver Oh, listen to you! Grovel, shmovel. I wish you'd find yourself a lover, you mightn't spread so much gloom and despondency around. You used to be good at that. What's the matter, isn't Patrick interested any more?

Chloe I haven't seen Patrick for nine years.

Oliver No. You can't achieve any kind of friendship with a man, it seems. You see sex in everything. If you did see him, you couldn't appreciate him, Chloe, you'd just fall down in front of him and open your legs as you did before and reduce everything about him to the banal and the ridiculous.

Françoise Oliver, I am afraid you are being unkind.

Oliver Shut up.

Chloe He's mad, Françoise. Take no notice.

Tears of rage and misery flow down her cheeks. He's smiling.

Oliver No, you're mad. Sitting here at my table when you're not even wanted any more. You have no place here. You don't even do the cooking. You embarrass everyone, hanging on the way you do.

Her hand moves to pick up a knife. She thinks she will kill him. He bangs his hand down on hers so that it hits the table with a thwack.

Oliver You want to kill me now. You murderess. You aborter of my children.

226

She runs from the room. The pain in her hand is intense.

Oliver (After her) And don't think you can have Imogen. She's mine legally, you know.

Inigo turns the television louder. He cannot hear his parents with his ears, but he hears them with his heart. There is a flickering before his eyes – the beginning of a migraine, he fears. He suffers from migraine, taking after his father.

I have heard it all a hundred times before, he thinks. The details are different, but the essence is the same. He looks forward to leaving home, and is glad for Imogen's sake – he is very fond of Imogen – that she goes to bed early.

fifty

Chloe lies on her bed and cries.

Chloe refrains from running back into the kitchen and uttering all the retorts, taunts and insults which she could so easily deliver.

Chloe is conscious of a certain sense of victory, having put Oliver so firmly in the wrong. Oliver has behaved badly. There is, for once, no possible doubt about it. Even he must see it. If she had not picked up the knife her conduct would have been perfect. Still, Oliver damaged her hand, thus neutralizing her offence. So long as he sees it like that.

It does not occur to Chloe that perhaps Oliver means what

he says. He has said it before, and hasn't meant it.

Oliver, poor Oliver, has cried wolf too often.

Chloe falls into a half doze. Her misery drifts with her; the house seems to fall in upon her, its beams eaten through with distress.

Grace once ran to Chloe and Oliver in the middle of the night, in such a state as Chloe is now, but with rather more reason.

Picture it. Oliver and Chloe in the front of the car – their first car, a Ford Anglia – reasonably rational and kindly people. A happy and loving couple, though with the pleasure of their days now disturbed by the distress of their friend, Grace, who huddles in the back of the car, gasping and sobbing with hatred and grief.

They are on their way to Christie's house in Kensington to retrieve Piers and Petra. Christie took them out of school that afternoon. Stole them.

Christie and Grace are separated. Grace lives with the children in a cheap two-roomed flat ('cooped up' Christie claims in Court. 'A normal home' Grace maintains, though through a free Legal Aid solicitor, who has not the flair of Christie's team of legal advisers). The battle over the children wages to and fro: files thicken; writs fly. He doesn't want the children. Grace maintains. All he wants is her unhappiness. She's unfit, he maintains. A whore. A criminal lunatic, she says, but who's going to believe that? He doesn't love the children, she repeats.

And indeed little Piers and little Petra, rocks in two languages, shrink even further back into themselves when

Christie appears, bearing gifts for which he expects to be thanked by formal letter. Christie believes in healthy discipline and a clear organizational framework as the key to successful child rearing. Their little anxious eyes peer out from beneath furrowed brows. Piers sulks and Petra whines. It is as if they have decided that their best defence against their parents' battles is to present themselves as a prize scarcely worth the winning.

Nevertheless Grace loves them immoderately.

Now he has stolen them. Grace has been to the police station but they will do nothing for her. That afternoon Christie, unbeknownst to her, became their legal guardian. He has already, forestalling her, been to the police and shown them the Court Order, properly signed, properly witnessed, properly come by. Grace can appeal if she wants. Another six months, at least, during which time Christie has care, custody and control.

Oliver, Chloe and Grace reach Christie's house. It is in a quiet, almost remote avenue in Kensington. Here the rich live, enclosed. The house is, allegedly, burglar proof. It stands on a corner, its windows set in a stuccoed concrete face, its garden enclosed by a high brick wall. It was built at the turn of the century by a dishonest industrialist with a paranoiac fear of thieves. As their car parks outside, guard dogs in the garden begin to bark.

Grace rings the bell. The dogs stop barking, begin again. No-one comes.

Oliver, standing on the roof of the car, can see into the high windows, brilliant with light.

He can see pictures on the walls and the backs of chairs and people moving inside. It seems warm, cosy and prosperous in there, and so it is. If the curtains are left undrawn it is from sheer indifference to the outside world.

Oliver, Chloe and Grace ring and ring the door-bell and bang upon the knocker. Still there is no response. Oliver goes to the corner phone-box and telephones the number Grace, her fingers trembling, writes down for him. When the phone rings, someone lifts the receiver off the hook. That's all.

The top window opens and closes again. Christie's hand, Grace swears. Something flutters down, and falls at Grace's feet, as she clutches the railings and screams and shakes her fist. No-one from all those other houses comes to see or intervene or help. They remain closed, and silent, and shut, as always, to the implorings and imprecations and dying desperations of those outside. All's well within.

Grace has tears pouring down her cheeks. She seems scarcely human.

'Petra, Petra,' she shrieks. 'You bastard,' she cries. 'You bastard. Christie, you murderer. I'll kill you.'

'If she behaves like this,' says Oliver wretchedly, 'perhaps Christie's right, perhaps she's not fit—' but he knows himself, how else can Grace behave?

What fluttered down is a narrow strip of yellow ribbon. Petra's hair ribbon. Christie's token of mirth and victory.

Oliver thinks Grace will have a heart attack. She has collapsed on the ground. She is screaming.

'Get an ambulance, for God's sake,' Oliver says to Chloe. 'That bastard Christie, it's too much. We'll all be locked up—'

Chloe phones. Grace picks herself up, crawls towards the house, scrabbling at the cream stucco until the walls and her hands are pink with plaster and blood mixed.

When the ambulance comes she seems surprised to see it.

'I don't need that,' she says. 'Why should I need that? I'm perfectly all right.'

The ambulance goes away. Grace stays the night with Chloe and Oliver. In the morning Grace seems composed, even cheerful.

'The children are much better off with Christie,' Grace says. 'I can have a much better time without them, can't I. That little flat is dreadful.'

And so it is, and so she can, and so she does. It's as if part of her brain has been burnt out.

Later, when Grace becomes pregnant by Patrick, it is Chloe who persuades her not to have an abortion. She believes vaguely that the burnt out parts will be reactivated, but of course they aren't – what's dead is dead, and childbirth may be a miracle for the child but it is not for the mother. And this is why Chloe now feels Stanhope to be her responsibility; her fault.

And indirectly, why Chloe feels responsible for Kevin and Kestrel, whose mother might still be alive, if it had not been for Stanhope's birth.

fifty-one

Mind you, Christie was right to be angry with Grace.

Grace slapped his face at a party, and humiliated him in public, and that was the start of their troubles. Petra was two, at the time, so such mad behaviour could not even be attributed to post-natal mania.

It was not because Christie was flirting with an elderly titled lady in a corner – that kind of thing seldom worried her – that Grace slapped Christie's face. It was because, having had a little too much to drink, she had decided all of a sudden that he had no business to be at the party at all.

'You murderer,' she cried, 'you mass murderer,' and Christie had to hustle her off home in a taxi. He couldn't even use his own car because the chauffeur had been instructed to circle the block until midnight, and was nowhere in sight.

A week previously one of Christie's hotels had fallen down, the day before its official opening, killing fifty-nine people, and injuring twelve. Amongst the dead were:

Two LCC Building Inspectors, called by the Manager to inspect the cracks which had appeared that day in the foyer ceiling.
The Manager himself.
Assorted interior decorators, florists, publicity men, developers, architects.
A conscientious pop singer supervising the setting up of amplifiers.

And the destruction was so total, and even the rubble so pulverized, that no amount of sifting the evidence proved anything much to anyone. And the architects' plans and Christie's specifications had to be dug up from all kinds of remote files, and that of course took time. The Inquiry was postponed.

Not one of *my* hotels, said Christie, to the Press and everyone. The architects' hotel, the owner's hotel, the public's hotel. Not *my* hotel, and besides, everyone knows it was a strategically placed bomb which brought the building down. And off Christie went, busier than ever; to the office, and to clients' meetings; and to parties and dinners, without, it seemed, a spark of grief or anxiety or remorse.

Christie's telephone bills trebled that week, however, and Christie drew several thousands of pounds from the bank in cash, and sent off many cases of whisky to all kinds of addresses. Grace knew, for she helped him at home with various accounts which he did not, he said, trust his office to do properly. She would transfer certain figures from one ledger to another under Christie's direction. Grace enjoyed doing it – she had an eye for the shape of figures on the page, and she wrote the numbers with all the delicacy of a Chinese calligrapher.

Now, at this latest party, as she watches Christie chatting up a blue-haired lady in a corner – wife of an LCC Alderman – she sees him as if with someone else's eyes. The dead Manager's wife, perhaps, or even a florist's widow. She slaps him. Slaps Christie, murderer.

On the way home from the party, in the taxi, she can feel Christie trembling. She is surprised; her own anger has been shortlived, springing out of nowhere, it seems, and vanishing as quickly. She is herself again. The spirit which possessed her, so momentarily but so effectively, has passed on.

'I'm sorry,' Grace says. 'I don't know what came over me. It was as if I was someone else. Of course it wasn't your fault that hotel fell down. And you only knew one or two of them, anyway, and only in a business sense.'

But he isn't satisfied. He is savage.

'Hold your tongue in public, you bitch,' he says. 'Or do you want me in prison? Is that it? It's costing me enough as it is; do I have to bribe you too? What do you want, diamonds, mink?'

She shrivels up. And things have been going so well, too. She is such an ornament in his life, she knows it, so loving, so happy, so pleased to be married, with her long slim legs and her wide cool eyes, running the house like clockwork, flattering the right guests, discouraging the wrong ones; loving the children, always there to admire her husband's resourcefulness and guile, his shrewdness and his wealth; to listen to his plans and sit out his indignations; never nagging when he's too busy to get home, confident that home is where he'd rather be than anywhere (and so it is – oh, marvel!). Never critical, never complaining, yet with a whole host of trivial likes and dislikes with which she regales and enchants him. Kippers she finds repugnant but she adores Velasquez. Wet leaves depress her, kittens cheer her up. A man without a tie is unmanly, braces are ridiculous, belts erotic. And so on.

And to think that he, Christie, owns all this rampant femininity, that he can take his pleasure in it as and when he chooses – even in the afternoons, if he wants; if only he could spare the time from work.

Christie is worth nearly a half-million, already.

Christie finds his children strange. The boy looks weedy and the little girl's nose seems to run a lot. He watches their antics curiously. He buys them expensive presents. Grace loves them, after all, and his clients and friends seem interested in them. He expects, in time, he will be too.

But now Grace slaps Christie's face at a party, and everything changes. He feels he cannot trust her. At this time more than ever, surely, he is entitled to her support. And what does he find? That Grace has not only joined his enemies, but heads them.

Christie sleeps apart from Grace, that night.

At breakfast she looks dreadful. Her eyes are puffy and her hair is unkempt and her skin blotched. He rather likes the sight of her. Does he have so much power over his wife? When Christie makes love to Grace she remains composed; she seldom loses control of herself. He had thought he liked her to be like that, but perhaps this is better, this malleable puffiness?

'Please forgive me,' Grace says. 'I'd had too much to drink. I behaved dreadfully.'

'Yes,' says Christie, 'you did.' He is cruel. 'It was not a pretty sight. I hate to see a woman drink, especially in public.'

'Of course that building falling down was nothing to do with you, how could it be. Everyone knows it was a bomb.'

'It's bad enough for me having to put up with an official Commission of Inquiry, without my wife holding one of her own.'

'Please don't go to work angry with me. Please don't.' Grace is panicky. The day stretches bleakly in front of her, overshadowed by his anger.

'I'm not angry,' Christie says, cold as ice. 'Let's forget it.'

'It's just that when people don't grieve for the dead, it's surprising.'

'How do you know what I feel?'

'You're my husband.'

'And what kind of wife are you proving to be?' he asks. 'Disloyal and treacherous. A wife should love her husband through thick or thin.'

'But I do, Christie, I do.'

'Do you? I wonder. Of course I can't trust you to do my books any more, you realize that.'

She cries again. The maid, coming with more coffee, is shocked. Christie waits patiently until the maid has gone.

'I don't believe in your tears,' Christie says. 'They are not honest. They are not tears of remorse, but of self-pity. You accuse me of not feeling sorry for the dead, but did you cry when your mother died? No. You were a heartless daughter as you are a heartless wife.'

Grace cries some more. He finds the sight of her increasing moral and physical disorganization more and more exciting, and beckons her back up to bed. She follows, meekly. Christie makes love to Grace without his usual sense of deference, of male lust bowing before the shrine of female condescension. In fact, the more she cries the more he slaps her. There is as much pleasure, he decides, in punishing her as in pleasing her. Possibly more.

And Grace, to be fair, takes to punishment as a duck takes to water.

All the same, Christie is disappointed in Grace. He had so hoped for something to worship, that would worship him in return. And all he has, after all, is someone and something quite ordinary.

The Inquiry into the hotel disaster neither exonerates Christie nor blames him. The plans, such as can be traced, are flawless, in design and execution. It seems that the members of the Inquiry simply do not like Christie – which is hardly fair but the kind of thing that happens – so do not expect themselves to clear his name. Christie deals with the situation by increasing the proportion of the day which he devotes to socializing. Not a glimmer of self-doubt must he show, he knows it. Thus he can convert the faint cloud of approbation which hovers over his head into a halo of fashionable success. To be noticed is the main thing, these days.

'All publicity is good publicity,' as he remarks to Patrick Bates, whom he engages to paint Grace's portrait, in the sanctity of her own home. 'I don't care what you make her look like, just so long as she's on canvas and you've signed your name. The medium is the message.'

Grace, reckless, is all too pleased to see Patrick again. She has quarrelled with Christie, again, that morning. Their rows are all one-sided, these days. He is icy, cold and rational. She is tearful, noisy, hysterical. He watches her, fascinated and unmoved, stoking the fires of her grief and rage.

Grace tells Patrick that she does not like coupling with a mass murderer. Not for nothing is he named Christie, she says.

Grace is showing off, as a wife will to a lover. She does not for one moment think that Christie was responsible for the disaster. Perhaps she imagined the phone-bills, the whisky and the bribes. She can't check, in any case, He no longer brings his books home.

But she cannot be unfaithful to Christie, she finds, not properly, however much she wants to, however much Patrick lies on top of her, trying to part her legs with his knee, telling her that art requires her cooperation, and asking her what difference does it make, since his sexual claim to Grace was prior to Christie's.

Really? The incident is long since obliterated from Grace's mind; it is only future events which will bring it to more precise recollection. Grace, these days, really believes she came to Christie a virgin bride, and that her secret passages belong to her husband alone.

It is not her mind, Grace finds, which rejects this adulterous lover; on the contrary, her mind welcomes him – she would be delighted to pay Christie out for his ill-treatment of her. Her body, however, seems to take a more serious and a less trivial attitude. Her legs remain crossed to protect that warm and pulsating mucous membrane from the strangeness of the intruder. It seems to expect familiarity and to reject what is unknown.

Ah, thinks Grace, and ah again, in Patrick's arms. This Christie of hers, who breakfasts with her in the mornings, quite normally, like any ordinary man, and makes telephone calls from the missionary position – not quite so normally, perhaps, but merely (he says) because he's a busy man and when he thinks of things he likes to see to them immediately – this daily and nightly Christie of hers, this father of her children, to outward appearances so honourable and efficient, to all inward appearances (she has this minute convinced herself, Patrick's warm breath in her mouth, her ears, her nose) is a villain, a devil, a monster, a criminally negligent constructor of unsafe buildings and she is entitled to be unfaithful to him. At whatever sacrifice to herself.

Patrick's mouth moves downward from her lips, while his hand moves upwards from her knees. Her legs capitulate, relax.

Patrick likes to paint women nude, or if they insist, wrapped in white bathtowels. Christie insists on the towel, and Grace has chosen the smallest she can find, such is her mood that morning.

Women who go to linen cupboards and find them neatly piled with clean, warm, sheets and towels, put there by other women, are given to such moods, says Marjorie. They have the time. Seduction is not for working women, or mothers, or earnest housewives – it is for the idle and absurd.

'This doesn't count,' says Patrick, 'it really doesn't. This isn't sex, it's pleasure.'

And so it is, and Grace moans and tosses with gratification, taken by surprise as she is by the unexpected nature of this event. Unexpected! By her, perhaps. But by Christie? For it is Christie who has led her to Patrick, almost by the hand.

Marjorie once told Grace of the urge ambitious husbands feel to render up their wives into the arms of the men they most respect and admire, as if in hopes that high achievement was an infection which could be venereally transmitted.

'Eskimos, perhaps,' said Grace, shocked. 'They lend their wives to passing guests. But not the kind of men we know. Really, Marjorie!'

Perhaps she was wrong? Perhaps Christie, her golden fiancé, her suitable husband, is more of an Eskimo than she thought? Grace, lying entranced by her own pleasure, and her

239

own wickedness, gains the strength to view her once golden fiancé, her once suitable husband, with impartial eyes. She must now believe the evidence of her unwifely ears, and unwifely eyes, and accept that her husband is a sadist, a mass murderer, and in matters of sex, an Eskimo.

For yes, he delivered her over to Patrick. He did. Believing first virginity and then fidelity in his wife to be as much part of his life and as necessary to his existence as the head on his neck, yet without a doubt Christie unclothed her, wrapped her in the scantiest of towels and pushed her towards Patrick, a man he greatly admires.

Indeed, Patrick Bates is much admired by everyone who's anyone. He is an artist, and he makes money out of artistry. Big money. His name is internationally recognized. He is accepted in palaces and hovels alike. He goes freely into houses where Christie, for all his money and connections, can barely scrape an invitation. And if he gets drunk inside them, and breaks up the furniture and the best vases, then Patrick is excused. (That he is seen as a kind of court fool, in these high places, escapes Christie the Colonial.) Women of all kind and conditions fall down at Patrick's feet. To be painted by Patrick Bates is to have slept with Patrick Bates, everyone who's anyone knows that. And what illustrious company to keep, albeit by proxy. What brothers and sisters in experience it makes of everyone who's anyone.

'Patrick and his fashionable cock,' as Chloe says sadly to Marjorie, who has been to see Midge, bearing clothes for the children and a kettle for the cooker, so Midge doesn't always have to boil the water in a saucepan – and brings back tales to

Chloe of desolation and poverty, much inlaid with protestations of undying and sacrificial love, like glossy marquetry on some shoddy old pine box.

Meanwhile Patrick says this doesn't count, and Grace allows herself to agree with him. This delicate intrusion, this deferential nibbling pleasure, his head between her legs in the most transatlantic of fashions, not eye to eye boldly, but servicing and being serviced, sight unseen, can surely be no more infidelity than masturbation is. No, it doesn't count.

Christie, returning unexpectedly, thinks on the contrary that it does count.

It is Patrick's belief – and experience has so far confirmed the belief – that if only he can appear suave enough, experienced enough, and rich enough, then husbands tend to be not just forgiving but appreciative of the interest taken in their wives.

He does his best, for he is fond of Grace, and when he says he loves her (for it is his custom, these days, to comfort women with the notion that he does) he almost means it.

Then the conversation goes: Christie advancing, Patrick retreating, Grace, still all of a tingle, covering her nakedness with cushions, and clearly panicking.

Patrick Why Christie! How good to see you! But how unexpected! Grace and I were renewing an old acquaintance.
Christie An old acquaintance?

Now Christie, remember, believes that Grace came to him a virgin (and so, in a way, does Grace herself). Why else the white wedding dress from an expensive couturier, the marquee, the champagne, and so on? Patrick's opening gambit stops him in his tracks.

Grace It's not true, Christie. Only this once today. I swear it. And we were only fooling about. You shouldn't be so unpleasant to me at breakfast. It's all your fault.

Christie knows she is lying. Grace, married to Christie, often lies, about how much she has spent on clothes, or what book she is reading: trivial lies, born of the fear of censure.

Christie Liar.
Grace I never lie to you, Christie, never.
Christie Don't think you'll get a penny out of me, you won't.

Worse and worse, what does he mean? Divorce? Later on in Grace's life, when it becomes clear to her that the worst can and does happen, and that no amount of lies or false evidence prevents it, she quite gives up disguising actuality and develops a taste for the truth, in all its most telling, trenchant and destructive forms. But now, caught in flagrante delicto, she is at her most absurd.

Grace Christie. I love you. I'd die without you. Patrick means nothing to me. I was angry because you let him paint me and you know what he's like, and I never wanted it—
Christie (*Ignoring her*) As for you, Patrick, get out of my house before I kill you.

Patrick I've nowhere near finished the painting. I need another three sittings at least—

Christie advances on the easel to destroy the barely daubed canvas, but prudence and a proper sense of value stop him.

Christie You can do it from photographs.
Grace Oh Christie, you've forgiven me—

But he hasn't. It is one thing to give your wife to the man of your choice, quite another to find she has done the choosing herself.

Patrick (Departing) For a man who conducts his business affairs from on top of his wife, you take a very humourless view of sex, Christie.

He shouldn't have said it, of course. If he'd kept quiet Grace might have been able to make her peace with Christie. But then Grace should never have whispered to Patrick the details of Christie's sexual habits. It was disloyal of her: she knew it at the time, and perhaps she deserved to lose her husband; and then again, perhaps she wanted to, and it was a healthy instinct which led her thus to disloyalty and ruin. That sadist Christie, that mass murderer; that monster of sex and status intertwined, rendered erect by notions alone – notions of beauty possessed, of virtue sullied, of business and sex rolled into one, and not a laugh, not a glimmer of a smile as Grace lay there waiting, penetrated, and Christie got on the telephone not his office

243

and his all-night staff, but wrong number after wrong number owing to a fault at the exchange. And not one person in all the world, not a friend, not a lawyer, not even Patrick, who only laughed, no-one to allow that she, Grace, was married to a monster. Later, they'd take her side, and sympathize, and encourage, as Christie the father revealed himself as villain. But Christie the husband, never. She should be grateful, they thought.

'I have finished with you, Grace,' says Christie.

And so he has.

He stops at the door,

'And don't think you will have the children,' he adds.

And she doesn't.

Christie divorces Grace for adultery, citing Patrick. Grace cannot deny the charge, since Patrick freely admits it. The judges look sourly at her, thinking her unfit to look after her children, being a self-confessed creature of low moral habits. But they do not like Christie much, either. His lawyers seem too clever by half, his vilification of his former wife too extreme. The children need a woman's touch: Christie is cold and sensible.

Grace gets the house in St John's Wood and, for a time, care of the children, though he has custody. He visits every second Sunday: he brings them expensive presents and hires a nanny for the day. They are confused and unimpressed. Grace, seeing him, is noisy, hysterical, and irrational. He is icy, indifferent, and powerful.

If they did not love each other, in their own dreadful ways, they might have left each other alone. As it is, they can't.

Christie marries Geraldine, the social worker. Faced with her, and photographic evidence of (1) the children crying at Grace's window, and (2) little Petra lying on the pavement outside Woolworths having a temper tantrum, (3) Grace dancing with a black man at a night-club – and a doctor's report that Piers has threadworms, the judges seem to have no choice but to award Christie custody of the children. Still they deliberate.

Grace could accept the divorce but not, it seems, the remarriage. Perhaps somewhere, somehow, she believed that she and Christie would be reconciled.

Christie is outraged by what he still sees as Grace's infidelities, and vengeful as ever. Christie has Grace's black boyfriend followed and framed (perhaps) by the police on a drug charge. Grace sends anonymous letters and makes obscene phone calls to his clients, his friends, and his family.

They never see each other. Her lawyers cringe when they see her coming. His rub their hands. More money! They present the judges with the obscene letters from Grace to Geraldine. Christie gets the children.

He steals them of course. Not content to have them decently handed over. It is the end. Grace cannot subject them to this, not any more. She loves her children. Christie does not. So, let Chistie have them.

Love can only damage them, she sees it now. She must give them up, and him up, and so she does. Piers and Petra, goodbye.

Piers, eventually, goes to Sandhurst, then Oxford, then the Guards. He always wears a tie, even on Sundays.

Petra goes to finishing school and then takes a secretarial

course. She is very good at flower arrangements and will one day have her photograph as the frontispiece of *Country Life*.

After their father dies in a car crash (on the day after his third marriage to California), they go back to live with Geraldine, his second wife, who is very good to them, although she does not really like them. California was never interested in Christie's children, in any case. She only cared about his money, and said as much, and Christie did not seem to mind.

Grace, at Christie's death, does not even inquire as to her children's whereabouts. Everyone says how heartless Grace is, what a selfish, unmaternal, unnatural woman.

Grace goes out to Golders Green, sometimes, where a plaque, marks (supposedly) his ashes, and sits placidly in the sun beside it, as if waiting for him to rise up and re-form again, and start another wrangle, and re-animate her.

Sometimes it is Patrick who drives her out there. He waits in the car, while Grace sits in the cemetery, and contemplates mortality.

fifty-two

Marjorie, Grace and me.

Fine citizens we make, fine sisters!

Our loyalties are to men, not to each other.

We marry murderers and think well of them. Marry thieves, and visit them in prison. We comfort generals, sleep with torturers, and not content with such passivity, torment the wives of married men, quite knowingly.

Well, morality is for the rich, and always was. We women, we beggars, we scrubbers and dusters, we do the best we can for us and ours. We are divided amongst ourselves. We have to be, for survival's sake.

fifty-three

After her evening's quarrel with Oliver – if so lopsided a conflict could be termed quarrel – Chloe lies crying and dozing on her bed, the quilt pulled over her. Oliver approaches.

Chloe is surprised. When she cries he normally keeps away from her. He does not like scenes. Afterwards, when she has regained her calm, he will renegotiate their marital relationship without reference to whatever incident has caused its temporary severance.

Now Oliver sits at the end of the bed, and strokes Chloe's hair. Chloe is exhausted by her grief. There is a luxuriant quality to her distress. He knows it, and capitalizes upon it.

'It's been a hard day, Chloe,' he says, and then, astonishingly, 'I'm sorry. But you shouldn't take on so. What's the matter?'

'The things you said.' To Chloe it is self-evident.

'Words,' says Oliver. 'You know I don't mean them. Why do you get so upset?'

There is something strange about this, Chloe thinks, pleasant though it is. She sits up. Gently but firmly Oliver pushes her back against the pillows.

'Stay there,' he says, 'I want to talk to you. I'll lie down beside you.' And so he does.

Oliver talks up at the ceiling thus:

Oliver You must have more confidence in my love for you, Chloe. We have been together for all our adult lives. We are part of each other. If I savage you with words, it is because you are an extension of me, and I say to you the things I feel like saying to myself. That's all there is to it. But you will react to words as if they were blocks of stone, coming hurtling down upon your head.
Chloe I'm sorry.
Oliver It's very damaging: it's no use just saying that you're sorry. You try and inflict a pattern of conventional married behaviour upon me which is alien to my nature. You want me to be nice. I'm not nice. People aren't nice, not all the time, just some of the time. You drive me mad, Chloe.
Chloe I'm sorry.
Oliver Never mind. I love you.

He takes her hand. He strokes it.

Oliver I hate it when we are estranged.
Chloe Then why estrange us, Oliver?

Oliver lays down her hand.

Chloe I'm sorry. I know it's me. Ever since Patrick—

He takes her hand again.

Oliver Oh yes, Patrick. I think it is time you forgot Patrick, Chloe.

248

Chloe How can I? You don't.

Oliver Dearest Chloe, you wrong me. See our marriage as a citadel, see Patrick ramming at the gates: he made a nasty dent in the walls, it's true. But as for me, I don't see the damage any more. He hurt himself more than us. He sent Imogen in, as a thief in the night, but Imogen has remained as our dearest ally. We have gained more than we ever lost, Chloe, you and me. And if the truth were told, I think Patrick has homosexual inclinations, and got at you to get at me. It was me he was interested in, not you at all.

Chloe I expect so.

Oliver Of course you, doing the actual betraying, feel worse about it than I ever did. It has coloured your behaviour for years. You have felt insecure and defensive – you've been no fun. You've stooped to jealousy. How ridiculous – what two – or three – people do to each other physically, what parts of each other they put into each other, can be a matter for pleasure, but hardly for pain. Patrick and I were friends – you couldn't let that alone, you had to come wiggling your pretty little arse between us. I don't think women understand the quality of friendship between men, and not understanding, resent it.

Chloe I have friends. Female friends.

Oliver Yes. You use them when you need them, discard them when you don't. Male friendship is of a different order – it gives as well as takes.

His hand has opened her blouse and is on her breast by now. Her nipples, in spite of herself, grow hard. She does not like to argue.

Oliver Darling Chloe. Darling hard-and-soft Chloe. Remember what it all used to be like?
Chloe Yes.

And so she does. Her body certainly remembers, turning easily towards Oliver's, with the same instinctive movements that a new baby makes towards its mother's breasts.

Oliver I'm sorry I made you cry. Put your arms round me.
Chloe What about Françoise?
Oliver Bother Françoise—
Chloe But you can't just—
Oliver I can, you know.
Chloe Poor Françoise, out in the cold—

Oliver disengages himself from Chloe, gently.

Oliver Very well. You are quite right. If you want Françoise you shall have her.

What does he mean? She is confused. But Oliver seems more than rational.

Oliver Take your clothes off, Chloe. Why have you gone to bed with your clothes on, in any case?
Chloe I was too unhappy to take them off.
Oliver My dearest Chloe, what would your mother say? You're falling to pieces, you must be put together again, at once, this very night.

250

Oliver helps Chloe undress.

Oliver Your lovely body. I never forget it.

Somewhere Chloe has heard these words before. Ah yes, the film his sisters thought so funny. Chloe went to a preview and told Oliver and everyone what a masterpiece it was. Only by clinging to that conviction could she escape the indignation she would otherwise feel.

Oliver It doesn't matter who I sleep with, Chloe, it's always the same. They turn into you. All-wise, all-seeing Chloe. I sleep with Françoise and I dream it is you. I punish myself, instead of you. It's a kind of superstition. I told myself that until I had finished the novel I wouldn't touch you. I'd feed on my frustration instead. I'm sure that's what went wrong with that last film – screwing you like fury all the time I was writing it. How could I stand enough away from myself to see my own life?

He's always denied it was his own life, but Chloe scarcely notices, so bemused, and so comforted, is she. As she says to Marjorie later, making light of it, 'I thought I'd been rejected on sexual grounds, but no, they were purely literary, after all.'

Chloe (Tentative) And will you be finished with the novel soon?

Or perhaps he has finished it? Perhaps that's why he's here, stroking her forehead, her breast, her tummy, between her thighs, with his familiar finger: her body is still warm and hopeful.

Oliver It's all madness, isn't it. I'm mad, I daresay. I don't know. Perhaps I'll never finish it. I have writer's block. I'll burn it. Be done with it. Go back to writing commercial crap.
Chloe You can't burn it, not after all this time.
Oliver Why not? What else can I do? You've taken to lying in bed with your clothes on, crying your heart out. I can't have you unhappy. It upsets the children. I've got to throw Françoise out, I have no choice, and she's so much connected with the novel, if she goes, it goes.
Chloe But Oliver—
Oliver Unless perhaps the three of us—

Chloe stares at him unblinkingly, neither assenting nor rejecting, too astounded to do either.

Oliver Lie there Chloe dear, don't move. I shall save us all, you see.

Chloe lies, dutifully. Oliver goes away and comes back with Françoise. She is bleary with sleep and wears an orange quilted nylon dressing-gown.

Oliver We shall have no more evenings like tonight. No more days like yesterday. The two of you must be properly friends.
Françoise We are most truly friends. Mrs Rudore is a most civilized and progressive person.

Oliver Mrs Rudore! It is ridiculous. Her name is Chloe. Say it, Françoise.

Françoise Chloe. But what of the respect due between servant and employer?

Oliver Françoise, I am your employer, and I would like you to love as well as respect Chloe. Take off that dreadful dressing-gown. You have a beautiful body. Hasn't she, Chloe?

Chloe, alas, can almost see her husband framing the scene in preparation for his next film. As Grace was to say later, unkindly, 'If he's going to try skin-flicks, he's wasting his time. Look what happened to Sebastian. Lost all his money and mine too. What the public wants these days is family entertainment, not scenes of lesbian delight. They're old hat. There's nothing left remarkable, not even pigs and fishes.'

It is, perhaps, this sense of being projected on to some future screen, and of the unreality of herself (thus at last revealed) through Oliver's eyes, which enables Chloe to lie at first without protest, and later with evident enjoyment, under Françoise's pressing lips and investigating hands. Françoise, Oliver explains to Chloe, is bi-sexual, and takes as much pleasure in the female response as the male. After the 1968 fiasco, tired of making coffee, thereafter, for armchair revolutionaries, she had joined a commune of insistently lesbian ladies.

Oliver And why not? The female is not treacherous, like the male. You women must learn to stick together. I'm sure you will. We men will be for decoration and to fill the sperm banks.

Well, why not, indeed? If this is what Oliver wants. Chloe feels she has all but grown, at last, out of motherhood. She feels safe in the knowledge that Imogen sleeps soundly through the night. Chloe can be woman again, not mother, not watchful, and if Oliver says this is what women are like, he may be right.

Françoise's breasts are white and heavy, marked blue where Oliver's fingers have pressed, the nipples are flat and pink. Her arms are dark with hair and are muscular, reminding Chloe of Oliver's. Otherwise she is as soft and hard mixed as the Cherry Cup in a box of Black Magic chocolates.

It has been a long and trying day, Chloe thinks. This is really no more remarkable than anything else, and better than crying alone on a bed. And has, besides, Oliver's approval. Perhaps indeed, like this, they could all three be happy? Françoise whispers French indecencies in her ears. Dimly, Chloe understands them. Her body, paying attention, Françoise's fingers probing, prepares itself to its surge of response.

Ah, but no.

Thus far, no farther, Oliver thinks (or as Helen once put it to Marjorie, spelling it out, with the jovial prudery of that earlier generation, thus far, no father!). Oliver intervenes between Chloe and Françoise separating them, bringing his orchestrations to a sudden, flat and silent halt. Françoise lies face down on the bed beside Chloe. Is she exhausted, overcome with emotion, or simply asleep? Chloe thinks it is the latter.

Oliver sits on the edge of the bed by Chloe and strokes his wife's forehead.

Oliver So, Chloe, now we see at last what your true nature is.

I have always suspected it. You do not really care for me, or for any man. Your true response is to women. To your Grace, or your Marjorie, or your mother. The maid, even. Well, why not? There is nothing wrong with being a lesbian, except that the degree of your hypocrisy has been damaging to me. All these years pretending to be something you weren't, blaming me for all our failures, throwing away our children. Of course your body rejected them. You have not been fair with me, Chloe.

Chloe Oliver, really, I am not a lesbian. Don't be ridiculous.

He bends and kisses her, indulgently. She sits up, pushing him away. Oliver goes and sits beside Françoise, running his fingers down her spine.

Chloe You are quite ridiculous. I don't care what you say, any more, or what you do.

And she doesn't. Her sincerity seems both to impress Oliver and take him aback. He turns Françoise on to her back. She has been crying.

Oliver You do care, Chloe. I'll make you care. You're not just going to sit there now and watch me and not care. You can't.
Chloe I can.

Chloe's head is quite clear. She is her own woman again. She can and she does. She watches Oliver go through the motions of intercourse with Françoise with as much dispassion as she watches her children bathe themselves. Françoise continues to

255

cry, from exhaustion and now apparently fright, turning her head this way and that to avoid Oliver's mouth, while Oliver takes what can only be termed his desperate and dubious pleasure in her.

Françoise, disengaged, continues to cry.

Françoise I am sorry to cry. I am so tired. Why is my life so wretched?
Oliver Because you're a silly stupid bourgeois bitch and not a liberated lady at all. Go back to bed, for God's sake.

Françoise goes. Oliver, Chloe sees to her amazement, has tears in his eyes.

Oliver I'm sorry, Chloe. I don't know what's the matter with me. I think I'm mad.
Chloe. So do I.

Chloe finds she is laughing, not hysterically, or miserably, but really quite lightly and merrily; and worse, not with Oliver, but at him, and in this she is, at last, in tune with the rest of the universe.

fifty-four

Working-class women, Grace believes, have a rather better time of it than the middle classes – apart from starvation, disease, over-work, miscarriages, exhaustion and so on, of course. But in their personal lives, they have fewer expectations and for that reason, fewer disappointments. They put up with their husbands in bed, take their weekly money in return, pack them off to pubs and football matches, and get on with their own lives.

Marjorie maintains that the great, gnawing, devitalizing vice of the middle classes is pretending to be nice when they aren't. Patrick, she says, in the eyes of women of aspiring gentility and/ or depleted nervous energy, smacks of the working classes, rumbling away with a raw, suppressed and vital energy, which must one day inevitably overwhelm and overcome, as the male overwhelms the female. Of course such women fall prostrate at his feet, welcoming the inevitable orgasmic defeat – and with it the expected punishment not just of their class presumptions, but for their female exploitativeness – which in turn is the product of their own exploitation.

'Marjorie sees Marx in everything,' Grace complains to Chloe, 'and from the point of view of a female who always lies beneath the male. I'm dreadfully sorry for her. Why doesn't she get on top?'

Her own long-drawn-out affair with Patrick, in and out of the ruin of both their days, seems to bring her little happiness – as Marjorie frequently remarks.

'Poor Grace,' says Marjorie, 'what a burnt-out case she is. Fancy putting your faith in sexual athletics. Grace uses Patrick as a memory of better times, of course, when she still had some feeling left in her. As for Patrick, he doesn't take her to Christie's grave because he adores her – as she tells everyone

– but to annoy Midge and because he likes the shape those dreadful headstones make against the sky.'

While Grace plays fast and loose through the sixties, her thirties, invincibly fashionable – in and out of water beds and topless dresses and the occasional acid-trip, into the occult, and flying saucers, astrology and force fields, and finding therein, of course, cosmic justification for her quite irrational persecution of the unfortunate Geraldine: taking up prison reform after a night in the cells for disorderly behaviour in a Chelsea pub (coincidentally called the Rose and Crown), vying with Patrick, one might almost think, in the number and variety of her sexual exploits – though unlike Patrick never putting brush to canvas, as she would have been better employed in doing, if only to demonstrate to the world that she, like him, suffered from the disease of artistic talent and did not merely exhibit its more disagreeable and anti-social symptoms; aborting frequently instead (an outer and visible sign of an inner and spiritual state, Marjorie maintains, underlining her determination to destroy and not create) – while Grace thus plays fast and loose with herself and her fate, Marjorie plays safe.

'Marjorie is very wise not to marry,' says Grace. 'She is the sort of woman born to be widowed five times. Her husbands would just drop dead one after another – you know how it happens – if not from poison then from sheer suggestion. Well, look at Marjorie's record. First her father, then her Ben, then her baby. She's best to stay where she is, putting the finger of death on television programmes.'

And it is certainly true that Marjorie appears to avoid any

personal commitment to anything other than a programme or a department. She battles with organizations rather than with people. She engages in a paper war of inter-office memos, fighting for position up the telephone list, to head first this section, then that, scaling the sides of the orthodox organizational pyramid the planners have made of the BBC; her name eventually there in leaded black, as near the apex as a woman can get.

'She only visits Patrick in the hopes of getting in touch with her younger self,' says Grace, 'when she was altogether more hopeful of life. Doing his washing makes her feel she's female. Well, what else is going to? She's the only woman in the world he doesn't fancy. It can't be very nice for her, though God knows these days he smells rather rancid and his feet are beginning to rot.'

Marjorie has her family, though. She acquires a set of homosexual friends. They cluster round her like a set of lost and earnest chickens: in the warmth of their chattering, clucking regard Marjorie acquires a kind of glow: the silence of her nights are punctured with gossip and laughter. They warm her little hands, admire her cleverness, bring her little gifts. Together, she and they make giggling, anxious excursions to junk and antique shops, collecting little goodies, little treasures, little bygones, bargains all. Forever, and how positive an act it is, rescuing what is good from what is past. Marjorie develops a visual taste: her bleak flat begins to be a place of interest. She talks knowledgeably about Victorian biscuit tins, Lalique and Tiffany. She learns how to cook coq-au-vin, and not just spaghetti bolognese. But presently her friends drift off as they have drifted in. The biscuit tins look rusty rather than quaint: she drops and breaks her best Lalique plate: she starts opening cans of baked beans again.

'Nothing good lasts,' she says sorrowfully to Chloe. 'After they passed that Consenting Adults Bill, and they could go about together openly, they seemed to lose their need of me. We'd quarrel and bitch properly, not just camping it up. And I began to feel they were mocking me and using me; they'd always pretended to, of course, but now it was for real. It was as if their lives had become serious at last, instead of just the play-acting it had always had to be, and so I couldn't be part of it any more. I'm glad for them, but sorry for me. I miss them. It was nice to have one's lack of bosom an asset and not a liability.'

As for Chloe, she grits her teeth and sticks to her marriage and children as a shoemaker to his last. The lives of the spiritually unmarried, and the spiritually childless, seem sad to her.

This morning Chloe is woken up by the sound of laughter. It frightens her at first, until she realizes it is her own, and not that of some stranger in her bedroom.

The sun shines through her window. It is another brilliant day. The winter has been short and mild – which is why, no doubt, the greenfly are so active so early in the year. If the climate is changing, thinks Chloe, should I remain the same?

It is eight o'clock. Chloe should get up and supervise the baking of Oliver's rolls. Françoise tends to forget them, and leave them in the oven too long, so they become dried out, and the crust a danger to Oliver's increasingly brittle teeth. Chloe lies in her virtuous bed a little longer. Then, when the smell of burning bread fills the room with an almost tangible cloud, she rises in temper, puts on her dressing-gown and goes into the kitchen.

Françoise, this morning, seems determined to deny her sex. She wears a white tee-shirt, faded jeans, and a pair of Inigo's sneakers. Her ripe female form, unintimidated, bulges alarmingly beneath. She is breathless with nervous distress, and wishes to ingratiate herself with Chloe, who merely throws open the windows in clattering and ill-tempered reproach.

Chloe Have you no sense of smell at all, Françoise?

Françoise Please, do not upset me. I have scraped the rolls. Oliver will not notice.

Chloe I am afraid he will.

Françoise On such a morning such things are not important.

Chloe You are mistaken. The morning is not important in the least, the rolls are. If you disbelieve me, take in Oliver's breakfast yourself, today.

Françoise You are cross when you should be loving. I want only to love and be loved. To be properly close to those I love most in the world. You and Oliver. And all your lovely family.

Chloe You should not get too close to Inigo's shoes, Françoise. He has chronic athlete's foot.

Françoise But I see I have upset you. I cannot forgive myself. I wanted only to make you happy. But your heart is closed to me. You believe that sex is for procreation. Therefore you can only conceive of it with the opposite sex. I disgust you. To you sex is something shameful. To me it is a sacrament; I grieve for you that you cannot share something so joyous with me.

Chloe I can only assume you are not familiar with athlete's foot, or you would not take it so lightly.

Françoise dissolves into hiccoughing tears, which turn Chloe cold with anger and embarrassment. She feels the desire to hurt Françoise as much as possible. Is this what Oliver feels? Why Françoise's breasts are black and blue? What pleasure there is in withholding affection, when it is both deserved and desperately needed.

Françoise You are unkind to me. I want to go home. But there is even worse than here. I lived intimately with my best friend the confectioner. She swore she loved me: she hated men, she said. When she made a wedding cake, she would drive a pin through the heart of the sugar groom. But then she eloped with my fiancé: she accused me to him of being a lesbian and seducing her, and so he hated me and married her. But the truth was the other way round. Why must people play when they should be serious?
Chloe Heaven knows.
Françoise I want to go home, where I am taken seriously.
Chloe I think Oliver takes you very seriously, Françoise. And I very much hope you will stay. I think you must, if only for the sake of literature. Only please will you try not to cry in front of the children? And will you now take Oliver's breakfast in to him?

But Françoise will not. Chloe goes. Chloe takes Oliver his breakfast tray, sits on the edge of the bed, and talks soothingly about crocuses, daffodils, and Inigo's athlete's foot.

Oliver I am not mad, Chloe. There is no need to humour me. I am sorry about last night.

Chloe Let us not talk about it. I am sure that what happens at night is nothing to do with our daily selves. I am sorry the rolls are burnt.

Oliver Françoise, I suppose?

Chloe Yes.

Oliver That girl will have to go.

Chloe No, no. She's useful.

And so Françoise is.

Oliver Perhaps I really should abandon the novel, and go back to film scripts.

Chloe Good heavens no. Not after all this.

Oliver If only one could control what one responded to sexually! I promise you, Chloe, that if I could you would head the list. It would save a good deal of trouble and effort, and putting up with really rather stupid people because one can't resist a hefty arse and heavy tits.

Chloe It must be dreadful to be a man, and so helpless in the face of one's own nature.

Is she laughing at him? Yes, she is. Her victory is complete.

She does not much enjoy her victory. Mirth cuts at the very roots of her life.

fifty-five

During the morning the telephone rings. It is Grace. And thus the conversation goes:

Chloe I thought you were in France, Grace.

Grace What, me? Topless beaches and dirty old men with cameras? You must be joking. I'm far too old to compete, anyway, in the beach girl stakes. Sebastian said so, and he should know, being Competition King himself in the Great Vulgar Life Game. Not that he'll get there, of course, his plane's going to fall out of the sky, thank God. We met a fortune teller at a party last night, and he said so, and he's never wrong about anything. If Sebastian wants to defy fate that's his business, I told him so at the time. Perhaps you're not life's Darling to the degree you think, I said. He didn't like that. But then I threw the teapot and put myself in the wrong, sod it.

Chloe Grace, is it wise to quarrel with Sebastian if he's got all your money?

Grace Quarrel? You call that a quarrel? I've been down to Out-Patients for stitches in my lip, and my ribs are black and blue. I don't care about the money. Let him keep it. It was Christie's anyway. Christie's last mean revenge, so I'd always be pursued by fortune hunters who defined a fortune as 50p. I'm glad it's all gone. I can earn, can't I?

Chloe I don't know, Grace. You never have.

Grace I must be mad, ringing you up. You're so pompous and respectable. Such a wet blanket. How's Oliver? Making you watch?

Chloe Yes.

Grace Wait till I tell Marjorie.

Chloe I'm sorry, I shouldn't have said that.

Grace Too late. Why do you stay so loyal to that monster? He outwore loyalty years ago. Did you know Marjorie's mother is in hospital?

Chloe No, I didn't.

Grace I rang Marjorie in the middle of the night when Sebastian was beating me up but she wasn't the slightest use, her mother had had a heart attack and that was all she could think about. She's in intensive care. She's going to be all right, though. The fuss Marjorie made, you'd have thought she was dying.

Chloe She's very fond of her mother.

Grace So was I fond of Sebastian. Chloe, I am really very upset. I can't go on like this for ever. There has to be a kind of truth about one's life, doesn't there? And Chloe, do you know what today is?

Chloe No.

Grace Midge has been dead for five years.

Chloe So?

Grace Do you think it was my fault?

Chloe Yes.

Grace I knew it. It's why you're so dreadful to me so much of the time. You don't blame Patrick?

Chloe No. Not any more. You can't hold men responsible for their actions.

Grace I suppose not. They follow their pricks like donkeys allegedly follow carrots. Though I've never seen it myself. Well, that's all over now. I'm going down to the hospital to be with Marjorie. Will you come?

Chloe Does she want me to?

Grace If you're going to be someone's friend, you have to intrude your friendship sometimes.

Chloe Really?

Grace Yes. Give my love to Stanhope, Chloe, you stealer of other people's children.

Grace rings off. The phone goes almost immediately. This time it is Marjorie.

Marjorie Chloe, it's mother.

Chloe Yes I know. Grace told me. How is she?

Marjorie Bad news, I'm afraid. It was malignant.

Chloe I don't understand. Grace said it was a heart attack.

Marjorie Grace gets everything wrong. It was a brain tumour. She might have had it for years, they said. The surgeon asked if she ever acted strangely. What's normal, I wanted to know, but he couldn't tell me. Anyway they've taken away what they can, and she's sitting up in bed with her head shaven and a great knitted scar on her temple, plucking her eyebrows. Is that strange or normal?

Chloe It sounds quite lively, Marjorie. And not as if she's in pain. Do you want me to come down? Grace said she was going to.

Marjorie Oh my God! Did she? Well, she might as well. And she did know mother, and so did you. Come this evening. I hate hospitals. I'm a perfectly competent person until I smell those corridors, then I go to pieces. They won't say anything. You're always asking the wrong person, anyway. I said is she going to die, and all they said was we're all dying, and she is an old lady. What do they mean? Poor little mother. She was always so brave, and

266

everything was so dreadful for her, but she'd always wring some sort of goodness out of the bad.

It doesn't sound at all like Helen to Chloe, but she says nothing. Poor Helen, she tries to think, but all she remembers is Helen's disparagement, all those years ago, of her social standing. Little Chloe, the barmaid's daughter. All those years! Has Chloe really borne this grudge for so long? Yes, Chloe has. It is not Helen's treatment of Marjorie which causes Chloe's animosity towards this poor, defeated, bandaged old soul, but this harboured, treasured slight.

Marjorie She's changed. I don't know whether it's sanity or madness, that's the trouble, but she's being so nice to me. She calls me my little girl, so proudly. She's never said anything like that to me before. And she takes my hand and pats it. You know how she usually hates touching anyone.
Chloe I expect it's sanity, Marjorie.
Marjorie But the nurse said 'they're often like this after brain ops.' I can't stand it, Chloe.
Chloe You have to stand it, Marjorie. You have no option.
Marjorie I could bring the cameras in, I suppose, and deal with it that way, through a lens darkly.
Chloe But you won't. Not this time.
Marjorie No. Thank you, Chloe.

Marjorie rings off.

Chloe does the ironing. She does not trust Françoise to do it with proper reverence – to take the time and trouble to get the corners of the shirt collars smooth, and the gathers of sleeves uncreased. Besides, Chloe enjoys ironing. She likes the smell of damp linen and hot iron; the dangerous sniff of scorching in the air, the growing pile of ordered neatness. Her hands move deftly and calmly.

So Gwyneth, Chloe's mother, damped and ironed in her day, with little Chloe watching, her nose peering about the ironing board.

So, while Gwyneth ironed, did Mr Leacock watch entranced, and stand behind her and put his arm around her waist, so that her hand first faltered, and then safely setting the iron on its end, leaned back against his male chest, her body folding gently against his, her head turning so her cheek rested against his shoulder, in a gesture of female submission – which, if the truth were known, and it never was made clear to Gwyneth, endeared her to him even more than her profitability to him and his wife (who never in all her born days rested her head in weakness anywhere). Let us not suppose Mr Leacock's romantic imagination was any less involved in Gwyneth, his employee, than hers was in him, her employer. The pity of it lay in the ending of the tale, not the beginning.

But let us perhaps be thankful that Imogen's nose does not peer above Chloe's ironing board. She is with the boys in the garden shed constructing a glider out of balsa wood, which is doomed never to fly.

Oliver works in his study.

Françoise plods about the kitchen, setting it to rights.

In the afternoon the phone rings. It is Grace.

268

Grace Chloe, can I speak to Stanhope.

Chloe (Suspicious) What about?

Grace I'm very upset, Chloe. Please don't argue, just go and get Stanhope. He is my son.

Chloe What are you upset about?

Grace Everything. I've got no money and no boyfriend and you tell me I'm a murderess, and I feel extremely old, and I've been to see Marjorie's mother in hospital – I must be mad – and that was a nightmare.

Chloe Why?

Grace That's how I'm going to end, I'm sure of it. Sitting up in bed with a shaved head and a bloody bandage, thinking I'm twenty and asking the nurse to take the baby away, it's too ugly. I've been dreadful to Stanhope, haven't I? Like Helen was to Marjorie.

Chloe How's Marjorie taking it?

Grace It's all very embarrassing. And Sebastian's plane landed safely after all so I might as well have gone. Please let me talk to Stanhope, Chloe.

Chloe What do you want to say to him? He's very busy. He's watching football on telly.

Grace You're being very wicked, Chloe. You're trying to separate us.

Chloe acknowledges the truth of Grace's accusation. It puts her at a disadvantage. It is Chloe's fatal weakness, her moral Achilles Heel. She ingratiates herself with other women's children, providing them with better biscuits, better treats, better bed-times, and a kindlier and more rational amosphere than any natural mother, even in the very best of circumstances, could provide.

The natural mother is ambivalent towards the child. The unnatural one behaves much better.

Grace Bring Stanhope to the phone, Chloe. Or I'll only write and say I rang and you wouldn't let him speak to me, and he'll never forgive you and neither will I.

Chloe fetches Stanhope from the television.

Chloe I'm sorry, Stanhope. It's your mother.
Stanhope I thought she was in France.
Chloe She changed her mind.
Stanhope Wack-oh.

He takes the receiver.

Grace Stanhope, I don't like to think of you staring at television all the time. You'll get square eyes. Why don't you play football instead of watching it?
Stanhope I'm tired.
Grace Stanhope, perhaps you'd better come and live with me as soon as I'm settled. Say the rain in Spain stays mainly on the plain.
Stanhope (*Baffled*) What?
Grace And you might as well go to a Comprehensive, come to that, for all the good that other place does for you. Stanhope darling, there's something I have to tell you. How old are you, dear?
Stanhope Twelve.
Grace Well, that's quite old enough. You know the facts of life and so on. Now listen. Are you listening?

Stanhope Yes.

Grace Your father was not that other husband of mine, the air-pilot, but a very important and talented portrait painter called Patrick Bates.

Stanhope But that's Kev and Kes's father. Only they never see him. He's mad.

Grace He isn't mad, he's very talented. If I were you I'd be proud of having such a famous father instead of finding fault instantly. Chloe will tell you all about it, she's good at explaining that kind of thing. Can I have her back now, darling?

Stanhope hands the phone over, and fidgets beside Chloe.

Grace I told him about Patrick, Chloe. You always said I should. And Stephen's always going on about being honest with children. Come to think of it, Stephen is Stanhope's brother as well as his uncle. Isn't life extraordinary. I'm glad I've told Stanhope. It's a weight off my mind. Supposing I died, or something, and someone else had to tell him? You'll have to tell Imogen some time, too, won't you? You shouldn't put it off, Chloe.

Chloe puts the phone down, and cuts Grace off.

Stanhope She says I can go and live with her in London and go to a Comprehensive. Do I have to?

Chloe I shouldn't think so.

Stanhope Is she a little bit mad?

Chloe I don't know, Stanhope. I think she's rather upset.

Stanhope The menopause, I expect. She said I had the same father as Kev and Kes. Does that mean I can't marry Kestrel?

Chloe I suppose it does. Why, do you want to?

Stanhope My God, no. Is that all? Can I go back to Match of the Day?

Chloe Yes. Unless you want to know more about Patrick.

Stanhope I'll think about it all some other time, if you don't mind. Could I change my name to Bob?

Chloe Why not?

Stanhope punches Chloe, exhilarated rather than depressed, and returns to the television. If such a thing had happened to me, thinks Chloe, such a revelation made between lunch and tea, I would have been finished for life. What saves these children? Television?

That sleeping bitch, Grace. Prod her awake and see what she does.

'You've missed your train,' says Oliver, 'if you're going up to see Marjorie.'

'No I haven't if I run,' says Chloe.

'I'll drive you,' he says, and does. She finds his new servility embarrassing.

'Give my love to Marjorie,' he says. 'I hope her mother's all right. What did Grace want?'

'Just to tell Stanhope who his father was.'

'Just like that?'

'Just like that.'

'People should get married and stay married,' says Oliver. 'It's less confusing for the children.'

But Chloe is not to be drawn back into the complacency of

former days, when Oliver and she, in spite of what Oliver called their ups and downs, were in the habit of congratulating themselves on the maturity of their ways, and their especial matrimonial superiorities.

fifty-six

Stanhope is Oliver's responsibility, as well as Chloe's.

It is Oliver, at Chloe's request, who drives Grace to the nursing home and prevents her from having her abortion. Grace is four months pregnant with Stanhope – not a safe time for a termination but Grace has told lies about the date of conception and the abortionist has not seen through them. Well, he is a busy man. There is always a queue in his consulting room on Saturday afternoons.

'I'll probably die,' says Grace, hopefully rather than anything else, to Chloe.

'Tell him the truth,' begs Chloe.

'Certainly not,' says Grace. 'If he can't tell by feeling then he's an incompetent and if I do die the police will prosecute and he'll go to prison, and it's worth dying to have that happen. Unctuous bastard.'

Abortion is still a criminal offence for both aborter and abortee. Grace's termination is costing all of two hundred pounds and is being performed by a top gynaecologist, who does six abortions a day, five days a week, in a Harley Street nursing home. Monday mornings he kindly reserves for charity cases – twelve-year-old girls and alcoholics in their late forties. The company which owns the nursing home takes seventy-five pounds a patient. The rest is the surgeon's due, except for twenty-five pounds per operation he gives to the anaesthetist – who, after all, risks imprisonment too.

The surgeon plays golf on Sundays, and on Saturday mornings he writes articles and makes speeches in favour of the liberalization of the abortion laws. He is a busy man. On Saturday afternoons, he arranges his next week's work. He believes (in a world which finds it hard to accept anything so simple) that women should have control over their own reproductive processes, and also in the law of supply and demand. How else justly regulate society? He is charming, kind, intelligent, immensely rich, and Grace hates him for the murderer and profiteer he is.

This will be the fourth time he has stood at the end of her bed, told her not to be afraid, that she'll wake up fit and well, and stretched out his scrupulously clean (well, one should hope so!) hand for the envelope containing the money. Cash, no cheques.

The anaesthetist accompanies him on his round of the beds, sizing up the patients in advance, to save time, rather as the hangman used to do.

Oliver provides the cash. Grace will be able to pay it back, but has difficulty in raising money at short notice. It is useless asking Patrick: his ashen pallor and the trembling of his hands when asked to provide cash is an offence against art, and indeed against human kindness. Oliver, rather than witness Patrick's distress, forks out.

On Tuesday evening Grace goes into the nursing home.

274

She's being done the next morning.

On Tuesday night Chloe weeps and carries on.

'Take the money away from her,' Chloe beseeches Oliver. 'You gave it to her. Go after her and get it back. It's murder.'

Chloe lies in bed after her latest miscarriage, pale and emotional. Only an eight-week foetus, not much – too soon for real grief, too late for indifference, though painful and messy enough – but with all her thwarted emotional energy now surging towards Grace's baby, which must, she tells Oliver, must be saved.

'Go and fetch her,' she stamps and screams as Oliver stands appalled, gaping at her. 'Fetch her! Tell her if she doesn't want it, I do. She can't do it! Oh, the bitch. The murderous bitch!'

And Oliver, helpless and adrift in the sea of maternal passions, goes, though every instinct tells him not to. Arguments he can refute; hysteria he can cope with – but when Chloe invokes the elemental forces of motherhood, Oliver does what he is told.

'What about Midge?' he asks, at the door.

'What about me, me?' shrieks Chloe. 'What about my baby?'

Oliver closes the door behind him, between him and her, and goes to fetch Grace home.

Grace gives birth to Stanhope at St George's hospital, some five months later. Midge, neglected, produces Kestrel in the next room. The two babies are laid, as it happens, in adjacent cribs in the nursery, and baby Kestrel's early eye infection – which was to linger for years – is laid, rightly, at Stanhope's door.

Meanwhile the traffic of London's Hyde Park Corner surges round the foot of St George's, as if everything in the world was prosaic, practical, and prone to forces well within our control.

Midge, betrayed, totters through the commendable motions of struggling wifehood and motherhood for another two years, before finally giving up Patrick, Kestrel's eye, love, duty and the ghost.

Grace blames Stanhope for it all, of course.

fifty-seven

St Stephen's hospital in the Fulham Road, where Helen has been taken, is overdue for demolition. Or so the taxi-driver tells Chloe, on her long journey across London from Liverpool Street Station, via St George's hospital, to the Fulham Road, in the very thick of the rush-hour.

'That place! It's alive with black-beetles. I lost an uncle in there. Collapsed in the street and they whipped out a kidney. When he came round the nurse asked him how he felt. "All right," he said. "Much better than when they took out the other one."'

Chloe is silent.

'No offence,' he says. 'Just a joke to cheer you up. No-one close you're visiting, I hope.'

'No,' says Chloe. 'Not really close.'

Marjorie's mother Helen. It was Helen's spite which drove

Patrick into Midge's arms, and so, though indirectly, drove Midge to destroy herself. Poor Midge, taken unconscious from her home, bound for St Stephen's too, but never getting there, dying in the ambulance instead.

It was Stanhope and Kestrel's birthday, though they were still of an age to prefer the wrappings of the birthday present rather than the present itself, having been in the world only two short years.

Marjorie's mother Helen. Trembling between youth and middle-age, back from Australia, loverless for an amazing moment, throwing Patrick out of Frognal. Motivated by what? A sense of property abused, or of flesh and blood defiled? For the big living room was stacked with portraits of Marjorie naked, and Marjorie naked, in Helen's view, was altogether too lumpy, bumpy, frizzy and pear-shaped an affair to reflect credit on her mother. Or was it merely a trivial irritation to find Marjorie thus not personally care-taking, but off at Oxford taking a further degree, and financed by sources well out of Helen's control, having left the Frognal house in the care of a man who did not cut his hair or do up his shirt, or use a fork if fingers would do, and wiped his greasy fingers on the mat made by the hair on his chin stretching down to meet the hair on his chest, reddish, coarse and curly – was it this irritation which led Helen to throw Patrick out, destroy the paintings, and put a padlock on the front door?

The door did not even close properly, and through the gap, narrow as it was, squeezed for several subsequent years a tide of cats, litter and leaves. Helen would have done better to have allowed Patrick to stay, and certainly not to have destroyed the paintings, which later would have been worth many thousands – although painted on too large a scale for the really perspicacious buyer. But of course Helen, and she was the first to admit it, was always prodigal with man-made works of art, seeing them as something presumptuous in the face of her own God-made female perfection, and a kind of challenge to it.

She threw Marjorie out as well. Thus, summoning her from Oxford, meeting her in the refreshment bar at Paddington, over bad coffee:

Helen Marjorie dearest, I am so distressed for you. How unhappy you must be to form an alliance with someone like that! And to think I was not here to protect you from it! To allow yourself to be painted, naked! To open yourself to such ridicule! What a tragedy it is that I could not bring you up myself, and develop your sensitivities. Esther Songford was a sweet soul, but so dull and so plain it would drive anyone to distraction, as you seem to have been. My dear child, I understand your desperation. We must face the fact that you're no beauty; but it simply is not true that any man is better than no man at all. Better to live in celibacy, believe me, than with a member of the working classes. It is not snobbery, simply that their attitudes to women are different from ours – they make use of their women, treat them as animals, as I am afraid that Patrick Bates has made use of you. I don't deny that to a certain sort of woman he might appear attractive, and he certainly made every effort to win my affections, Marjorie, I may say, in the hope of further free board and lodging, but he mistook his woman. I know what I have to offer a man, I don't need the likes of Patrick Bates to tell me so. If you are to survive as a woman, Majorie, and not to shrivel up into the blue-stocking you seem determined to become – what is all this Oxford nonsense? – you must develop a little more pride in your femininity. And that does not mean flaunting your nakedness in front of the working classes like some kind of prostitute. What are we to do with you?

Marjorie But mother!

Helen I have tried and tried to be a good mother to you, and you always let me down. Look at the state of the house—

Marjorie I did my best—

Helen But you did not. Any more than you did your best when your poor father died. I should have been there, and I was not.

Marjorie I sent a telegram—

Helen A telegram which did not arrive. Well, we will not go into that now, or your callousness, or your spite in trying to keep me away. It hurt me very much at the time, but my friend Peter Smilie – he runs the Department of Education in Sydney – has explained the resentments which apparently children – God knows why – hold against their parents. And I am sure your father's death was sufficient punishment to you. I am just surprised you hold his memory so lightly, Marjorie. It would break his heart to think of you sunk to such depths.

Marjorie But I'm not, mother. It's not like that. We're just friends. And poor Patrick, where's he going to go?

Helen You really think more of him than you do of me, Marjorie, I'm afraid. And don't tell lies on top of everything else.

She's quite right. It is a lie. An empty bottle of Grand Marnier, kept beneath Marjorie's bed, bears witness to it. Guilt depletes Marjorie's strength.

Marjorie It's not a lie, and I'm sure Father wouldn't mind Patrick staying at all. He loved paintings.
Helen Good paintings, dear, not bad painters. You're so naïve.
Marjorie (*Tearful*) And I don't want to be there by myself. It's haunted.

She had determined never to mention it, too. Rightly. See what happens when she does? Helen is affronted. Haunted? The happiest days in her life – before Marjorie put an end to them – were spent in that house. How can it possibly be haunted?

Helen But you're supposed to be so clever, Marjorie, how can you talk such nonsense? Haunted! If that's what you feel about that poor house, we had better lock it up, close it altogether, and I'll try and find a buyer. It's too much responsibility if you won't help me.
Marjorie But where will I go in the vacation?
Helen Stay in Oxford. Such a pretty place.
Marjorie I can't afford to. I only get a small grant—
Helen Take a job. You're not too grand for that, I hope, but please not as an artist's model. You simply haven't the figure, or the skin. There is to be a portrait of me in this year's Summer Exhibition at the Royal Academy. Isn't that exciting? And Marjorie if you don't mind me saying so, you simply must not wear your hair like that. It's so bad for the shape of your face. You always just thrust it back behind some old scrap of ribbon. I know it's frizzy and discouraging but you have to work at these things, you know. Good heavens, you've drunk your coffee. How could you!

Helen goes off first to the hairdresser, leaving her coffee

untouched, and then to buy a padlock and order a carter to transport Marjorie's things from Frognal to Oxford. Generously, she bears the cost herself. At the Summer Exhibition she meets a man from Newfoundland who owns a trawler fleet, and goes off with him to Northern climes. She looks better, these days, muffled up in sailor's sweaters than sunning all but naked on the deck of someone's yacht, and knows it.

Helen does not marry again. She invested the total of her commitment, as women will, who have little to commit, into that first marriage, and the return on the investment proved, in the end, so disappointingly small, that she prefers not to repeat the experience. Like Grace after her, Helen never seems to be short of money. Dim male figures lurk in the background of her life, dispensing riches, kindnesses, holidays. What they get in return is not passion, but a kind of unkind condescension, a grudging parting of the legs, and such a total absence of orgasm as seems to fascinate rather than repel. And so fastidious is she, that to be allowed so much as to admire her is to these suitors a matter of self-congratulation.

Oh messy, modern Marjorie. Living in college at term-time, working in a pub during vacations, sleeping in a room above the bar, looking out at closing time, as once Chloe did, upon those reeling scenes of male depression and debauchery: waiting, as if she knew, for Grace's wedding and her own fate to come together on the same day.

And Patrick, sent off by Helen into what she thought and hoped would be a wilderness, and which in fact was Midge.

Midge the Mason's daughter, dead.

Whose fault?

fifty-eight

Marjorie, Grace and me! How do we grow old? How shall we die?

Marjorie has her pension fund, her insurance policies, and perhaps, presently, the inheritance of her mother's Frognal house. She does not let her mind go further than that – she keeps it trained on practicalities. Her epitaph will be the affection of her friends, the regret of her colleagues, and a shelf or two of tapes in the library of the BBC – until eventually, in the interests of economy, they too are wiped for re-use. She hopes for nothing else.

Grace hopes to die suddenly, and soon, or so she says, before the shame of physical inadequacy overtakes her. She will not grow old serenely. She fights against it. Already she drinks too much. She is used to being admired, and only her looks are admirable. When they go, she goes, Grace says.

I, Chloe, put my faith in children for my immortality. When I die, they will remember me, as I remember my own mother – and Esther, who, like me, saved other women's children, stealing them in passing. Of such maternal warmth, I think, legal or illegal, is immortality made. It seeps down through the generations, fertilizing the ground, preparing it for more kindnesses.

fifty-nine

The corridors of St Stephen's hospital are long and green, lined with pipes, echo to the clanking of metal food containers and are foggy with steam, disinfectant and age.

Helen is in a small ward, with four beds. Three are empty. Helen is in the fourth, propped up against pillows. She seems to be asleep, or in a coma. Her eyelids have fallen over her large eyes, as if by gravity and not from any muscular intent. Her old mouth droops. They have taken out her teeth. Her head is bald. Only the wound on her temple, too clearly seen beneath a thin skull cap, jaggedly cobbled together, as if very little in the way of service was expected from the stitches, demonstrates anything of her old vitality. It pulses; or does Chloe only imagine it?

Her old enemy, brought so low. Chloe finds that there are tears in her eyes. Marjorie sits beside her mother, stroking the limp but still graceful hand. They who in good times so seldom touched each other. Helen would certainly not have allowed it in life, as she does, perforce, in this half-death of hers.

Marjorie It was good of you to come. And Grace was here earlier.
Chloe Of course we came.
Marjorie No of course about it. We were none of us all that much help to each other.
Chloe (*Surprised*) We do what we can.

She whose garden rings with the oaths of Inigo, Imogen, Kevin, Kestrel and Stanhope.

Marjorie We should interfere more in each other's lives, and not just pick up pieces. I should go and shoot Oliver, and you should

283

commit Grace to an insane asylum, and as for me, you should have got me to a marriage bureau a long time ago. See how it all ends—

Marjorie indicates her mother, and snivels.

Marjorie They say she can go on for weeks like this. I've got a taping today and I'm just not at the studio, am I?
Chloe Of course you're not.
Marjorie I just don't care about it
Chloe You will again.
Marjorie I don't think so, somehow. How am I going to live without her, Chloe? I have no children. She's all the family I have.
Chloe There's always the BBC.
Marjorie What's the point? Mother never even had a television, you know. I'm sure it was in case she saw my name on the screen.

As if in affirmation, Helen stirs and opens her eyes. She withdraws her hand from under Marjorie's and relapses again into quiescence. Marjorie endures.

Chloe Why don't you go home and sleep, Marjorie? I'll stay.
Marjorie She might wake up and miss me.
Chloe You'll go on wringing and wringing, won't you, trying to squeeze a drop of affection out of an old dry bone. No wonder you take in so much washing.

Marjorie smiles, pleased at the notion, and lies down on one of the empty beds, and closes her eyes.

284

Marjorie I've been thinking of Midge.

Chloe So have I.

Marjorie We just stood back and let her die.

Midge the Mason's daughter. Patrick, turned out of Frognal by Helen, goes to live with Midge. Who'd have thought it?

Not Midge's parents, Mrs Martha and Mr Mervyn Macklin, stationer and Master Mason. Midge is is their fourth child and their only daughter, and at the age of fourteen winner of the Luton Child-Artist-of-the-Year competition.

Mrs Macklin is a worrier. She worries about Midge's health and happiness, and Mr Macklin's secret Masonic rites. Mervyn keeps no other secrets from her; what is this disloyalty? Martha tries to break into the locked suitcase in which Mervyn keeps his robes: Martha wheedles, Martha begs, Martha cries, to no avail. Mr Macklin keeps his secrets. Midge his daughter aids and abets him. Daddy's girl, not Mummy's.

Mrs Mahonie next door tells Martha that what Masons do is to kiss the arses of goats in secret conclave. 'What children men are,' she says. 'Like little boys, always trying to piss higher than anyone else. To see who can make the ceiling stink, as well as just the walls.' Midge is not allowed to speak to Mrs Mahonie.

Midge is the triumph of the Macklin family: she is what they have worked and lived and bred for over generations; someone who will step out and away from the world of small streets and corner shops, and into something rich, grand and strange. Their offering to the middle classes.

Mervyn and Martha see Midge off to Art School, fearful for

her virginity, her future, her sanity. She seems such a frail offering, this thin childish creature, with her stick-like legs, her mousy hair, her sparse bosom and her fierce loyalties.

They do well to be afraid. Midge takes an attic flat in Camberwell – unheated, unfurnished, and cheap, as two Doberman Pinschers roam the floor below – and within a month Patrick is installed there with her.

The female turtle wades out of the sea and on to the shore; digs a hollow and with infinite effort lays some six hundred eggs, covers them with sand, and dies, exhausted. The eggs hatch; the infants scramble for the sea. A thousand sea-birds lie in wait. Perhaps one turtle escapes, and reaches the waves. The quickest, the liveliest, the fittest to survive – or just the luckiest.

Is Patrick good luck or bad? Midge to her dying day – not long removed – maintains that it is good. Stubborn to the end.

Why then is she always crying? Is it her nature, or is it Patrick, or is it her nature making Patrick what he is?

Mr Macklin comes to London to rescue his daughter.

'It's my life,' Midge says. 'Let me lead it.'

'You're thin and ill,' says Mr Macklin, 'and wasting yourself and your talent – our talent – on that man. I'll go to the College authorities. I'll get him sent down.'

'He's left college already,' says Midge, 'and so have I. It was a waste of time. What can Patrick learn? He's painting portraits and doing well. I'm perfectly all right.'

But she isn't. Patrick cannot bear to give her money. He wants Midge to live with him for love, not for what he can provide. She does.

Midge is taken off to hospital suffering from malnutrition. How she cries, missing him.

Mr Macklin conceives a plan to poison Patrick. He sends him chocolates through the post, which Patrick prudently feeds to the Doberman Pinschers. They do not die, but their diarrhoea leaves dead patches over a wide circular area of Camberwell Green, to be seen to this day. (The park-keepers insist the dogs be kept on leads, so the owner takes them out on reels of kite string.)

Midge goes home to recuperate, stays three weeks in impatience and misery, in the room above the shop, and then goes back to Patrick, who marries her; to be revenged, he says, on Mr Macklin for his murderous attack and the wilful damage of Camberwell Green.

Midge, asked to leave the flat while Patrick paints his portraits, discovers he sleeps with his sitters. Everyone else has known for a long time. She goes home. She comes back. But to what? How Midge cries.

Patrick has taken a studio in London and is having an affair with Grace, who does not care whom he sleeps with or how so long as it's only art; and he has smart ruthless friends, amongst them Oliver and Chloe, who terrify Midge. Midge, mousier every day, snivels and sniffs in her lonely sleep.

Midge gives birth to Kevin. Patrick, entranced by the visual aspects of motherhood, moves back. It is a dreadful time. Midge does not mind going hungry herself, or wearing jumble-sale clothes or Grace, Chloe, and Marjorie's cast-offs, but when the baby cries from hunger and she has to borrow money from Chloe, while Patrick loses hundreds every night at poker, she is distressed, and cries, and the baby cries, and Patrick can't stand it, and moves back with Grace.

Patrick oscillates between Grace and Midge. Weeks at the studio, weekends at the flat. Years pass. He buys bones for Midge to boil. There's lots of nourishment in bones, he says.

Midge can't go home any more. Her father has had a stroke and her mother nurses him and takes in lodgers and says to Midge 'if you don't mind I'd rather think of you as dead.'

Patrick impregnates Grace one drunken night, quarrelling with her the while, gets out of bed and goes home to Midge who has forgotten to take her pill and impregnates her.

Women conceive more easily when they're crying, Patrick observes.

Grace, distraught, embarks on the abortion from which Oliver, at Chloe's instigation, rescues her.

Oliver knocks on the door of the clinic. A pretty Irish nurse with steely eyes opens the door a crack. Does he have an appointment? No? Then he can't come in.

But Oliver can and does, and the staff bundle Grace out of the building, sniffing trouble in the wind. Even though she doubled the money in the surgeon's envelope, they would not touch her now. They are superstitious, as well they might be, dealing with death. Trouble breeds trouble, they all know that.

If your aircraft's delayed, don't board it. Bomb scares breed engine failure, and vice versa.

Grace proceeds with her pregnancy with an ill-will. She smokes, drinks, takes tranquillizers, tells Chloe if it's a mongol, if it's deformed, then it's Chloe's fault. Grace won't see a doctor, won't book a hospital bed, goes out shopping on the day the baby's due, and in the labour ward encounters Patrick on his way to visit Midge.

Patrick stays with Grace, to watch the birth, and afterwards goes back to live with her. He admires her spirit. Midge keeps crying.

Grace calls the baby Stanhope, the name least likely to please, and parks it with Chloe most of the time.

Midge tries to get National Assistance and can't. She is entitled to money from the State only if she starts divorce proceedings. Divorce Patrick? How can she? Patrick is her husband. Her children's father. She loves him. One day, surely, he will settle down. Age and impotence, if nothing else, will eventually effect a cure. Or Grace will lose interest in him.

Grace sees Midge's love for Patrick as nothing to do with her. Such singleness of spirit, in Grace's post-Christie eyes, is nothing but masochistic and destructive folly. Midge should divorce Patrick, oblige him through the courts to support her properly, and set him free to follow his own nature. By what right, she asks, does Midge demand fidelity from Patrick, who is not equipped to give it? She, Grace, demands nothing. She enjoys what there is to enjoy, and has ironed physical jealousy out of her soul. If she torments Geraldine it is for fun, and not from any sense of despair. Grace says.

She sends Kevin and Kestrel presents, however. She has some sense, or so Oliver says, of having deprived the children of something, if only a father.

Oliver takes fatherhood seriously.

Chloe, in Midge's company, feels neither natural nor comfortable. She longs to take up a scrubbing-brush and scrub

Midge's floors, make up curtains for the bare windows, provide a toy-box for the children's toys, a private doctor for Kestrel's eye, handles for the chest of drawers. But she does not. She does not wish to offend Midge, by seeming to offer so simple a solution to her misery, and ignoring the greater, inner cause of it. Besides, she feels humble in the face of Midge's devotion to a cause so vital yet so hopeless.

'Humble! I can't think why,' says Marjorie. 'With Oliver bringing home clap.' Chloe had to tell Grace, in case Patrick as well as Oliver had been infected from the same source, and of course Grace had told Marjorie. 'You show the same absurd devotion to Oliver as Midge does to Patrick. And Oliver isn't even an artist.'

'That's altogether different,' says Chloe. 'Oliver doesn't deny by word or deed that I'm his wife. Patrick's every waking breath is a denial of Midge.'

And she believes it, too, like Midge. One day, one day, Oliver will calm down, stay home, acknowledge her own sexual supremacy over all the rivals he has found for her, and watch television with her through the evening of their years. That Oliver, as Christie did to Grace before him, will take it into his head to push this neglected looming wife of his into Patrick's arms – in what can only be seen as an attempt to assuage his own guilt, or an excuse for further unpleasantness, or just a liking for emotional escalation, she is not to know. All she knows now is that Midge seems in some vague way her, Chloe's, moral superior. And that she cannot ask her to her dinner parties, because how would Midge fit in amongst all the film people (who have sunken baths and marble front-door pillars) she must ask to dinner for Oliver's sake. And how can she, with so much on her mind, be forever traipsing over to Acton in order to cheer up Midge, and listen to her tales of woe?

As for Marjorie, she is at work all day, and recovering from work all night. Marjorie can't be much help. Marjorie uses Midge, as tactfully as possible of course, in a documentary about women with wasted lives. Marjorie feels that Midge cramps Patrick's style.

'Everything changes,' says Marjorie. 'You have to accept that it does. Because you had good times once doesn't mean you have any right to have them now. Midge should never have had the children. It was selfish madness.'

Meanwhile, Kevin and Kestrel tug at Midge's skirt and cry, and pester and mess. Kestrel's eye gives constant trouble. It is always inflamed and weeping.

Midge is behind with the rent. She is given notice to quit. She goes to a phone-box and rings Grace's flat, and asks for Patrick, but Grace spends so much time fetching him, that by the time he gets to the telephone Midge's money has run out, and all he can hear is the dialling tone.

Midge has no present to give Kestrel for her second birthday, although Chloe, Marjorie and Grace have all sent little packets through the post. That's something.

'If anything ever happened to me,' Midge once said to Chloe, 'would you look after the children?'

'Of course,' said Chloe, not thinking. 'What do you mean, if anything happened?'

'An accident,' Midge replied.

Midge takes all the sleeping pills the doctor has ever given her – she has been saving them over the years – on the eve of Kestrel's birthday. In the morning she does not wake, and the children tug and pester in vain.

Marjorie, passing by on the way to an outside location, calls in, finds her thus, gets the ambulance, summons Chloe, and goes on to work. Well, what else is to be done?

No point in sitting around, letting grass grow under bridges.

Grace says what kind of future did Midge have anyway, if she'd been saving sleeping pills she must have had a suicidal nature; and was clearly looking for a scapegoat, and she, Grace, hereby refused the role. And what kind of woman did a thing like that to her children? Suicide, says Grace, is an act of hostility, and the murderer/murderee deserves censure, not pity.

All the same, from that time on, she seemed to lose her interest in Patrick.

Chloe took Kevin and Kestrel home. Patrick made no protest. But later, when Oliver suggested that he and Chloe might adopt them formally, he shook his head. In that case, says Oliver, pushed for money at the time, although paying Patrick some £2,000 to paint Chloe, you might pay towards their upkeep. Chloe, clothed only in her towel, on the very last sitting, all others having been completed without Patrick making a gesture other than purely artistic towards her, or she to him, brought up the subject of maintenance out of loyalty to Oliver, of course; she could never have done it for herself. But Oliver spending so much on her! £2,000 for a portrait. His brothers-in-law having just publicly paid a thousand each towards the cost of a forest on Mount Sinai.

Patrick Chloe, try and understand. If I give money away I can't paint.

Chloe It's not giving money away. It's spending it on your own flesh and blood.

Patrick That's what Midge said. She was never faithful to me. She was having an affair with the man who owned those Doberman Pinschers. That's why I tried to kill them.

Chloe That's absurd. Don't say such things about Midge. She loved you. Why do you always have to make matters worse than they are?

Midge's funeral was a desolate affair. Midge was buried, not cremated. Mrs Macklin pushed Mr Macklin in a wheelchair to the side of the grave. Mr Macklin tried to leap at Patrick's throat but only succeeded in falling out of his chair on to the ground. Patrick, who seemed drugged or drunk or both, and quite out of his mind, had come to the funeral with a fifteen-year-old heroin addict, whose industrialist father wanted her committed to canvas while still presentable.

Grace did not come at all. Oliver, Chloe and Marjorie were there.

Patrick danced a kind of horn-pipe on Midge's grave, until forcibly stopped by Oliver, who put out a leg so that Patrick tripped and lay on the earth where he had fallen, behind a large tombstone. He and the girl then attempted to have ritual intercourse there and then, for the sake, Patrick said, of the harvest, but both passed out before achieving any such thing.

Fortunately the Macklins had gone by then, off in their black hired Rolls-Royce, and only a younger and more forgiving generation remained.

Patrick Then don't ask for money for the children. If Oliver can afford to get me to paint you, he can afford to keep my children. Besides, it gives you something to do, Chloe.

Chloe I have quite enough, thank you Patrick.

Patrick Really? Wouldn't you like another baby?

Chloe Yes. But I keep miscarrying.

Patrick That's Oliver all over. The most uncreative character I ever met. He puts the finger of death on everything. Scripts, women, booze-ups; babies, now.

Chloe, accustomed as she is to the daily sacrifice of herself on the altar of Oliver's creativity, is quite shocked. And the miscarriages his fault, not hers? It is too much to take in.

Patrick Would you like me to give you another baby, Chloe? Since I can't give Key and Kes any money, the least we can do is offer them a sibling.

Chloe How do you know I'd get pregnant? It's nowhere near the middle of the month.

Patrick Of course you would.

Chloe I didn't last time.

Patrick You held that against me?

Chloe Yes.

Patrick How you women do bear grudges.

And there Chloe is, intertwined after all these years with Patrick, conceiving Imogen. It does not occur to her that Patrick will tell Oliver that he is the father of her baby, but of course, when Oliver repeats his demand for money for Kevin and Kes, and holds up payment of Chloe's portrait, Patrick is driven to. And Chloe does not miscarry, which is proof enough.

Oliver forgives Chloe. Chloe does not forgive herself, or Patrick.

sixty

Chloe dozes by Helen's bed. She is short of sleep. She wakes with a start.

'Poor little Midge,' Marjorie says from the bed where she lies, as if she too were a patient. She is crying.

Chloe Why don't you cry for yourself, for a change? Why choose something ten years old?

Helen's eyelids flutter but do not open.

Marjorie If I started I might never stop. All the things I should have done, and didn't do. Wasn't it strange the way I called in at Midge's flat that morning making myself late. I never had before. Too late to help, all the same. I drove round and round the block first, like some kind of zombie. If I'd only obeyed the impulse, and not struggled against it.
Chloe It's always like that when people die. If only.

Marjorie And poor little Kevin opened the door. He could just reach. There was nothing I could do, except what I did. Call the ambulance and wait for you. But I think something else was expected of me, and all I did was just go back to work.

Chloe What do you mean, something else?

Marjorie I don't know. Just being there. Or at least finding out for certain whether she was going to live or die. I didn't really want to know. Such cowardice. And I shouldn't have used her in that documentary. It can't have helped. All the things one does, and shouldn't.

Chloe What else?

Marjorie Handing Ben that light-bulb. I was angry with him. He was going to see his mother and I knew she didn't like me, so I made him reach too far. I hoped he'd fall off. And the other thing, the awful thing – I didn't send mother a telegram when father came home. I don't think I did. I went to the post office to send it, and I know I wrote it out, and then I think I just screwed it up, Chloe.

Chloe Think?

Marjorie You know how every penny counted, in those days. It was send the telegram, or buy the butter. I hated margarine. Everyone called me Marge at school, especially you, Chloe.

Chloe I'm sorry.

So she had. Her own name, Chloe, rare and strange, had elevated her from common status. To call Marjorie Marge was to demote her, and when she could, she did.

Marjorie Too late now, I just thought I'd mention it. Anyway it wasn't that. I wanted father for myself. I thought mother would be bad for him. And he died.

Chloe Marjorie, have you told Helen's friends that she's in hospital?

Marjorie (*Ignoring her*) And the other thing, the Frognal house. I should never have stayed there. Patrick was right, it was me haunting myself, sending myself messages. Get out, forget it, forget everything, start again. Stop trying to wring blood out of stones. My blood, staining those stairs. How strange it all is. I should have been glad when mother changed the locks and kept me out, but I wasn't.

A house, thinks Chloe, a home. If I only had somewhere to go, would I take the children, leave Oliver? No.

Chloe (*Persistent*) Marjorie, who else have you told about Helen being here?

Marjorie No-one. Just you and Grace.

Chloe opens Helen's crocodile handbag, which stands on the bedside locker, and searches it for an address book. What sacrilege! Rifling mother's handbag. Will Chloe grieve for Helen when she is dead; and if then, why not now? Or will it be pity for herself she feels; another's death, by implication, being her own. We must live in the expectation of death, Chloe thinks, for ourselves and others. Only in the light of our ending, do our lives make any kind of sense. Helen's handbag is neat and clean. A little vanity case; powder-case and rouge. A lace handkerchief, amazingly white. A note-case, decently filled. A suède purse, unscuffed and unstained. A sachet of eau-de-Cologne. A dentist's card. The address book, with a tiny pencil tucked down the spine, and the pages neatly filled with tiny writing. An old lady's handbag, but full of expectation.

Marjorie accepts the address book.

Chloe Marjorie, when I was sleeping just now, did I snore?
Marjorie What a funny thing to ask. No, of course you didn't.
Chloe It's the kind of thing one never knows.

Marjorie leaves the room in search of a telephone. Chloe is left alone with Helen, and is afraid. And indeed, as if relieved of the weight of Marjorie's presence, Helen's eyelids flutter, and lift, and Helen stares full at Chloe. She speaks, in a lilting fashion, in the manner of some thirty years ago.

Helen I wish you'd do something about your hair, Marjorie. Why can't you be more like Chloe Evans? She's always so neat.

Her eyelids fall again. She sighs, exhausted. Two nurses, one black, one white, both tired, come in with a trolley and set about transferring Helen from her comfortable bed on to its uncomfortable surface.

Chloe Where are you taking her?
Nurse Are you the next-of-kin?
Chloe No.
Nurse Well, I don't suppose it matters. Just down to X-ray.

Helen's bed is empty when Marjorie returns. She brings Grace with her. Grace has been visiting Patrick. She wears faded blue jeans, a navy shirt and a denim jacket. Her eyes are still puffy from the outbursts of the morning, and her face seems lax and flushed. She is growing old, thinks Chloe. But Grace sits on the edge of the bed and swings her legs like a girl, and is undaunted.

Grace I'm sure it's all right, Marjorie. They wouldn't be X-raying her if they thought she was going to pop off any moment. Patrick says people live for years with brain tumours. He says he thinks perhaps he has one himself. I wouldn't be surprised. What an excuse for bad behaviour! Please sir, it's me tumour. He's looking dreadful. I'm sure he's got scurvy. He's living off kippers and tea and has at least six chains on the door to keep out robbers. You should see the ulcers on his gums. He wants his washing back, Marjorie, clean or dirty. He doesn't trust you.

Marjorie I have other things to think about.

Grace I only told you to amuse you. I nearly brought him with me. You know how he loves hospitals.

Marjorie Yes, well he never loved mother.

Grace I suppose not. Why are you looking so glum, Chloe? Do you want me to go away?

Chloe No. I wish you'd be more responsible about Stanhope, that's all.

Grace Truth is truth, you're always saying so. Actually, I have to agree with you. Patrick isn't much cop as a father. I'd forgotten. His legs are in a dreadful state. His varicose veins have ulcerated. He's drinking much too much, but at least it should lower his sperm count. Anyway I hope so. Tell Stanhope I made a mistake, or something. I'd got my months muddled up. Set him free to marry Kestrel.

Chloe Why should he want to do that?

Grace Well, you know what life is like. It's the kind of thing that happens.

Chloe You don't want Stanhope to live with you?

Grace Good God, no. I'm not fit. You're always saying so. Anyway Sebastian's on his way home. The beach was awash, he says. I wish he'd rung this morning, before I'd seen Patrick. Marjorie, Patrick says if the Frognal house is ever unlocked, can he move back in?

Marjorie No.

Grace He's angry because you haven't returned his washing. He thinks you've stolen it. He can't go on living down there. He needs some help.

Marjorie He won't get it from me, any more. Life's too short.

Grace Why not? He's been in such a state since Midge died.

Chloe Good.

Grace You think you're a saint, Chloe, but really you're a devil. If anyone's to blame for Midge dying, it's you.

Chloe Me?

Grace Yes. If you hadn't said you'd look after the children, Midge couldn't have done it. She'd be alive and grizzling today. You're a very dangerous, person, Chloe. People who stand about waiting for other people to fall to bits so they can pick up the pieces ought to be locked up. They encourage disintegration. It's time you learned to enjoy yourself, Chloe; you're too dangerous as a martyr.

Do what you want, not what you ought. Isn't that what Chloe once shouted at poor Gwyneth? What progress can there be, from generation to generation, if daughters do as mothers do? Will Imogen anguish over Chloe, as Chloe does over her own mama? To understand, forgive, endure. What kind of lesson is that for daughters? Better to end like Helen, unforgiving and unforgiven. Better to live like Grace, at least alive.

A nurse, pale and shaken, comes to summon the next-of-kin, identified after some confusion as Marjorie, not Grace, to the social worker's office. Chloe barely notices. She, Midge's destruction, not her salvation?

Grace Mind you, I'm only the girl who got sent to her room for hoping that Hitler would win the war. Anything for a change. I have at least kept my energy, by caring about nothing, or not for longer than a couple of hours. Morality is very devitalizing, Chloe. Look what you've done to Oliver, by being so much better than him. He hasn't done a decent day's work since you married him.

Marjorie comes back from the social worker's office, ashen. She smooths the pillows of Helen's bed and replaces the counterpane tidily. Helen is dead. Her heart stopped on the trolley on the way to the X-ray department, and whether motivated by kindness or enervated by exhaustion, no-one ran for the resuscitation equipment. They walked instead, and by the time help came it was too late.

'They should never have moved her,' says Marjorie. 'You should have stopped them, Chloe. Poor little mother.'

Marjorie cries, for herself.

sixty-one

Chloe sits with Marjorie and Grace at the bus shelter outside the hospital. It is raining. There are no taxis. No bus appears. Chloe's blue suède shoes are wet, and darker blue around the sole. Her feet are cold. She shivers. They are silent for a time. Grace is feeling the top of her head.

'I'm sure I'm pregnant again,' says Grace presently. 'I have that funny feeling. And the top of my head is tender when I press. Remember when we saw the baby moving in mother's tummy? Wasn't it dreadful? I wish it had been a girl. A girl wouldn't have killed her. I'm better with girls, anyway. I wasn't really interested in Piers, actually, only Petra.'

'It will be a boy,' says Chloe, 'if it's anything. You're wanting too hard.'

But she doesn't doubt that Grace is pregnant. Marjorie holds her mother's handbag in her lap.

'What shall I do with it?' she asks. 'I can't bear to go through it.'

'Leave it in the waste bin,' says Chloe.

'Just like that?'

'Yes. Someone who needs it will find it.' Marjorie puts the handbag in the waste bin. Later, remarkably, someone honest finds it, takes it to the police station, and Marjorie is traced and asked to collect it, and does, and grieves afresh, and blames Chloe, but at the time the gesture holds good.

'That's that, really,' says Marjorie. 'I wish a bus would come. I'm cold. What a dreadful country this is. There's nothing to keep me here, now, is there.'

'If you only believed in the transmigration of souls,' says Grace, 'as I try very hard to do, you wouldn't feel so dismal. Helen was at her best in a beautiful body. If I'm pregnant, I daresay her soul will enter the baby. That's what it was all about.'

'God help us all,' says Chloe.

'She didn't say anything before she died?' asks Marjorie. 'I should never have listened to you, Chloe. I should never have left her.'

'She stayed asleep,' says Chloe. Is she right to lie, or wrong? She will never know.

'If you want the Frognal house,' says Marjorie, 'you can have it.'

'What for?' asks Chloe, surprised.

'To live in without Oliver,' says Marjorie. 'With the children but without Oliver. You can let off the top and live off the proceeds.'

'She'll never do it,' says Grace. 'Give it to Patrick instead.'

'Certainly not,' says Marjorie.

A bus arrives. They board it, and sit in a row on the seat next to the door. Marjorie and Grace get off at Earls Court. Chloe goes through to Piccadilly Circus and changes on to a 13 for Liverpool Street. She lies awake most of the night. Neither Oliver nor Françoise disturbs her. Everyone, that night, sleeps in his own bed.

Who'd have thought it?

sixty-two

Marjorie, Grace and me. What can we tell you to help you, we three sisters, walking wounded that we are? What can we tell you of living and dying, beginning and ending, patching and throwing away; of the patterns that our lives make, which seem to have some kind of order, if only we could perceive it more clearly.

We have only our own small patch of experience to relate, we three. If there are lessons to be learned by others, I would be glad, but also surprised. For who bothers to learn by another's experience? When the booby-trap is sprung, who lives to tell? We all know that.

Female bodies lie strewn across the battle-field, of course they do, gaunt dead arms upflung towards the sky. It was an exhilarating battle, don't think it wasn't. The sun shone brightly at the height of it, armour glinted, sparks flew. And the earth receives its blood with gratitude. The seasons are renewed again.

Pretty little sister, on your feather cushion, combing out your silken hair, don't discredit what your elder sister says. Much less your grandmama. Listen carefully now to what she says, and you may not end as tired and worn and sad as she. Be grateful for the softness of the cushion, while it's there, and hope that she who stuffed and sewed it does not grudge its pleasure to you. The sewing of it brought her a great deal of pain and very little reward. But for her, and you, and all of us, says grandmama, it is much the same. The good times come, and no sooner here than gone. And as they go, they come again.

304

So treasure your moments of beauty, your glimpses of truth, your nights of love. They are all you have.

Take family snaps, unashamed. Dress up for weddings, all weddings. Rejoice at births, all births. For days can be happy – whole futures cannot. This is what grandmama says. This moment now is all you have. These days, these nights, these moments one by one.

As for my friends, my female friends. Grace does a soft-shoe shuffle amongst the bodies of the fallen, and keeps the vultures off a little while. She has her baby, keeps it, calls it Hypatia to annoy, lives with Patrick for a little, goes back to Sebastian, whom she presently declares, rightly or wrongly, to be Hypatia's father. Sebastian gives up the film industry and goes into advertising, under the patronage of Esther's son Stephen, who, being now responsible for a slimming food account, presently loses some five stone. As Grace remarks, improvement in the human condition is always possible. She herself is a good mother to baby Hypatia, quite a lot of the time, and in her domestic life with Sebastian recaptures a little of the languid chocolate-box flavour of her earlier life with Christie. Stanhope visits once a month. She makes him cucumber sandwiches, and otherwise leaves him alone. And once a week she goes to Bournemouth to visit her old father, and keep the tomatoes in his window boxes watered.

Who'd have thought it?

Hypatia, fortunately, is a patient and obliging baby, who never cries if she can help it, and is not in the least like Helen, but more like Chloe's former self.

Marjorie, patched up, removes herself from the conflict

altogether, and finds another, healthier battle-field in Israel. 'I was my father's child and not my mother's,' she says. She and her camera crew court death daily up and down the cease-fire zone, waiting for violation incidents. Without her womb and without her mother, she seems cheerful enough. She is brown, weather-beaten, and handsome at last, in a country where to be devoid of juices is not remarkable, and to be alive, male or female, is commendable.

As for me, Chloe, I no longer wait to die. I put my house, Marjorie's house, in order, and not before time. The children help. Oliver says, 'But you can't leave me with Françoise,' and I reply, I can, I can, and I do.

Maggie O'Farrell